THE MEDDLER

A Series of Worthy Young Ladies
Book One

Kate Archer

Dragonblade Publishing, Inc. is an imprint of Kathryn Le Veque Novels, Inc.
P.O. Box 7968
La Verne CA 91750
ceo@dragonbladepublishing.com

Produced in the United States of America

First Edition January 2022
Trade Paperback Edition

ARE YOU SIGNED UP FOR DRAGONBLADE'S BLOG?

You'll get the latest news and information on exclusive giveaways, exclusive excerpts, coming releases, sales, free books, cover reveals and more.

Check out our complete list of authors, too!

No spam, no junk. That's a promise!

Sign Up Here

www.dragonbladepublishing.com

Dearest Reader;

Thank you for your support of a small press. At Dragonblade Publishing, we strive to bring you the highest quality Historical Romance from some of the best authors in the business. Without your support, there is no 'us', so we sincerely hope you adore these stories and find some new favorite authors along the way.

Happy Reading!

CEO, Dragonblade Publishing

Additional Dragonblade books by Author Kate Archer

A Series of Worthy Young Ladies
The Meddler (Book 1)

The Dukes' Pact Series
The Viscount's Sinful Bargain (Book 1)
The Marquess' Daring Wager (Book 2)
The Lord's Desperate Pledge (Book 3)
The Baron's Dangerous Contract (Book 4)
The Peer's Roguish Word (Book 5)
The Earl's Iron Warrant (Book 6)

PROLOGUE

Number 38 Grosvenor Square
1811

T HE SIX WOMEN who gathered in Lady Featherstone's richly furnished drawing room were past that time when they might find themselves with child. From afar, they appeared extraordinarily fortunate—they had married well, and to acceptably genial lords, and they had kept up their end of the marital bargain. All six women had produced an heir. Some of them had gone on to deliver a spare. One of them had supplied the world with a distressing number of spares and was rather relieved that they'd stopped arriving.

What none of them had held in their arms, though, was a daughter. A dear, darling girl had failed to make an appearance.

As the ladies became better acquainted throughout the seasons, the whispers of this grave disappointment grew more insistent. Conversations crossed card tables and were had in quiet corners. There were sad and knowing nods at some other woman's bright young girl at the pianoforte.

The ladies' husbands were delighted with the circumstances of their lives—they had heirs and no dowries to put aside. The ladies were not so sanguine and the loss they shared had bound them to one another.

When they'd first begun welcoming sons, the idea of a girl had been ever-present. Some beautiful little thing would make her appearance and they would dress her in fine lawn and soft silk. There would be quiet teas, company at sewing, carriage rides in the park, and someone to read to them on dreary afternoons. The darling girl would grow and there would be a full year's preparation for her launch. Even after she was married, this adored daughter would write for advice or to relay interesting news about her own children.

How was it that this perfect little being had never arrived? How was it that their houses were sadly empty, their sons at school or carousing the Town with friends, and their husbands forever at their clubs?

The ladies, being so little used to disappointments of any sort, began to form an idea. Letters flew across England from estate to estate with growing rapidity. All manner of suggestions were examined, not the least of which were the charming pictures painted of maternal felicity. Their notions of daughters they might call their own were added to with delightful abandon and they imagined being showered with girlish gratefulness and affection. It began to feel as if they must go forward, they could not put aside the dream.

And so, this first meeting was the result.

The women fiddled with their fans and reticules and barely contained their excitement over the inception of The Society of Sponsoring Ladies. They may not have *born* daughters, but they could still launch a few.

Of course, at that exciting moment in their history, none of them could have foreseen that their lives would shortly be turned upside down, their households thrown topsy-turvy, or that handwringing would become a new and frequent habit. They could not predict that the worthy young ladies they would sponsor might not be the meek and demure creatures of their fevered imaginations. They could not know that at some later date they would turn to each other to inquire whose idea this had been in the first place.

That was only to be expected—one never *does* anticipate such things.

CHAPTER ONE

A NNE BUXTON, KNOWN in the wider world as Lady Feather-stone, poured tea and handed it out to the five ladies gathered round her prized pink marble table. She deliberately stayed silent until the doors to her drawing room were firmly shut. Handing the last cup to Lady Redfield, she said, "The first meeting of our society has officially commenced. We shall, over the course of the next few years, launch a series of worthy young ladies."

The Duchess of Stanbury set down her cup with firm deliberation. "Through our diligent and, if I may say it, *noble* efforts," she said, "we shall be the means of these disadvantaged girls' entrée into the society they were rightfully born to."

Lady Featherstone nodded in acknowledgement, knowing full well that Theodosia would not be satisfied until she had worked in the idea of nobility.

"We are agreed, then," Lady Easton said, "that we look for girls who are disadvantaged through no fault of their own? What I mean to say is, their parents or guardians, though eminently respectable, are not in possession of the necessary...funds."

"Oh, I think we must be of the same mind as to that," Lady Redfield said, always liking to be in agreement. "That way, their parents must stay behind in the country, and it will be just as if we ourselves are the girls' mamas."

There were long and gentle sighs over this idea, as that was the shining purpose of their newly-founded society—to find themselves acting as mamas to any number of charming young ladies.

Lady Featherstone instantly noted that one lady amongst them did not join in the gentle sighing. She was not the least surprised by it. Though Lady Heathway could not know it, she had long ago been tagged by society's wits as Lady Naysay.

"We ought to have rules and procedures, though," Lady Heathway said. "How we open a meeting and such."

"I just opened it, Penelope," Lady Featherstone said with some aspersion. Though she had known Lady Heathway since they were girls and was very fond of her, the woman was diabolical in her efforts to complicate things with procedures.

"Yes, let us not get twisted up in endless rules," Lady Easton said. "We have all known each other forever, I expect we can manage our meetings well enough."

"But we have not even discussed the particulars," Lady Heathway said. "We've only thought of how pleasant it will be and that is not at all sufficient. For instance, if we introduce a girl into the marriage mart, what do we offer? Her parents will not have the means of providing a suitable dowry. There may not be a dowry at all if the family's circumstances are particularly dire."

Lady Featherstone's brow wrinkled just a bit over this question. She had to admit to herself that though Penelope *was* an awful naysayer, she was also often the most practical among them.

"We will add two thousand pounds to whatever she comes with," the Duchess of Stanbury said. "The final amount will surely not be the largest dowry dangling and may well be the smallest, but respectable all the same. Further, the marriage will have *our* stamp of approval, which must be worth thousands on its own."

"Two thousand pounds," Lady Featherstone whispered. "My lord will have a lot to say about that, and none of it pleasant."

"As will the duke," the duchess said, waving her hands as if this were an inconsequential point. "It is of no importance, Anne. I will run over my duke, you will run over your viscount. We will pummel down and barrel past any objections. After all, can we not make life miserable if we so choose? Would our lords not have had to pay out far more if they had their own daughters? Do we not *require* these funds for our own happiness?"

Lady Featherstone slightly squinted, as if attempting to peer into a future conversation with her viscount. Such a sum would severely curtail his gambling habits for a year at least, which would not put him in a cheerful frame of mind. However, Theodosia was right. They had no choice.

Lady Mendleton suddenly leapt up from her chair, sending the crumbs from a recently eaten biscuit flying in all directions. "Oh, I cannot even sit still. I must speak."

The ladies all turned in her direction. Lady Mendleton smiled and said softly, "I have found my girl. Miss Georgiana Wilcox, Baron Manley's daughter. Her lines are very good, as he is a cousin. At least I believe he is, though it is rather distant. The mother is not ideal, of course, she is the daughter of a local tradesman of some sort. Well, you know how those things happen—leave a young gentleman to his own devices... But no matter, the girl takes after her father, I am sure. I have written him, and he has written me, and she is everything I could wish for—pretty, well-mannered, modest, and so very grateful."

"What luck, Louisa!" Lady Featherstone said. She was not particularly surprised that Louisa Stapleton had jumped in headfirst. She was a cheerful and impetuous sort of person.

"Luck, you say? Where is the investigation?" Lady Heathway cried, setting her cup down with a clatter. "Naturally, a father seeing a chance for his daughter will praise her to the skies. You do not have the first idea of what you get yourself into. She may take after the mother! She may be coarse."

Lady Mendleton, well used to Lady Heathway's habit of naysaying, ignored her warnings. She clapped her hands together. "The girl arrives on the fifteenth."

"Goodness," Lady Featherstone said, "that is only a fortnight from now. There is so much planning to be done. Louisa, what preparations have you made? Has a modiste been secured? Have the right balls and parties been accepted? I understand the queen is foregoing presentations this year on account of the poor king's condition so you can at least strike that off your list, but will you have your own ball?"

Lady Mendleton slowly turned a pale pink and it was abundantly clear that nothing at all had been done. "I have thought of which room she might occupy," she said softly. "And ordered some new wallpaper for it."

Lady Featherstone sighed. Louisa was a darling, but not much of a planner.

Lady Heathway shook her head sadly and whispered, "Willy-nilly is what this is. I predict a disaster, just see if I am not right."

"Nonsense, Penelope," the duchess said. "*I* am involved and I do not involve myself in disasters. Therefore, ladies, we must all pull together."

The ladies nodded eagerly, Lady Mendleton herself perhaps the most enthusiastically.

MISS GEORGIANA WILCOX, daughter of Baron Manley, had always done just what she liked in her corner of England. She was perfectly aware that her upbringing was not as it should have been, and that her family's fortunes had been in slow decline for the past three generations.

She had resigned herself to the idea that her mother, a rather silly creature whose primary activity was gossiping in the village, had been completely unequipped to supervise her education. Her dear father, though well-spoken and cultured, had not the funds to hire a governess or tutors. This circumstance had left her to teach herself in a rather haphazard fashion. She could vaguely play the pianoforte, but not in a manner that anybody would like to listen to—she did not read music and if she could not remember the proper key, she just chose one. The chosen key was invariably wrong, as she did not have a natural ear. She could sew, or at least look like she was sewing, though the results were a conglomeration of ragged stitches that came apart with remarkable ease. She was an excellent rider, though only astride, and that was perhaps her highest accomplishment. She had learned that way and there had been every intention of purchasing a sidesaddle when she was fully grown, but somehow it had never appeared. She supposed it did not signify as she only rode through her father's extensive wood and took a carriage to the village. There were whispers of it, occasionally, but in a neighborhood so limited nobody was eager to break with the local baron over his daughter's habits.

She adored reading, at least, and the house had a decent library. Of all the things that her father had sold off over the years, he would not sell his books. The books had given her whatever education she had acquired. Georgiana had done her best, though she often wondered if it had been good enough. She was well-aware that she ought to have read more history and philosophy and read less about horses and horse breeding.

For all that, she was not an unhappy person. Once she had been old enough to understand her circumstances, she resolved to make the best of it. She would never be dressed in finery and slay the gentlemen at an elegant ball during a London season. It seemed a bit of a shame, as the one thing her mother *had* given her was a pile of wavy black hair that might look charming set off with a sparkling tiara. However, with no tiaras in sight, she would settle for marrying a dashing soldier who might turn up at the local assembly. At least, she hoped so, though she was not unaware that she could sometimes frighten even a soldier. She'd garnered a reputation of being exceedingly direct. Too direct, as some of the local matrons kindly hinted. As she was not particularly inclined to be less direct, she supposed she'd better find herself a gentleman who could stand up against it and who better than a soldier?

As was her habit, she'd taken her father's horse for a morning ride. It was well that her father was in possession of a great deal of woodland, as her skirts rode up rather shockingly on either side of his saddle. Fortunately, the only creatures to view her ankles this fine morning were those that lived in the forest and were not prone to gossip.

Georgiana had just reined in Mischief at the stream that ran nearby the stables so the horse might get a drink before she took him in.

Though it might be her own habit to rise with the sun, it had never been her mother's inclination. Lady Manley preferred something rather nearer to noon. Therefore, Georgiana was surprised to see her running down the lane toward the stables. She was also surprised to note that the lady had not paused to dress and was still in her bed gown.

"Where is Georgiana?" she shrieked into the air.

Matthew, one of the stable hands, came out to investigate. The boy did not look particularly alarmed, as all on the grounds were used to Lady Manley shrieking quite often.

Georgiana gently spurred Mischief, who seemed not very enthusiastic about leaving the vicinity of the stream, to discover what Lady Manley was shouting about this time.

"I am just coming, Mama," Georgiana called.

Matthew tipped his cap to her and retreated gratefully into the stables. Georgiana trotted Mischief to her mother, who was fairly jumping on the lane.

"Has Marta set the kitchens on fire again?" Georgiana asked playfully.

"Not that I know of, but she might be doing it this minute to vex me," Lady Manley said. She was a short woman and the rosy cheeks that had once defeated Lord Manley and convinced him to marry a tradesman's daughter had long fled. The rosiness had been replaced by a rather dough-like countenance that spoke of too many cakes and biscuits. Georgiana would tower over the lady, even if she had not been on her horse, which was a constant source of aggravation, though nobody was clear why.

"That diabolical woman who poses as a servant is not why I've roused myself so early in the day," Lady Manley said.

Georgiana could not imagine what *had* roused the lady, but it was clear enough that it had not been a pleasant circumstance.

"Your father has been in receipt of a letter for two days while I have been kept completely in the dark! I found it while looking...well never mind where I was looking. The point is, I found it and demanded an explanation!"

Georgiana, well-used to her mother's particular brand of disordered thinking, waited patiently to be told more so that she might make heads or tails of it.

"Then, I discover it was not the only letter! There has been a back and forth for weeks!"

Georgiana patted Mischief's neck to keep him steady, as the horse did not have as much patience for the lady's roundabout stories.

"Here. Read the last of them for yourself!" Lady Manley said, pulling a letter from one of her robe's pockets.

Georgiana bent down and took the letter. She thought she ought not to read her father's personal correspondence. She also thought she did not have much choice—once her mother was fixed on an idea...she was fixed.

She suppressed a sigh and unfolded it, certain it would be some risky investment with whatever funds her father had left. His desperation to rescue the family fortunes and his seemingly bad luck with stewards often drove him to wild ideas.

My dear Lord Manley,

I cannot tell you how delighted I am that we are in agreement on the arrangements. Let me assure you, Georgiana will have every advantage and I will personally step in and act as her mama. She will be well-dressed, well-protected, taken to all the

right places, and introduced to all the right gentlemen. She will have her proper place in society!

I will send a carriage and my maid, along with two grooms and an armed coachman, to retrieve the dear girl on the fifteenth.

Louisa Stapleton

Though Georgiana was still attempting to parse the meaning from the letter, her mother barreled on.

"Of course, you notice, there is no mention of *me* getting into that carriage!" she shrieked.

"But I do not understand," Georgiana said. "Why should any of us get into the carriage? Who is Louisa Stapleton?"

Lady Manley sniffed, as she did when she meant to say she was not impressed. "She is the Countess of Mendleton and some kind of distant relation of your father's. She thinks she will whisk you off to London for a season. Oh yes, I discovered the whole scheme when I confronted your father with that letter. She says *she* will act as your mama! And what am I, I wonder? She does not even mention me, it is as if I am dead!"

The whole of what was being proposed slowly dawned on Georgiana. The Countess of Mendleton, for reasons only known to herself, had decided to sponsor her for a season. The question was not whether her mother would allow her to go. The question was would her father allow her, and according to this letter, he would.

She would go to London. How extraordinary. The idea had been ever so far out of reach that it had been relegated to dreams and fantasies. Without warning, it had become a reality. The illusive soldier she'd had a mind to marry could jump off a bridge—Georgiana Wilcox was going to Town.

Georgiana leapt off Mischief and called for Matthew. As the stable hand took the reins, she said, "There is so much to do!" She picked up her skirts and ran toward the house.

Lady Manley, left behind on the lane, only shouted, "I am

against it! Or else I should go! I put my foot down—it is one or the other!"

JASPER STAPLETON, VISCOUNT Langley and eldest son of Lady Mendleton, straightened his already perfectly straight cuffs and pretended he did not notice his mother's pacing. They were in the drawing room at the house in Mayfair and he once again thought he'd made a mistake in agreeing to live in it. The country was one thing—he'd done up a hunting lodge remarkably comfortable and suitably removed from the main house. The low season in Town was equally acceptable and he happily ensconced himself, alone but for his valet and a few day maids, in its rambling rooms.

He had been in the Mayfair house alone for the past few months in service to the queen, it being close enough to Richmond to come and go. Though his destination was so often Kew Palace, the queen preferred to use its older name—The Dutch House.

Now that the regency had finally been made official, things should have settled and quieted. Rumors and speculation should have died out. Yet, they had not. There was a viper in the queen's midst, spreading lurid news of the king's infirmity, and Jasper had been tasked with discovering the culprit. So far, he could not determine whether this person was part of the staff, a courtier, or even one of the endless array of doctors called in. There were plans to move the king to Windsor, as Jasper had become suspicious of some of the staff at Kew and the grounds were not so easily secured.

He might have rented a house closer to Windsor if he'd been sure where the queen intended to settle. She at once thought she ought to stay by the king's side, but that she did no good in her attendance. She preferred Buckingham Palace and she also thought that showing herself in society would calm the people's nervousness at having her wastrel of a son named regent.

When Jasper's mother wrote that she was on her way to London, he ought to have moved mountains to rent his own house, despite not knowing where the queen would place herself in the longer term. He'd even told his mother that he would. But then, she was an affectionate sort and wheedled and cajoled that she might at least have his company when he did not go out. He'd not seen the real harm in it until just recently.

For the past three days, the countess had been nervous as a cat. There was something she wanted to say to him, of that he was certain. He was equally certain that she'd developed a plan. He very much feared it would be on the subject of marriage, and that she would revisit the idea that she had her heart set on a particular lady.

His mother was impetuous, and a bit of a meddler. She had taken one look at a certain female and become infatuated with her father's title and the girl's insipid blond locks.

Jasper sighed as he glanced at Lady Mendleton. She was on her way to wearing a hole in the carpet.

"Mother," he said, "you'd best just come out with it."

Lady Mendleton stopped in her tracks. "Come out with what?" she asked, her tone a bit higher than usual.

"Whatever it is you want to say," Jasper said. "Though, if it is about some lady you wish me to marry, I must point out I do not have the time to think of such things at the moment. I am far too taken up with the queen's business."

Lady Mendleton hurried her plump figure to her son's side and sat down next to him. "It is not that at all!" she said. "Though, since you ask, there is something you ought to know."

"Will I be made happy in knowing it?" Jasper asked drily.

His mother seemed to consider this question and only shrugged. "I do not see why you should be made *unhappy* to know it."

"Just tell me," Jasper said.

"It is only this," Lady Mendleton said, "you of course know

how much I adore you and your brother. Never has a mother been more blessed with such fine sons. But, I did so pine for a girl..."

Now, Jasper was beginning to be alarmed. He hoped the dear lady was not under the delusion that she was with child—it was far too late in her history for that. He had no wish to be forced to point out that her expanding waistline was a result of the silver trays of marzipan found on every table.

Suddenly, a far worse idea came to Jasper and he clutched the armrest. Had she adopted some waif without bothering to inform anybody? It was not out of the realms of possibility—the estate was overrun with at least eight dogs of varying sizes and uncertain parentage that had been taken in, one by one. By the fourth dog, Lady Mendleton had garnered a reputation for rescuing, and dogs began to get dropped off on the doorstep under cover of darkness. For all he knew, there were more dogs there by now.

She collected servants just the same way—every hard case that came to her notice was taken in and never left. It was still of some amazement to him that Mrs. Ripperton had been employed as the estate's housekeeper. Her claim on Lady Mendleton's affections was two-fold—her husband had died in a tragic accident and she was in the habit of praising Lady Mendleton to the skies. The housekeeper was decidedly lazy, particularly unskilled, probably a drunk, and generally useless. She had not even come to Town, claiming the London air was bad for her chest, though she had wept when Lady Mendleton had suggested hiring someone in her stead. The end result was that there was no housekeeper in the London house and Perry was left to manage it all as best he could.

His mother brushed at her skirts, as if to give herself courage for whatever she was ginning herself up to say. "You know of my friendships with Lady Featherstone, Lady Easton, Lady Redfield, Lady Heathway, and of course the Duchess of Stanbury?"

Jasper nodded. How could he avoid knowing? That gaggle of

ladies were like a cabal. They haunted drawing rooms and card rooms, the arbiters of what was acceptable or not—especially Lady Heathway and the duchess.

Good God. He had never thought of it before, but none of those ladies had daughters either. Had they *all* adopted female orphans?

"Well, we have formed our own society," Lady Mendleton went on. "It is The Society of Sponsoring Ladies. We will each sponsor a worthy girl, you see."

Jasper was not certain he did see. "What do you mean by *sponsor,* exactly?"

Lady Mendleton patted her son's hand. "Nothing to disturb your peace, darling," she said. "The girl will only move in here and I will dress her and squire her about, and of course if you could help me squire and make introductions, well, I can only say, the society would be in your debt."

Seeing her son was rather speechless at this announcement, the countess hurried on. "I ought to host a ball. Lady Redfield says I really ought. And you see, it is just that I really, really wished to have a daughter. They are different, you know. They depend upon a mother as a son does not. And this way, it will be as if I do have my own daughter. Is that not delightful?"

Jasper could hardly think of anything less delightful. "How has father received this remarkable news?" he asked.

"Oh, him?" Lady Mendleton said with a nervous giggle. "I cannot be sure. He is still at his shooting, you know, so I wrote him a letter." There was a long pause, and then she said, "The only real expense will be her clothes and the ball and...her dowry."

"Her dowry!" Jasper nearly shouted.

Lady Mendleton twisted her skirt in her hands and, "Theodosia says it must be two thousand pounds and it's quite necessary and that we are to run down, pummel and barrel our way through it."

"I bet she did," Jasper said.

"She must be right though," Lady Mendleton said. "A girl does need a dowry and your father has escaped that inconvenience twice on account of having sons."

Jasper could perfectly well imagine his father's complete and utter amazement in becoming apprised of this development. Especially that he was to provide a two-thousand-pound dowry for some person he'd never met in his life.

Then again, once the old man got over the shock, he just might go along and put a good face on it. The amount would not kill him, after all. Further, they all knew that when Lady Mendleton was set on something, she was rather like a badger about it. A smiling and kind badger, but determined all the same. Over the course of years, what once would have elicited strong protests from Lord Mendleton now only drew quiet groans and a glass of brandy to soothe himself.

Jasper supposed he'd better at least pretend to go along with it—let his father put up a fight if he had the fortitude. It was a ridiculous scheme, but she seemed very keen on the idea and they should all be grateful she had not adopted an orphan.

At least, he assumed so.

"And who is this new daughter of yours? She's not an orphan, is she?" he asked.

Lady Mendleton appeared exceedingly pleased to be asked, as if it indicated all problems had been satisfactorily disposed of. "She is Miss Georgiana Wilcox. She is not an orphan, she is the very charming daughter of Lord Manley. She comes on Tuesday next."

"I see. May I assure myself that you have no plans to throw her *my* way?"

"Gracious, no!" Lady Mendleton said. "I had not even thought...well, you know who I have in mind for *you*, dear. No, that would not do at all—you must promise not to be overcome by Miss Wilcox no matter how charming she is!"

Jasper nodded. "You have my solemn vow."

Whoever Miss Wilcox was, he was in no danger of being

overcome. He would do what he could for his mother's sake, but he was in no way prepared to throw himself into the project. He was far too busy and lately it had been one thing after another. His valet, who'd been with him for years, had taken himself off to America to do he knew not what—something about land and cows. His new valet, Marcus, had not quite got the hang of things yet. A chimney on the east wing had begun to crumble and needed repair, and a shelf in the wine cellar had collapsed, taking with it some of the house's best wine.

Those were all the sort of minor annoyances that took up one's time and he did not have extra time to give away. Miss Wilcox would have to shift for herself—the queen had need of him.

CHAPTER TWO

L ORD MANLEY PACED behind the desk in his library while
Georgiana patiently waited for him to speak. Lady Manley
had carried on for days, each new idea sending her into a frenzy.
She was offended that she would not go to Town and that the
countess wanted only Georgiana. She decried the idea that she
was to be thrown over as a mother, though prior to this moment
she had never been interested in the state. She named Lady
Mendleton a terrible snob and claimed she was only ignored
because her father had been in trade. That one might well be true
but was rather beside the point.

A woman had arrived some days ago, sent from Lady Mendleton to take Georgiana's measurements. There were to be
various gowns and day dresses made and, alarmingly, a riding
habit. Georgiana took this to mean that it was assumed she was
accustomed to a sidesaddle. She was not certain what she ought
to do about that, but there was hardly time to think of it between
her mother's various hysterics.

The idea of new clothes, in particular, sent Lady Manley into
fits. She took to walking down memory lane and recalling all the
fine dresses she deserved but never had. The poor seamstress had
done the fitting with alacrity, furiously writing down measurements and making samples in muslin. She had firmly declined the
baron's offer to spend the night.

Doctor Wade had finally been called to Manley Hall and Lady

Manley had been dosed with her oft-received and very favored calming draught—a mixture of lavender water, apple wine, and a good helping of laudanum. It'd had a good effect and the lady had been taken down from high dudgeon to merely querulous.

"Father," Georgiana said, "do sit down and rest. It has been a...distressing time."

The baron did finally sit down. "And will be again, as soon as that draught wears off. But you will be out of range soon enough, my dear, and I am happy for it."

Georgiana nodded and thought if she would miss anything about this house, it was only her father. He was a kind and sensible man.

"Well then," her father said, "we ought to talk about Town. Though, I have not been since I was a young man and much will have changed."

"Tell me what you remember, though," Georgiana said. In truth, she did not know what to expect. Certainly, it would be different, though she could not say how.

"What I remember most, I suppose, is that things in Town are a little more...boxed in. More formal, that is. There will be a lot of rules on how one is expected to conduct oneself."

"What sort of rules?"

"Hmm, I cannot be entirely certain, things do change so rapidly. But for instance, I am sure it will not be right to ride astride. Of that I am absolutely sure, as it is not even quite the thing *here*."

Georgiana was not surprised as that had been in her thoughts before now. She had never tried out a sidesaddle and hoped it was as straightforward as it appeared to be.

"I really ought to have seen to a proper saddle," the baron said. "I fault myself and hope it does you no harm."

"Sidesaddle cannot be so hard, Papa," Georgiana said reassuringly. "I am certain it will be no trouble—Margaret Hardy uses one easily enough and she is prone to trip over her own two feet."

Baron Manley nodded gratefully at being let off the hook on that particular subject. "Then of course," he continued, "it is even quite usual in our little corner of England that only the gentlemen stay behind for port and that all the ladies retire to the drawing room. Though we may run things looser in our own house…"

"I've always enjoyed our conversations after dinner, Papa. And port for that matter."

"Yes, but that's the sort of thing that only goes on with us. Nobody else will do it. In general, I think your good instincts may steer you. Though, perhaps it will not always be right to say what is on your mind."

The baron stared at the far wall, as if he were thinking hard. After a gentle sigh, he said, "I suppose what I mean is, I have been lax in your education and I hope it does not result in any difficulties, my dear. Perhaps suppress your natural…enthusiastic honesty. At least until you get the lay of the land. Lady Mendleton will guide you and she will expect you to wish to be guided."

Georgiana smiled, finally understanding her father's meaning. "What I think you say, Father, is do not set London afire with my forthright opinions."

"Just so, Georgie."

SIX DAYS LATER, the Countess of Mendleton had been as good as her word. Georgiana had heard the carriage rolling up the drive to Manley Hall as she sat at breakfast with her father. It was all too evident that her mother, still abed above stairs, heard it too. She glanced at the ceiling and the distant wailing heard over their heads.

The baron had thought it wise to make some prior arrangements for this particular day. Writing back and forth to the countess, he had expressed the idea that the carriage ought to stop the night before at an inn nearby so that the horses were fresh and Georgiana's departure might be made speedily. The countess was left to think this was on account of Lady Manley's distress at parting from her daughter. Everybody else knew this was to avoid whatever scene Lady Manley had planned to express her vexation over not being included.

Georgiana's trunks, such as they were, were packed and by the front doors. There would be no dilly-dallying in her leave-taking, lest her mother have time to dress and come down and say or do nobody knew what.

She took a last bite of toast and leapt up, her father already heading for the door. Marta helped her into her traveling cloak and bonnet, and Georgiana hurried out the front doors and down the steps.

The carriage that stood on the circular drive was well-appointed, with a coat of arms emblazoned in gold paint on the door and pulled by four fine chestnuts. It was driven by a burly coachman, the type one suspects has a pistol in each pocket and would not hesitate to use them. Two tall grooms had leapt off the running boards and a pert lady's maid popped her head out the window.

Georgiana had been prior informed that the woman was to be her companion on the journey. Her name was Jenny and she was a surprisingly bright-faced girl who could not be much older than herself.

The grooms loaded the trunks, though they did not appear over-awed by the looks of the house or the state of her luggage. All the while, her father glanced nervously at the above-stairs windows.

Jenny threw open the door and said, "Good day to you, my lord! I been told we're to cut and run like chickens ahead of a fox."

The baron did not answer this unique phrasing, but only nodded and helped Georgiana inside the carriage.

The door was shut, the grooms leapt onto the running

boards, the coachman tipped his cap, and the carriage set off. Georgiana thought not even Queen Mary fleeing Lochleven Castle had got off so speedily.

She poked her head out the window to look back and give a last wave to her father, just as Lady Manley opened her own window and shrieked.

Georgiana sat back and was grateful that the coachman did not pause upon hearing the outcry, but put distance from it by way of the horses' spirited trot.

"Ah," Jenny said, nodding knowingly, "just as Lady Mendleton predicted, your ma is distraught that you leave her."

Georgiana nodded, as she supposed her mother was indeed distraught, though not for the reasons the maid suspected.

"I expect you been told I'm Jenny, but if you wasn't, I'm Jenny."

Georgiana smiled. "You may call me Georgiana," she said.

"I may not!" Jenny said. "You are to be Miss Wilcox. Lady Mendleton will fret if I don't get it right."

Georgiana supposed this was part of the more formal rules in Town. Or everywhere but her own house. Nobody in it ever called her Miss Wilcox.

Jenny leaned back comfortably and said, "It ain't so much she is such a stickler, mind. It's them friends of hers. The duchess and Lady Heathway, to be exact. *They* are real sticklers. *They* would say, Jenny you got to know your place!"

Jenny scratched her cap, as if her mind itched with a new idea. "No, that ain't right," she said. "They wouldn't say nothing to me directly. They'd say, Louisa, that maid of yours has got to know her place!" Jenny paused and said softly, "They probably don't even know my name."

"Well, Jenny, *I* know your name," Georgiana said.

Jenny seemed to find great comfort in that idea and nodded enthusiastically.

Georgiana found herself rather delighted with Jenny. She had expected a staid middle-aged woman who would sit silent and grim for the entire journey. In truth, she rather wondered at Lady Mendleton sending a maid so young to be a chaperone. For all that, though, Jenny was certain to be a more interesting companion.

"So you're the very first girl...just think of it," Jenny said.

"The very first girl?" Georgiana said, wondering if Lady Mendleton had invited a whole slew of ladies to stay. She might not mind it, if that were the case. Now that she was on her way, she'd begun to feel too...something. Too singled out, perhaps?

"You're the first girl of that society they've slapped together," Jenny said confidentially.

"Society?" Georgiana asked. She had not heard her father mention a society.

As Jenny rarely needed prompting to tell all that she knew, and perhaps some she only thought she knew, the next hour was taken up with everything she'd gleaned about The Society of Sponsoring Ladies.

As Georgiana listened, her head fairly spun. She now understood that a group of six ladies, longstanding friends and all without daughters, had come together in a plan to launch girls who had not the means to launch themselves. And, God help her, she was the first.

She was rather touched when Jenny talked about how poor Lady Mendleton always had her heart set on a daughter and never got one. How she'd heard that in the early years, Lady Mendleton had secretly bought all manner of lovely things for a baby girl and they were locked up in a trunk in the attics now.

"A course," Jenny said, "yesterday, when she sprung the whole plan on Lord Mendleton, there was a bit of a ruckus over the dowry. The earl was stupefied, if you understand me. But Lady Mendleton said she was directed by the duchess to run over, pummel, and barrel ahead and that's what she did. The lord's an easygoing sort anyway so he eventually gave up and poured himself a brandy."

Georgiana gripped the seat. "Jenny," she said, "what dowry?

Nothing of the sort was discussed with my father, of that I am certain. It cannot be right."

"Oh, it's right. Two thousand pounds of right," Jenny said.

Georgiana felt herself color. This had all seemed a wonderful romp, but two thousand pounds? Did her father know how indebted he was?

Before she could question Jenny further on that particular matter, the maid was off to describing Lady Mendleton's son, Lord Langley, who appeared to live in the residence.

"His given name is Jasper and he's always got the look of ease about him, like he knows what's what. He's ever so tall and he's got his mother's light hair—sandy colored I'd call it. Tis a blessing *that's* what he got from her, as she's on the short and plump side which suits her ever so well, but wouldn't do him any good. He's persnickety about his clothes and he's got a new valet and there seems to be some bumps in the road there. Anyway, he's a mysterious sort, always running off to the queen's side."

Georgiana could not help but think Lord Langley sounded rather dashing. Perhaps even mysteriously dashing if he were a confidante of royalty. "He is often found at the queen's side?" she asked.

"The very one, that poor love. Can you imagine, being married to a king and life is roses, then he goes all funny on you?"

Of course, Georgiana could not imagine any such thing, but she understood Jenny's meaning well enough. Though the king had always managed to recover from whatever malady he suffered from, it had begun to seem that he would not this time.

"I heard they locked the poor old king up right and tight. Though, nobody understands what the queen needs Lord Langley for, at least I don't, as he don't tell his valet anything and so we don't hear it at the servant's table. Shame, as I'd like to know it. I suppose there's ladies all over London who'd like to know it. I heard from Meggy, who is lady's maid to Lady Featherstone, that Lord Langley is thought of as quite the catch who won't be caught."

Georgiana was beginning to realize that she walked into a far more complicated situation than she had thought. In her mind's eye, as she had prepared for London, she had envisioned parties and balls, escorted to all by a rather non-descript, faceless lady. Now, she was hearing of all these people! Real people, and a society that had been formed. As well as a dowry? She felt she carried more responsibility on her shoulders than she had envisioned. Or that she would like.

Jenny finally wore herself out and fell asleep, despite the rocking and shaking of the carriage over rough roads. Georgiana gazed out the window, feeling entirely unprepared for whatever she was walking into.

They had passed through Hounslow and neared Kew, making alarmingly good progress. Georgiana wished the coach would slow down, that she would have more time to think. Or just to delay. She and her father had held a rather brief and fact-less conversation about the rules of Town. She'd not concerned herself overmuch about it and thought she would approach it as she did a gallop on a horse—she would jump that fence when she got to it. Now, she was fast approaching that fence and she wished she knew more than she did!

As if God had heard her prayers, the coach came to an abrupt halt on a shaded country lane.

Jenny opened her eyes and said, "Are we there already?"

"No," Georgiana said, "we have suddenly stopped." Though she had wished for a delay, now that she thought about it, it was odd that they had suddenly come to a standstill. She hoped they were not on the verge of being robbed. She had not much to take, but she understood those sorts of encounters could be violent.

"Stand aside, sir, you block the road," the coachman shouted.

It did indeed sound as if they encountered highwaymen. Who else deliberately blocked the road? Georgiana carefully opened the window and peered out. Ahead of the coach was an odd-looking older gentleman. His bottom half seemed dressed richly and he wore highly polished boots. His top half did not match, though. He wore some sort of odd waistcoat with undone buckles swinging everywhere.

"No need to rush off, you rascal," the man said to the coachman, "I am only trying to do you a service. Do you not see that if you plant this carriage you will end with two of them? There is a likely field just ahead. You'll need a shovel, though."

Georgiana sat back, away from the window. The man was stricken with madness. She understood well enough the unpredictability of the state. Mr. Jenner's nephew suffered from the condition—one moment he was a jolly enough fellow and the next he was weeping, terrified he'd burned down the barn. Even showing him the barn still standing might not always be enough to soothe him.

The sound of hoofbeats sounded in the distance and grew ever closer. Georgiana turned her head to see three men reining in their horses. The largest of them dismounted. He tipped his hat to Georgiana and approached the man. She could just hear him say, "There you are, sire, let's just get you back now."

Georgiana took in a sharp breath. The old gentleman was no ordinary man. He was the King of England. How did she not know it instantly? He was rumored to be tucked away at Kew Palace, which was not a half mile off. Apparently, he was not as locked up right and tight as Jenny had thought.

Jenny peered out the window and murmured, "The poor queen, having a husband go all funny like that."

A carriage that must have been following the men on horseback pulled up behind their own carriage. As the burly man walked the king to it, the king paused at her window. He said, "I was just trying to help. Sometimes I perceive things other people can't see."

He walked on and Georgiana was struck by how downcast he seemed that their coachman had been unwilling to bury his coach and receive two in return. It was sad, really. How frightening it must be to live in a world where one's own mind betrayed in such a manner—where everything that seemed real was not real to anybody else.

"Poor fella," Jenny said.

"Indeed," Georgiana said. "I think we should not speak of what we have seen here. It will do nobody any good. And, it seemed a rather private moment."

Jenny nodded vigorously. "Right you are, Miss Wilcox, nobody likes a gossip. I'll tell the boys and Carstares that it's to be lips buttoned shut."

>>>><<<<

JASPER WAS IN his bedchamber, attempting once again to demonstrate to his new valet how to properly arrange his neckcloth, when the ruckus reached his ears.

The front door had been thrown open with a bang that reverberated through the house and his mother was on the pavement crying, "My dear Miss Wilcox!"

"Leave it for now, Marcus," he said, putting aside his neckcloth and making his way to the window. He would very much like to get a look at his mother's latest project. Lady Mendleton had been extolling the young lady's charms for days, though nobody had yet set eyes on her. He sat on the window bench and pulled aside the curtain.

Jenny had come out of the carriage first, laughing and seeming as flighty as she ever was. A lady with a rather remarkable head of dark hair peeking out from under a charming blue bonnet had followed her.

She momentarily glanced up at the house and he could see that she was quite lovely. She was not one of those round-faced girls with dimples, rather her features were more sculpted. Perhaps it was the dark hair and dark eyes that gave her a more refined, classical look than many of the ladies he encountered. So often they were fair-haired with the sort of plump cheeks that made them look as if they were barely out of the schoolroom.

They tended toward light blue eyes, which he did not care for, though his own were only a shade or two deeper.

He smiled to himself, as he realized he had given the matter some thought, and likely developed his aversion to that sort of girl from personal experience. His mother was intent on making a match between him and Lady Annabelle Rumsford. That she was the daughter of a marquess was the only thing to recommend her, as far as he was concerned. She was short, and very pale. Pale hair, pale eyes, pale skin. Her conversation was equally pale—she relied on angling for compliments, as if her pale looks demanded to be commented on. It had been tiresome in the extreme the last time he'd been seated next to her at a dinner.

She'd said things like, "Goodness, I do not know what the Town air does to my hair, it is such a fright." Then, he would be forced to respond that no air in England could mar her locks, though he really wished to say, "It is not only your hair, miss—you are a fright in general and do not blame it on London."

He had not told his mother of his low opinion, but only dodged and weaved when the lady was mentioned. However, he would have to tell her sooner or later. He could no more imagine waking by the side of Lady Annabelle for the rest of his life than he could a goldfish. A tiresome goldfish endlessly swimming after compliments.

Miss Wilcox appeared to be a different sort altogether. He could not guess how his mother's latest scheme would unfold, but at least she would be exceedingly pleasant to look at.

Though, he must not spend too much time looking. For one, he would not wish to encourage the girl. For another, he was far too busy.

He watched his mother fuss around Miss Wilcox as they made their way inside. The countess had assured him that the lady would be a shy and retiring sort who would need endless encouragement. He thought she might be wrong about that. There did not seem to be anything especially retiring about the lady.

"Well, I must not get caught up in it. There is no time for it."

"My lord?" Marcus asked, still holding the neckcloth.

"Nothing," Jasper said. "Do give me a new cloth and I will arrange it. I will be late to see the queen as it is."

As Marcus hurried to retrieve a fresh cloth, he said, "How does the poor king do? The people really feel for him and miss his presence."

"He does well enough, I suppose," Jasper said.

He would be endlessly grateful if his valet spent more time on his craft and less time inquiring about the king. "Hurry now, if you please."

LOUISA STAPLETON'S DREAM had finally arrived and been made real. Miss Wilcox was everything she could have possibly wished for. Well, of course, there were *some* things she had not anticipated. The girl was not quite as shy and nervous as she had envisioned, for one.

In anticipation of Georgiana's arrival, Lady Mendleton had paced the drawing room and peeked round the curtains for over an hour. Finally, she'd seen her carriage roll to a stop and had flown out the front doors to see a very comely girl helped down to the pavement. Her father had told no tales—she was tall and well-proportioned, with a delightful amount of dark hair. Her features were rather regal-looking—a fine straight nose and dark eyes—and she gave Louisa a very pretty smile. Despite Lady Heathway's grim predictions, this lovely young lady would do very well. Very well, indeed.

Louisa had rushed forward to greet Miss Wilcox. The girl had made a sweet curtsy, though when she rose, she looked Louisa straight in the eye without even a blink. There were no blushes or demurs or lookings away. She really had thought the girl would be a bundle of nerves and need assurance just to get up the front steps. But Miss Wilcox had fairly marched up them with no assistance at all.

Since then, Miss Wilcox had been settled in her room and come down for tea. It was to be just the two of them together. Though her husband and son had both promised to at least turn up for dinner, Lord Mendleton was off to his club and Jasper had already left to attend the queen.

For now, they would be two ladies together—mother and daughter—just as Louisa had rehearsed so often in her imagination.

Louisa glanced at the pianoforte and said, "Would you play for me, my dear?"

Miss Wilcox had looked critically at the instrument. "I am afraid you'd regret it."

Louisa could not help but be pleased. What modesty! It was just as she had expected, and exceedingly charming. Some girls could not wait to display their prowess and though they sought to hide it, pride always did show itself. They would gaze longingly at the instrument or circle round it or pose questions about it until they were asked. Miss Wilcox was no such creature. She would need encouragement, just as it should be.

"Nonsense," Louisa said kindly. "Do indulge me."

Miss Wilcox rose to do as she was bid. "Might not you call me Georgiana? It feels very formal to be Miss Wilcox all the time."

Louisa clutched her handkerchief to her heart lest it pound out of her chest. "Of course I will, Georgiana." In a softer voice, she said, "I would not mind being called 'Mama'...but I suppose that would not be right."

Louisa had almost held out hope that the dear girl would *insist* on calling her Mama, despite what anybody might say about it, or that she might do so when they were alone. However, Georgiana only looked a bit perplexed over the idea.

Well, perhaps over time...

The girl sat down at the pianoforte and Louisa took in the picture. She had so often imagined sitting by a tea tray while the lyrical stylings of her daughter wafted about the drawing room. And to see how she looked so finely seated and how elegant her slim and graceful hands appeared! Finally, Louisa could hold her head up at a musical evening, when all the young ladies played for an admiring audience. She'd be a real part of it and be congratulated on her girl. It was all coming true.

As Georgiana began to play, Louisa gripped her teacup and then set it down with a clatter. With every note...if it was a note...something was going terribly wrong. Louisa began to feel as if the air in the room had become thinner and hard to breathe.

Perry came in with a tray of fairy cakes and nearly stumbled, looking toward the instrument in alarm. Georgiana's playing was...Louisa was not even certain how to describe it. Each moment, she would be convinced the girl's fingers would go one way but they went the other way. The tune was at once familiar but not the same. The strength of her assault on the keys was...perhaps that was it. It was an assault rather than a delicate dance between player and instrument.

Georgiana stopped and said, "Now you understand the truth. A rather awful truth, I suspect."

CHAPTER THREE

"M Y LADY," MR. Perry said to Louisa, looking with horror at the pianoforte that had just recently filled the room with dissonance and discord, "I will call in a tuner and rectify the matter at once!"

"Oh, yes," Louisa said, grasping at the straw her butler held out, "certainly it must be tuned."

"I am afraid, Mr. Perry," Georgiana said, "that there is no tuner on God's green earth who can make me sound any better."

As far as Louisa could tell, it was just now dawning on her butler that the fault of the racket was not to be laid at the instrument's door. He seemed mightily confused, as his mistress had made the point, repeatedly, that the girl who was coming would be an angel on the pianoforte. Louisa had been entirely convinced of it.

Perry nodded, set down the cakes, and fled the room.

"I am certain you are disappointed," Georgiana said, leaving the pianoforte and coming back to the sofa.

"Oh no, not at all," Louisa said. She was *very* disappointed, as it happened, but she would not for the world wish to bruise the girl's feelings.

On the other hand, she could not let this development get out. Lady Heathway would crow about it endlessly.

"I only think, my dear," Louisa said, "that perhaps you will not wish to play in public just yet. Some of my friends come on the morrow to be introduced to you and you might refuse to play, no matter how urgent the insistence. And then on other days, you could practice! When nobody is about."

Georgiana nodded. "Of course I will, I will do as you wish. You have been so kind to me, how could I refuse? I am sure I can get better if I practice."

Louisa nodded enthusiastically. It was as if she were a drowning sailor and somebody had thrown her a rope—she grasped the idea with both hands and held on tight. "Of course you will. My goodness, you will be expert in no time at all. In any event," she said, "not all girls favor playing. They might be better at other things. Do you sing, I wonder?"

"In church, but not loudly as it would disturb the congregation."

"Well then, I suppose your needlework is something to behold?"

Georgiana bit her lip. "Nobody would behold it willingly, not even myself."

"Oh dear," Louisa said, quite at a loss. "Drawing, perhaps?"

Georgiana shook her head.

"Netting a purse? Painting a fire screen? Knitting? Feather work? Papier mâché? Growing orchids?"

The girl had shaken her head at all of them. What had the baron had her doing all day? What would Penelope say when she became apprised of the circumstance?

A sudden, and a hopeful, idea came to her. "Now, I know you are an expert in one thing in particular. Do not be modest about it, your father told me you really are an accomplished horsewoman."

Georgiana nodded. "I do not deny it."

"There, you see?" Louisa said. "We will show ourselves in the park. I will ride in the carriage and you will ride a horse alongside and you will look exceedingly fetching in the riding habit I've ordered made."

Louisa found herself rather relieved to have hit upon something the girl was accomplished at. She must simply play up that aspect and change the subject if Penelope or the duchess brought up music or embroidery work. Or any other possible thing.

Goodness. Becoming a mother to a girl was turning out more complicated than she had expected.

MR. ALDOUS PERRY, longstanding butler to Lord and Lady Mendleton, was determined that his staff catch no hint of his trepidation regarding Miss Wilcox.

All along, he'd thought it a rather harebrained idea! The ladies had thrown together a society and they were determined to ensconce young women from who knew where in their very houses. It would have been preferable had another of the ladies tried out the idea before it was laid at *his* doorstep. Let Lady Heathway, that unrepentant harridan, conduct the experiment. Let Lady Heathway bring in a girl to assault her own pianoforte.

But of course, it had been Lady Mendleton who'd jumped in headfirst.

Still, it was not his role to pronounce judgment on the mistress or her way of going about things. Did he comment when yet another flea-bitten mongrel arrived at the estate's doors? Did he rail against it when some unqualified person was taken on as a servant and he was left to manage the idiot? Did he throw up his hands when a housekeeper was hired who couldn't keep house for a family of mice and spent most of her time dipping into the sherry? Did he allow his eyes to roll when Mrs. Ripperton claimed the London air would kill her? Did he allow himself to say: "Not if I kill you first?" Did he at all betray his feelings when their good, old English cook retired and *a Frenchman* was brought in? Did he not keep himself expressionless when he spooned a sauce with a name nobody could pronounce?

Espagnole, indeed.

No, he met all these challenges suitably stone-faced, and he would do just the same with Miss Wilcox.

As he gazed round the servants' table at tea, he pretended he did not hear Jenny's endless opinions on the matter. She had been detailing her journey with Miss Wilcox for the past ten minutes.

"Now," Jenny said, "I get to the good part. You will never, not in a thousand years, guess who we saw on the road."

One of the maids ventured that it must have been Mr. Brummel. This was met with the usual jeers from the footmen. Peggy fancied herself in love with Mr. Brummel though she'd only seen his likeness in a newspaper once. The footmen thought this was both silly and rude, as Peggy was a comely girl and they took exception to Mr. Brummel being held above them.

"It was never Mr. Brummel," Jenny said.

"It was Tom Cribb, I reckon," one of the junior footmen said.

Benjamin, who considered himself very wise to the ways of the world said, "Don't be daft, Jack. If it were Tom Cribb we would'a knowed it straight away. Carstares would'a told us."

"It was the king himself," Jenny said. "They say he's gone funny and he *has* gone funny. He told Carstares that if he buried the carriage, he'd get two in return."

Perry did not know if Jenny were inventing the tale or no, but he did not think it very seemly, even if it were true. He also did not think the new valet's apparent interest in the matter, as evidenced by his leaning forward, befitted a senior servant. Marcus was always interested in the king because his new master was interested in the king. Perry had already explained to him, repeatedly, that servants did not take on the interests of their masters. Good Lord, was he, himself, to start chasing after fox and shooting at birds because Lord Mendleton favored it? The notion was absurd.

"What exactly did he say, Jenny," Marcus asked.

"Just *that*," Jenny said, appearing to take pride in everybody's interest in the story. "Bury the carriage, get two back, there was a likely field just ahead. Oh, and we would need a shovel."

"How did he look when he said it?" Marcus asked. "I am sure Lord Langley would wish to know it."

"The poor fellow was what I would call disheveled, the buckles on his waistcoat were all undone and it was an odd-looking thing anyway, I never did see the like. Also, his hair was mussed, it's a reddish-brown color if you was wonderin' over it."

Perry held up his hand, "Nobody at this table shall dare have the temerity to wonder about the king's hair."

All at the table were silenced after that and carried on with their tea. Perry could at least congratulate himself that when it came to Lord Mendleton's household staff, *he* was the king and he had *not* gone funny.

GEORGIANA HAD TAKEN her time getting dressed, or rather Jenny had taken her time helping her. She had been sent above stairs to change a full hour before she was due back down for dinner. It was so different from Manley Hall! There, she did most things herself and then Marta, who also acted as diabolical kitchen maid, would straighten her hair into some semblance of order and do up whatever buttons she couldn't reach—the whole operation taking less than a quarter hour.

Jenny had quite different procedures, including using a pair of hot tongs to take a curl that was already there and curl it another way. She could not say she was opposed to it, as she did not think her hair had ever looked better. It had gone from verging on unmanageable to extremely orderly, which was some feat considering how much hair there was to subdue.

As Jenny chattered on about a certain absent housekeeper named Mrs. Ripperton who was alleged to be just now in the country house relaxing with a bottle of the lord's sherry, Georgiana could not help but reflect on her very sad lack of accomplishments. Of course, she recognized she was not particularly talented on a pianoforte, but to see Lady Mendleton's surprise...or was it shock? She had not comprehended that she was *that* awful. Then the poor lady had searched her mind for anything else she might hold onto and eventually settled on horsemanship. Georgiana had allowed her to do it as she could not bear to disappoint the lady one more time, though she had some misgivings about riding sidesaddle while pretending she'd been doing it all her life.

"Well," she said softly, "I must just figure it out."

"Figure out what, miss?" Jenny had asked.

Georgiana had smiled and said, "Most everything, I am beginning to think."

Now, she had gone down the stairs and entered the drawing room. She had been made aware that she would dine with the family this evening and it felt like yet another gauntlet to get past. She now understood that she would cost Lord Mendleton two thousand pounds were she to marry and she could not fathom what he thought about it. Well, perhaps she *could* fathom some of his feelings—Jenny had said he'd been stupefied by the news and drank brandy to calm himself. Then, there was the son who Jenny had described as rather dashing and an intimate of the queen.

Lady Mendleton rushed to her side and took her by the arm. Two gentlemen stood together near the window, one older and distinguished and one...very dashing indeed.

He was tall and fair-haired, though there was nothing insipid about the color—in fact there were different shades running through it from blond to light brown. He had lovely blue eyes the shade of a deep lake in summer and a firm jaw. The whole resulted in perfectly regular features. She supposed describing somebody as perfectly regular did not sound the highest praise in the world, and yet it was. His lips were the right size for his nose and his nose was the right size for his eyes and his cheekbones were rather prominent and spoke of eschewing indolence. His face was lightly tanned, which she found highly superior to some of the pasty-white faces she had encountered in her own neighborhood. He was a gentleman who went about on horseback and not hiding himself in a carriage.

"My dear," Lady Mendleton said, "allow me to introduce you to my husband, Lord Mendleton, and my son, Lord Langley."

Both gentlemen bowed and Georgiana curtsied. Thinking to leap over the fence ahead of her rather than tiptoe round it, she said, "Lord Mendleton, I am aware that I am already a great deal of trouble to you."

Lord Mendleton at first seemed taken aback by this direct assault, but then rather captivated by it. "Think nothing of it, Miss Wilcox," he said gallantly.

"Oh I do think quite a lot about it," Georgiana said. "It is impossible not to, really."

"Now you see how charming she is," Lady Mendleton said, as if attempting to steer Georgiana away from the fence she was currently jumping.

"Miss Wilcox is very direct," Lord Langley said. "That is not something we are used to encountering in Town."

Georgiana knew there would be a faint stain of pink on her cheeks, as there always must be when somebody thought to point out her most glaring fault.

"It is true," Georgiana said, "I am often guilty of it. I must work harder to be…indirect?"

"I do not see why," Lord Langley said.

"Nor I," Lord Mendleton said. "I don't like to talk in circles myself."

Mr. Perry interrupted this very interesting conversation. "My lord and my lady, will you go through?" he said.

This, as far as Georgiana could gather, was the manner in which dinner was announced. A far cry from Manley Hall's housekeeper, who only ever said, "It's ready."

THE DINNER HAD progressed very satisfactory to Georgiana's mind. The house was grand enough to have two dining rooms—one for parties and one for the family. As they had been led into the smaller family room, the set up was quite cozy.

Lord Mendleton had been delighted to talk of horses through several courses and equally delighted that Georgiana knew enough to keep up her end of the conversation. There was a rousing discussion of the Byerly Turk and his sired line, the lord most enthusiastic as he'd recently purchased a young stallion sired by the Turk's descendant, Selim.

Georgiana's travels through her father's library may not have ended in a well-rounded education, but as she had read every book on horses that he owned, she found she could keep up very well. Lord Langley was equally engaged, and it was only Lady Mendleton who had nothing to add.

As the last course came out, Lady Mendleton said, "That is quite enough of horses, if you please. We are not dining in a stable, after all."

Lord Mendleton nodded, but did not appear too put out about it. Georgiana suspected that he often indulged in such talk, knowing that at some point his wife would put a stop to it.

Lord Langley said, "You are right, Mother. Especially since we have a guest. We should engage in more usual conversations."

Lady Mendleton said, "Exactly what I would wish for."

"I will ask Miss Wilcox about her journey," Lord Langley said. "There cannot be a more commonplace topic."

"It was most commonplace," Georgiana said, "as the best journeys are."

"Now we have abruptly come to the end of *that* conversation," Lord Langley said. "Really, you must think of something, Miss Wilcox. Was there not a broken wheel or a moment when you were stuck in a muddy ditch or even a passing by of someone suspicious-looking that sent you the shivers?"

"I am afraid there was nothing at all," Georgiana said. Of course, there had been something. A very great something, by way of encountering the poor king. However, she had told Jenny they ought not mention it to anybody and she thought she was right in it. It had been as if they had peeked around somebody's curtains and viewed a private and embarrassing moment.

"Well, what now I wonder?" Lord Langley said. "I suppose we could move to the weather. It is always very reliable to predict rain."

"I am certain Lord Langley has far more interesting things to talk about," Georgiana said. "I understand you are a confidante of the queen, surely that must be fascinating."

Lord Langley suddenly did not seem as jolly as he had been. "I would not be so bold as to raise myself to confidante, Miss Wilcox. I am only at Her Majesty's service."

"What is it you do for the lady?" Georgiana asked.

"Oh don't bother inquiring into that, my dear," Lady Mendleton said. "I have asked and asked and still know nothing."

"It is of a confidential nature," Lord Langley said. "Now," he said in a more cheerful voice, "we'd best go back to horses, much to my mother's chagrin. Father, what about this new stallion of yours?"

And so the subject was changed, and very deliberately, Georgiana thought. What *did* he do for the queen? What could it be that was so secretive?

She did not know, but she could not claim it in any way diminished him. In truth, it might make him even more dashing. He was handsome, and was engaged in something confidential for royalty, she supposed there could not be anything more interesting than that. She only wished she could have heard what it was.

The conversation never did drift back in that fascinating direction, though it *had* landed on which horse must be given over for Georgiana's use. Lord Mendleton had suggested an older and very sedate mare named Biscuit that even Lady Mendleton was comfortable riding. Without thinking, Georgiana had claimed she would prefer something more lively and Lord Mendleton was not to think she could not keep her seat on even his most spirited horses. Minerva was quickly settled on, a young mare with an enthusiastic if sometimes unruly nature.

She wished she had not been so quick to speak! It was all well and good to manage her father's horse while riding astride, but she had yet to be on a sidesaddle. As that was the case, she would have done better to have gone with the sedate Biscuit.

EVER SINCE HE'D worked for the queen to uncover the viper in the king's midst, Jasper had made it his habit to have every newspaper in Town brought to his father's library. There, first thing in the morning accompanied by coffee and rolls, he would scan each page, looking for news of the king.

All too often, there was some vague report somewhere. Usually, it was just speculation and that was not what he looked for. He sought descriptions of events that had actually occurred and would not be known unless somebody close to the king had told of it.

This morning, he had read an outrageous account and had set off to Dutch House to confirm if it were even true. He'd sent for Gerard, the king's senior handler.

Gerard lumbered into the room and sat heavily on a chair. Jasper had learned long ago that there would be no bowing and scraping from this fellow. Gerard had no respect at all for rank and had years ago punched the Earl of Wainscot over a remark the fellow had made about the king's coat—that remark having had the bad luck to be overheard in a corridor of the palace. Another servant might have been at least dismissed, if not jailed. But Gerard did love the king and he was valued because of it. He was loyal and would lay down his life for him and that was far more important than toadying. Or punching an earl. Wainscot had been told to apply ice to his eye and say no more about it.

"This report," Jasper said, laying the page of the paper down on the desk, "of the king stopping a carriage and suggesting the coachman bury it to get two. Did this really happen?"

"Aye, though I didn't think to see it in the papers," Gerard said. "He's getting more and more clever about getting out. He waited until food arrived, knowing his buckles would be undone to eat. Then, he switched his cup with the handler overseeing his meal and so the handler took the calming draught and fell asleep while the king sauntered out. It is not secure enough here, we ought to make the move to Windsor soon."

"But why did you not alert me at once?"

"Why didn't you know all about it from your own people?" Gerard asked. "T'was your own carriage that he stopped."

"*My* carriage?" Jasper asked.

"T'was your pa's coat of arms on the door," Gerard said.

Jasper sat back. That would mean that it had been Jenny and Miss Wilcox in that carriage.

"And nobody else saw him? Not a farmer in his field, not anybody passing by?"

Gerard shrugged. "Could'a happened, I guess."

"But if not, that would mean…"

"Aye," Gerard said. "The report came from your own household. Seems anybody that *can* will tell tales of my poor king. If I could discover the rotter, I'd knock his eyes out of his head."

Since then, Jasper had left Kew and returned home. Carstares confirmed the case, though he said it was a short encounter and ought not be spoken of. Jasper then collared the two grooms who had been with the carriage. They did not in the least deny it and reported that the footmen had claimed that Jenny had told the story at the servants' table. He now understood that, thanks to Jenny, it could be anybody who had passed the tale to the newspapers.

Though, when he thought about it, he decided he could safely rule out the grooms and the footmen, all who would have seemed a deal more nervous had they been guilty. The coachman, Carstares, had been with them for fifteen years and rarely spoke to anybody, much less a newspaper. Jenny was too silly to have managed such a thing and would have kept the story to herself if she planned to sell it. Perry was out of the question, as he'd rather die than besmirch the family's honor. Marcus was a keen admirer and defender of the king. That left some of the other servants, though none of them seemed very likely.

And yet, there had been one person in that carriage that he knew little about. That one person had denied anything unusual occurring on her journey. Why had Miss Wilcox pretended that nothing had happened? Why had she kept the encounter a secret?

Where had the lady come from anyway? Would it be plausible, or even possible, that the king and queen's enemies had sent one of their own into his very house? In the guise of an innocent-seeming young lady?

It seemed farfetched, but then little of what had happened in the past few years sounded within the realm of reasonable. There was a game afoot and he could not know what these people would stoop to. He did not even know who they were or what they wanted. Was it someone merely disgruntled over some matter, or was it the young pretender's grandson, Charles Edward Stuart, Count Roehenstart, with a more devilish plan in mind?

It would seem dubious that there would be another Stuart run at the crown, but that did not mean much—every upheaval in history had seemed dubious before it actually happened. If the Stuart did have some hopes, might he not attempt to show the king's madness in a thousand different ways before positing that it was an inherited condition, and the British people might look forward to many more mad kings?

The man was reported to be in Russia; could the Tsar have initiated some kind of plot? Alexander had only recently broken with Napoleon and lifted the blockade against the British—was that part of a grander plan? If it were, how else to depose the current royal line than claim they were not fit?

There had been whispers for years, since the very first bout of madness, that it might be inherited. Stuart would be in his late twenties by now. If one planned to stage a coup, this would be the time to do it.

Jasper did not know if that was the scheme, but it would be helpful if the regent would present himself as a stable and judicious man, rather than acting the indulgent fool.

Still, could Miss Wilcox really be involved in any of it? Or was he allowing his imagination to run away from him?

He supposed the one thing he had learned this past year was to trust his instincts and that things were often not what they seemed.

He would have to find out more about Miss Georgiana Wilcox.

CHAPTER FOUR

As JASPER SAT in the library debating how exactly he would find out more about the lady, Perry brought in a coffee tray and set it down on the table.

Behind the butler, a loud cacophony suddenly erupted from the drawing room. It seemed as if it might be the pianoforte, but not as he had ever heard it before. Had a housemaid fallen on it? But then why did it go on as it did? Why did it not stop?

Perry swung around and stared at the open door. He hurried toward it and closed it.

"What is that racket?" Jasper asked.

"It is Miss Wilcox," Perry said. "She must be unaware that you are home."

"Miss Wilcox? But what can she be doing?" Jasper asked. It sounded as if the lady was having a boxing match with the instrument.

"Practicing, my lord," Perry said, with a keen look of disdain. "*That* is how she plays. Lady Mendleton suggested she practice when nobody is about. Shall I tell her to cease?"

"No," Jasper said, "do not bother. I am on my way out soon enough."

Perry nodded and left, closing the door firmly behind him. As Jasper drank his coffee and attempted to ignore Miss Wilcox's dreadful dissonance, he wondered what sort of young lady came at an instrument with so little skill. She seemed to know an awful lot about horses and not a thing about a pianoforte. Whatever she was, she was not the usual lady come to Town for her first season.

Though, despite her lack of musical skill she would be a hit, he was sure. Nobody who viewed that lovely face would fail to feel the allurement of it.

Was that part of the game, then? It was not unknown that a courtesan might be in the employ of secret sponsors. A man's downfall over a pretty face was a tale as old as time. It was known widely that he often visited the queen, how much easier to slip a spy into this house then the palace. But the daughter of a baron? That would certainly put a new spin on it.

On the other hand, if somebody were looking for an easy mark, they might not look further than his mother. She was enthusiastic, and very kind. But she was dreadfully naïve.

If there were such a scheme, would not Miss Wilcox be the perfect lady to send into it? She was remarkably pretty and had a very charming way about her. There was nothing simpering in her manner, and she did not fish for compliments. He'd found he quite liked looking at her face and listening to her voice over dinner, and he had been sorry when it had ended.

On the other hand, while another lady dining with him might have concerned herself with gathering praises, *she* had been inquisitive about his work for the queen. *She* had failed to mention encountering the mad king.

He straightened his papers and stood up. He did not have enough information and he did not have the time to come to any conclusions this instant. He needed to see the queen and explain how the story of the king and the buried carriage had ended up in the newspapers, possibly through his own household.

GEORGIANA MIGHT NOT have been so nervous to be presented to

Lady Mendleton's society of ladies, had the lady been at all calm herself. She was just now pacing the drawing room like a trapped tiger.

"Perhaps you might tell me something of the ladies before they arrive," Georgiana said, hoping to distract her hostess. "What are they like?"

"Oh yes, well, let's see," Lady Mendleton said, "Lady Featherstone is rather practical I often think, but not as…strident about it as are some others. Lady Easton is a dear, really, as long as things end up done properly. Her house runs like a clock! Lady Redfield is a bit of a marshmallow, which I find very charming. She's always very agreeable."

Lady Mendleton fell to silence and began pacing again.

Georgiana was aware that there were five ladies coming, though she had only heard described three. "And the last two ladies?" she asked.

Louisa froze mid-pace. "The last two?" she said, her voice sounding as if it had gone an octave higher.

"Yes," Georgiana said, beginning to be alarmed by Lady Mendleton's alarm.

Lady Mendleton collapsed into a chair and said, "It's just that Penelope, Lady Heathway, well, she can be frightening if one listens closely to what she is saying—rather like a general directing troops. And then of course Theodosia…well, she is a duchess, and you know what they can be like."

Having never met anybody so elevated, Georgiana had not the first idea of what a duchess could be like. She waited for Lady Mendleton to elaborate.

"Rather imperious sometimes," Lady Mendleton said. "Though I do so admire her confidence!"

The clatter of a carriage coming to a stop interrupted Lady Mendleton's rather concerning descriptions of her friends. The lady ran to the window and peeked out.

"Good Lord, it's her. Why is she never late?"

By *her*, Georgiana supposed it was either the duchess or Lady

Heathway, as those two ladies seemed to unnerve Lady Mendleton the most. She leapt up from her own chair, now filled with trepidation.

Two footmen, seeming to have been waiting for the moment, swept in and laid the tea. A minute later, Perry led in the recently arrived guest.

"My dear friend," Lady Mendleton said, grasping the lady's hands. "Here she is, here is Miss Wilcox."

As Georgiana swept down into a low curtsy, she realized that she had not the first idea if this was Lady Heathway or the Duchess of Stanbury. What was she to say? Your Grace or Lady Heathway?

She decided that if she were to go wrong, it had best be in naming a lady a duchess who wasn't, rather than insulting a duchess who was.

"Your Grace," she said.

By all appearances, she had guessed right. Nobody commented on her address. Rather, the duchess circled her and eyed her in a critical manner. Georgiana began to feel as if she were a horse being examined at Tattersall's.

"Good height, regular features, clear skin, rosy cheeks, not plump but not too thin, you know I cannot abide a girl who eats too much or too little, very fine head of hair and plenty of it. Perfectly acceptable, Louisa."

Lady Mendleton clapped her hands. "Did I not say she would be perfect?"

"Of course you did, what else would you say? I will presume the girl is accomplished?"

Though Georgiana had felt it uncomfortable to be spoken of as if she had no ears, she found herself rather grateful to be left out of the current conversation. She stared at Lady Mendleton to see what she would say of Miss Wilcox's rather thin accomplishments.

"Accomplished? Oh, naturally," Lady Mendleton said in a hurried voice. "Most particularly, she is an exceedingly talented horsewoman. Quite renowned in her home county. We plan on parading her through the park in the most charming new riding habit you can imagine."

"Ah, excellent plan," the duchess said. "What young gentleman fails to admire a lady who's got a good seat? I am quite certain the duke took notice of *me* on a certain similar outing."

"So you have often said," Lady Mendleton said. "I knew you would understand the charm of the scheme."

"Now, the park is all very well, but I have a scheme of my own. I am to have a musical evening on Tuesday next which will be simply ideal in showcasing the girl."

"A musical evening?" Lady Mendleton said, sinking down into a chair.

"My dear Miss Wilcox," the duchess said, "do me the honor of sampling your talents while we wait for the other ladies to arrive. I insist on being the first to hear, as I do think my rank entitles me to it."

"Oh, I..." Georgiana said, trailing off.

"Do not be modest!" the duchess said.

"It is not modesty, truly," Georgiana said.

"To the pianoforte this instant," the duchess said in the imperious manner that Lady Mendleton had previously mentioned. "Another of the ladies may arrive at any moment and I *will* be first."

Georgiana slowly made her way to the instrument. Exceedingly slowly, as if her feet were sunk in mud.

"Hop, hop, Miss Wilcox!" the duchess said, clapping her hands energetically.

There was no getting round it. Georgiana sat down at the pianoforte and stared at the keys. Certainly, her diligent practicing must have helped. She was likely feeling nervous over nothing. She might not ever be acclaimed for her playing, but she at least would not shock, as she had on her first try in front of Lady Mendleton.

She chose a lively Irish tune that she thought suited whatever little skill she had. While the slower tunes allowed more time to move between keys, the faster airs were less likely to highlight any misplaced fingers on the wrong keys. As she was in the habit of misplacing fingers whether fast or slow, she thought speed more likely to cover her mistakes.

Georgiana gained confidence as she played and found herself rather relieved to near the end of it. That was, until she noted Perry out of the corner of her eye.

The butler was just coming in with a tray of cakes and biscuits. His brows were knit together as one, he had gone slack-jawed, and his eyes held the sort of dread one might see in a rabbit caught in a field with a hawk circling overhead.

She stopped playing and slowly turned round to the ladies.

Lady Mendleton lay back on the sofa, fanning herself vigorously. The duchess gripped the edge of her chair and her cheeks puffed in and out like a bellows.

Certainly, she could not have been that bad?

Goodness, she *must* have been that bad. She had not ever thought her playing would pose a physical risk of harm to anyone, but the two ladies were indeed laid low.

"Miss Wilcox," the duchess said, nearly gasping, "do not ever do that in public again. Not even under threat of death."

Georgiana bowed her head. "I know it's dreadful. I have been practicing and I had hoped—"

"Hope no more in that direction," the duchess said, taking a deep breath and seeming to regain some of her composure. "I do not suppose you favor another instrument? Harp? Lute?"

"She does not even sing," Lady Mendleton said sadly, waving her fan slowly over her cheeks.

The duchess tsk-tsked and said, "Very strange."

The sound of carriage wheels stopping from out of doors caused Lady Mendleton to drop her fan and fly to the window. "Oh God," she whispered, "it's Penelope! What will *she* say?"

The duchess drew herself up and said, "Lady Heathway will say nothing at all. This unfortunate circumstance is to be kept strictly under wraps! *I* said we would not have a disaster on our hands, and I will not give Penelope a reason to crow over me—my rank as a duchess and my noble feelings recoil from the very idea."

The duchess turned and faced Georgiana. "If she or anybody else asks you to play, Miss Wilcox, you are to claim a sore finger. Sprained, badly. Now, as to my musical evening, thank heavens I've not sent the invitations out, as that is most definitely *off*. Nothing remotely musical has been heard in this room."

Georgiana should have been abashed at finding herself the cause of the duchess calling off her musical evening, but she was far more relieved than anything else. It was well that her abominable playing had been caught out now, rather than in the duchess' drawing room in front of dozens of people. As it was, it seemed it would remain a closely guarded secret between the three of them.

LADY HEATHWAY WAS, as Lady Mendleton had explained, rather like a general. She'd attempted to grill Georgiana on her accomplishments as if she were a soldier in the ranks, though thanks to the duchess she did not get very far. Lady Heathway was even more determined to inquire into Georgiana's mother and father and Manley Hall in general. Georgiana was suitably vague, as she did not think Lady Heathway would spend more than two minutes in conference with Lady Manley, nor would she likely see the charms of Manley Hall, crumbling as it was.

Lady Easton's interests seemed to lay more in the direction of Lord Langley being in residence and wondering if that was quite the thing. Though none of the ladies said so, it was clear enough that great things were expected from Lord Langley and that Georgiana was not one of the great things. Who *was* one of the great things, apparently, was Lady Annabelle Rumsford, daughter of a marquess.

It seemed Lady Mendleton was quite settled on the lady as the perfect choice for her son, if only he would get on with it. All the ladies approved of Lady Annabelle and there was much talk about her lovely flaxen hair and her pretty manner. Lady Annabelle, if these women could be relied upon, was perfect in every way—she played beautifully, she was said to have a particularly fine hand at landscape drawing, and she had that certain way about her that spoke of fine breeding.

While the ladies waxed on about Lady Annabelle, Georgiana could not help but be both grateful to get a reprieve from being the focus of their attentions, and a little irritated by this paragon.

Lady Annabelle, indeed.

What was so wonderful about flaxen hair? Was flaxen even a color, or just a farmer's crop? Did not Georgiana herself have a pretty manner? At least, when she was not being overly direct she must have. And why should anybody draw landscapes when one could drive out to the countryside and simply gaze at them with their own eyes? As for fine breeding, that was all well and good for a horse…

She paused her silent attack on Lady Annabelle. She had never even met the woman and should not have the slightest enmity toward her.

Still, the lady sounded a weak cup of tea for Jasper Stapleton. He was, well, he was very interesting! She had thought quite a lot about the dinner the evening before. There had been times when he'd looked at her across the table as if there was nobody else in the room. It had sent a flutter in her stomach that she very much enjoyed.

Georgiana quietly sighed. She supposed Lord Langley sent flutters through quite a few ladies. She supposed Lady Annabelle fluttered. Or perhaps not, as Lady Annabelle sounded insufferable, and it would be just like her not to flutter.

"Well," Lady Heathway said, rising, "we will see how we get on tomorrow evening. Lord Ryland's ball will tell the tale of this venture."

"I am certain Georgiana's card will be filled instantly," Lady Mendleton said.

"That would be a happy circumstance, would it not?" Lady Redfield said.

Georgiana sat calmly with a pleasant expression. In truth, she was not at all calm. Of course, she had known she would be taken to balls. Thanks to Lady Mendleton, she had a wardrobe full of gowns suitable for a ballroom. She had just not known it would be so soon. Tomorrow evening!

She wondered if Lord Langley would attend. And if he did, would he put his name down on her card? Perhaps the astonishing Lady Annabelle would be too taken up with playing the pianoforte beautifully and drawing landscapes to have it on her own calendar.

"Will he have one of those funny dinners, though?" Lady Redfield said, a note of concern creeping into her voice. "I never do feel clever enough for it."

"I am certain he will," the duchess said. "Why do I think so? Because he always does."

Georgiana did not know what was meant by a *funny dinner,* but she supposed she was to be served some sort of exotic fare. She was not at all sure she would like it, though she *was* sure she would pretend to. She also thought poor Lady Redfield need not fear being clever enough for it—when one was served something ghastly, which was not unknown at Manley Hall, one simply moved it around in circles and cut it into ever smaller pieces and then ate biscuits in one's room later.

JASPER STOOD IN the hall waiting for the others to come down so they might set off for Lord Ryland's annual ball.

He had been to see the queen and relayed the unwelcome news that the most current report of the king's madness had possibly emanated from his own household. He had, of course, mentioned that it was also possible that it had not. While it was true that his own carriage had encountered the king during his unfortunate ramblings, there might have been somebody else about who he'd encountered beforehand. The king had been missing for three quarters of an hour, giving ample time for that to occur. Then, there was the further speculation that people working for the newspapers haunted the environs of Kew in hopes of gaining a glimpse of the king. It was not out of the realm of possibility that one of these fellows had been lurking at the right place and time. And of course, the king might have told the same story about burying a carriage to anyone he encountered. These days, when he got an idea into his head it tended to stay there until another idea arrived to push it out.

Queen Charlotte had been gracious in considering that his household ought not to be condemned on such thin evidence. She had been adamant on one point, though. The newspaper's report reeked of a woman's eye. There had been too much detail paid to the king's personal appearance, his mussed hair and his unbuckled waistcoat, for it to have been a man. Even the color of his hair had been noted.

Jasper did not know if the queen was right in her assessment or not. After all, *he* was a man and took a deal of care with his own appearance and noticed when others did not. Or even if they achieved something superior to his own dress. Had he not eyed Wainright's neckcloth quite closely just the other day at Brooks's, and wondered how he might force that gentleman's valet to educate his own?

Still, the queen's insistence that there was a woman's hand in it had chilled him. He at once thought it was impossible that a charming lady like Miss Wilcox could be the culprit, and that all signs pointed toward her.

Ryland's ball was this evening and his mother had pressed him to come and help squire Miss Wilcox. He had not really needed to be pressed, though his feelings on the matter were grossly conflicted. On the one hand, it would be very pleasant to squire Miss Wilcox. On the other hand, was he squiring some sort of spy or informer?

As it was Ryland's ball, there was sure to be some kind of murder mystery to solve over dinner. Lord Ryland was a rather renowned criminologist who enjoyed studying grisly murders, audacious robberies, and highly skilled forgery schemes. He'd even put together a club of sorts, *The Society for Advancing Criminal Knowledge*, that met weekly during the season. It was attended by both keen criminologists like Ryland himself and those who merely enjoyed the titillation of horror-filled reports. Lady Featherstone was of the second type and was forever regaling his mother with some blood-soaked story that gave the lady nightmares.

Jasper had sometimes wondered if he ought to bring Ryland into the investigation of who was giving information to the newspapers, but the queen had insisted that nobody else be made aware that they were looking into the matter. Queen Charlotte was a wise woman who often said something that struck him as a truth all could see once it was pointed out. At that particular suggestion, she'd said, "A secret known by two is a quiet sparrow on a leafed branch, a secret known by more is a parrot screeching to get out of its cage."

Tonight, Ryland's penchant for murder and mayhem might be an opportunity in disguise. If Jasper were to take Miss Wilcox into dinner, he could examine how she approached the inevitable mystery that would be thrust upon them. Perhaps he might glean how clever she was, or how criminal-minded she was. The usual young lady at these annual affairs read through the description of the murder and then fanned herself, squealed about how dreadful it was, claimed she had no knowledge of the sort of low neighborhoods where a murder might occur, and vowed she would never sleep again. What she never seemed to do was solve it. Perhaps Miss Wilcox might give away that she was not so innocent.

Or, perhaps he wished to take her into dinner because she was very nice to look at.

He was so rarely of two minds over anything! It was really very irritating.

"Oh my dear," his mother said, coming down the stairs, "you do look well turned out, as always."

"That brocade suits you, Mother," Jasper said. He was not certain it was true, but recently the lady had become enamored of the sort of heavy fabrics he might himself favor as curtains. He suspected she was influenced by the Duchess of Stanbury, to whom every female of a certain age would follow despite her questionable taste. He would never say it, but it had resulted in flocks of middle-aged ladies appearing as waddling and well-padded furniture.

"Your father has managed to wiggle out again," Lady Mendleton said, smoothing the brocade of her skirt. "He claims his gout has flared, though I know perfectly well he does not have the gout. He cannot even decide which foot—last time it was the right, now it is the left. He shall be down in the library with a brandy as soon as we leave the house. Though, I will not harass him over it, as he has been very agreeable about Miss Wilcox."

Jasper smiled. He knew as well as his mother did that wily Lord Mendleton did not have gout. In fact, during one of his fatherly talks with his son he had laid out how when one reached a certain age, one might excuse oneself from almost anything by claiming a gouty foot. Lord Mendleton, if he understood his father at all, was a gentleman keen on having his way when he could manage it, though very much not keen on having any sort of battle over it.

His attention was called to a movement at the top of the stairs. Miss Wilcox descended, carefully picking up the hem of her gown as she did. She wore a blue silk gown, the color reminding him of the sea at Dover. It was embellished with darker blue rosettes at the hem and the sleeve, and the neckline was graced by a simple sapphire necklace chained in silver. Her color was high and her glorious dark hair artfully composed in soft curls, complimenting her delicate features.

My God, she was smashing.

Though he silently warned himself not to be so easily taken in by a pretty picture, he *was* fairly taken in.

"Goodness," Lady Mendleton said, "you take my breath away, Georgiana. You are simply lovely."

"Miss Wilcox," Jasper said, "charming."

The lady's color rose somewhat higher and she said, "If there is any real compliment to be given, it is in your generosity in dressing me so."

Jasper watched his mother nearly swoon over the sentiment. It was prettily expressed and yet might it not also be exceedingly clever? Lady Mendleton had ever had a soft spot for any being that was grateful to her, as evidenced by the strays both canine and human that she was forever collecting. A clever interloper would have picked up on that quality in less than a day.

"We should set off," he said.

Perry, who seemed to be always lurking nearby and on hand when he was needed, opened the front doors. The carriage was waiting—the footmen stood by ready to help the ladies in, two grooms were poised to leap on the running boards, and Carstares held the leads with his dependable scowl.

As the carriage made its way the short distance to Berkeley Square, Jasper waited for some moment when Lady Mendleton might pause in her speech. His dear mother had been rattling on ever since the door closed.

Finally, she did pause, and he leapt into the momentary silence.

"Miss Wilcox," Jasper said, "this will all be new to you as you have so far been introduced only to my mother's friends. I think I ought to take you in to supper for this first outing. As a practical matter."

Miss Wilcox had only nodded, though he thought she seemed not ill-pleased with the idea.

Lady Mendleton clapped her hands. "What a capital notion, my darling. You know absolutely everybody and can explain to

Georgiana who is who, and who is the right sort of gentleman and who is…perhaps not."

Though that was not Jasper's intent in squiring Miss Wilcox to supper, he understood his mother perfectly well. There would be some she would not approve of, for varying reasons. Skeffington was rumored to have a mistress he was none too discreet about. Clamarin was a member of Ryland's criminal society and was sure to attend. Though he was a large landowner from somewhere in the north, Lady Mendleton distinctly disliked him, though she could not say why. There would be others that his mother would feel not precisely up to snuff. Though she liked Harry Vance exceedingly and he was to inherit a barony, she could not entirely get over the idea that his grandfather had been in trade. Lady Mendleton would conveniently ignore the fact that Miss Wilcox was only the daughter of a baron who had married a lady from a family in trade.

Jasper paused, stealing a glance at Miss Wilcox. He thought it was not only his mother who would ignore Miss Wilcox's not-particularly lofty credentials.

With a face like that, a lady might start a war.

CHAPTER FIVE

G EORGIANA KNEW VERY well that she'd blushed violently when Lord Langley had suggested he take her into supper. Her complexion was both a blessing and a curse. With naturally rosy cheeks, she always appeared in perfect health. However, when she was taken off her guard, that rosiness could begin to look like a fever. She had high hopes that the darkness in the carriage had hidden her flush.

He had asked for her supper! She had all but convinced herself that Lord Langley would escort the much talked-of Lady Annabelle into supper.

She had been wrong! It was not Lady Annabelle who was to be taken in, it was herself. Of course, she understood it was only a courtesy. She was new to Town and this was her first ball—it was only natural that she would be guided properly.

Still, it would be very pleasant.

They had entered the house and been introduced to Lord Ryland. The gentleman was urbane and had what seemed to be a rather confident manner. What he did not seem like was a gentleman who would serve what Lady Redfield had worried would be a *funny dinner*. Georgiana could only wonder what would be offered, though she speculated that the gentleman had probably been to India and brought back some rare spices. That would be a deal better than the funny dinners that had been served at Manley Hall, which were usually gone funny because

Marta had made a mistake somewhere. Nobody in that house would soon forget the mustard in the custard incident—it had been an interesting Christmas dinner with Marta the worse for drink in the kitchens and each dish coming out more bizarre than the last.

Lord Langley had fetched her card and put his name down for supper, just as he'd said he would. Georgiana found a great amount of relief and satisfaction in that, as she had begun to fear that the lord might spot the flaxen-haired Lady Annabelle and forget all about his suggestion.

She scolded herself for being a ninny, and for spending as much time as she had already, silently insulting Lady Annabelle who had done no crime against her.

As they made their way into the crowded ballroom, they were fairly rushed at. A line began to form, as one gentleman after the next waited to be introduced and put his name down.

Georgiana was near-overwhelmed and glad their names *were* written down as she was sure she would not remember half of them. And also, exceedingly grateful that her card had filled. In the darkest hours of the night before, she had allowed herself to imagine what it would be if nobody asked. After all, who was she? Just another girl, in from the countryside. There would be other ladies there who would outshine her, they would be beautiful and have the further allurement of being the daughters of dukes and marquesses and earls and viscounts. She saw herself sitting at the edges of the ballroom, attempting to ignore the pitying glances of bystanders. Or worse, ignoring the disappointed looks from Lady Mendleton's friends regarding the failure of their latest project.

As it was, the duchess was nearby and looked on approvingly. Lady Heathway was across the room and seemed satisfied enough, though Georgiana was not certain she was ever entirely satisfied with anything. Lady Redfield caught her eye and smiled encouragingly, while Lady Featherstone and Lady Easton nodded in unison.

A younger lady near Georgiana's age approached and said,

"Lady Mendleton." She was petite and very fair, the sort Georgiana thought resembled drawings of forest fairies. The lady held her card out ever so lightly from her gown, as if at the ready should someone wish to grab hold of it.

"Lady Annabelle," Lady Mendleton said with real enthusiasm. "How well you look! How is your dear mother?"

Of course it was Lady Annabelle, and she *was* a divine little creature.

"My mother is very well," Lady Annabelle said to Lady Mendleton, "and already in the card room, I think." She lowered her eyes and then glanced up under her lashes. "Lord Langley."

Georgiana noticed the lady had edged her card in his direction. She supposed Lord Langley noticed too. He took it and said, "Lady Annabelle."

As Lord Langley glanced at her card, Lady Annabelle adopted a particularly coquettish tone. "Now you see the awful truth, Lord Langley—Lord George has taken my first. He swore he would take my first *and* supper too if he could be allowed. Naturally I scolded him and my supper remains free. The silly creature would go on about my eyes, though I am sure I do not know what he means by it."

Lord Langley put his name down and said, "Hopefully he means something complimentary by it."

Georgiana worked to suppress a giggle as she was quite convinced that Lady Annabelle had hoped Lord Langley would demand to know and attempt to top whatever compliment Lord George had invented.

Lady Mendleton appeared a bit flustered and said, "I have often heard my son mention your eyes, dear Lady Annabelle."

Lady Annabelle seemed somewhat mollified by this gambit, though Lord Langley only raised a brow at the idea.

As Lady Annabelle took her card back, she said softly, "Oh, I see, the second."

"Well now," Lady Mendleton said, "you are already taken for the first and Jasper is escorting Miss Wilcox to supper because she is my guest, really more than my guest, I am her sponsor and will act as mother to her while she is here, we have a society you see, and naturally, well, it is her first ball...in any case, Lady Annabelle, allow me to introduce you to Miss Georgiana Wilcox. I expect you will be great friends!"

The two ladies curtsied to one another, but despite Lady Annabelle's smile, Georgiana could almost feel the enmity coming from her. She was beginning to think it was not only Lady Mendleton who wished for a match, it seemed likely Lady Annabelle did too. There could not have been a heavier hint dropped that Lord Langley ought to take her into supper. She could not blame the lady, he was so very dashing.

As for Lord Langley, she could not guess what his feelings might be, though he did not seem particularly overcome by Lady Annabelle.

Georgiana was very satisfied to note it, though it was certainly none of her affair.

GEORGIANA HAD THOUGHT that a ball in London would be remarkably different from the assemblies at home. It was true that the surroundings were far richer, down to the carefully chalked mahogany floor and the superiority of the orchestra. The ladies' finery was a deal more costly and there were some who she was certain wore her father's yearly income on their dresses. However, when it came to dancing with a gentleman, it was much the same as it ever was.

Some gentlemen struggled to make conversation, some made too much conversation, some were confident, some only pretended they were. Some spoke of topics that might interest her and some spoke of a particular topic that interested *them*.

Lord Blackwood, the duchess' son, had just bought a horse and it seemed that no subject was to be more interesting than that creature. Lady Easton's nephew, Lord Bertridge, was friendly but on the stiff side and Georgiana thought he very much resembled his aunt in that regard.

Lord Gresham was exceedingly agreeable, but in his effort to find common ground he'd informed her that he was Lady Heathway's nephew. He did not seem at all like her, but Georgiana found herself guarded, lest she say anything that might be repeated to the lady and frowned upon.

Lord Asturt was recently come to Town, having spent some years in Ireland. He was polite enough, but his accent was strange and held hints of the continent. It mattered little what she thought, though, as he was far more interested in Lord Langley than her. He seemed to take a deal of pride in noting that he had referred Lord Langley's new valet to him and wished to know how the fellow got on. Georgiana was quite at a loss as to how she was to know how a valet got on.

Mr. Vance was rather a delight. He was exceedingly jolly and the son of a baron. Georgiana wondered if that was why he was so jolly—just like herself, he did not carry over-high expectations on his shoulders. She did think that he, or someone like him, would be suited to her. They were of the same rank and he seemed to admire country life. It was only a shame that there was no particular spark between them that hinted of more than friendship.

It was all very amusing. That was, until she danced with Lord Langley. While none of the previous gentlemen had at all discomposed her, Lord Langley did. She felt herself flustered, which was the silliest thing in the world.

Georgiana Wilcox did not fluster. She rather disdained ladies who did.

His hand was firm in guiding her and he had some sort of hard to define presence. A manly presence that made the other gentlemen seem younger. There was nothing at all unusual about their conversation, it centered on commonplaces such as the lord inquiring how she was enjoying her stay in Town. Yet, when he looked at her, that was when she became flustered.

She began to see that she must be more careful around him. She wondered how she did not see it before. What else had all that silent condemnation of Lady Annabelle been about?

Though her father had not come out and said so, she must understand that she had a job to do while she was in Town. She was to get herself married to somebody suitable. It was her one chance, and another chance would not come again.

Lord Langley was not suitable. For one, he was the son of her sponsor and that dear lady had already chosen for him by way of Lady Annabelle. For another, she was certain *he* was not equally flustered. It would be the most idiotic thing in the world to have any hopes in that direction. It would be pointless, and she would not allow herself to be pointless. She had deemed him attractive the moment she'd laid eyes on him, but that shallow sentiment was where it must stay. Nothing more.

Her father had not had the means to launch her properly. From out of the blue, a heaven-sent opportunity had come her way. She must not be stupid about it.

"You seem pensive, Miss Wilcox," Lord Langley said as the dance ended.

"Do I?" Georgiana said. "I was only reminding myself not to be stupid."

Lord Langley laughed. "Are you in the habit of it?"

"Not usually," Georgiana said quietly.

"Well, you must gather your wits for the next bit of this evening, as you will need them."

It was an enigmatic thing to say, and Georgiana had no idea what he meant by it.

He held out his arm and led her toward the dining room.

Georgiana had expected the supper, *funny* as Lady Redfield had claimed it would be, to be much like other suppers at other dances she had attended. That was not the case.

First, Lord Ryland's dining room was of such dimensions as to make Georgiana certain that he'd knocked down some walls that would have originally been other rooms. It was cavernous and just as big as the ballroom. Then, rather than a long table, there were smaller, square tables to seat just four people scattered about the room. It was rather like an enormous and opulent common room at an inn.

It seemed they had also been assigned where they were to be seated, as dozens of footmen were on hand to take a name and lead one to their proper place. It was the oddest set-up imaginable, at least to Georgiana's eyes.

As soon as Lord Langley said his name, a bright-faced young footman led them to a table on the far side of the room. A table that also contained Lord Bertridge and...Lady Annabelle.

Neither Georgiana nor Lady Annabelle seemed particularly enthusiastic about the arrangement, though if anybody noticed it, it was not Lord Bertridge.

"Lady Annabelle," he said, "Miss Wilcox is sponsored by Lady Mendleton. You will have heard of The Society of Sponsoring Ladies? My aunt, Lady Easton is also a member. Very worthy cause."

Georgiana knew her rosy cheeks must be flaming to hear herself spoken of as a cause. Especially in front of Lady Annabelle.

"Indeed?" Lady Annabelle said. "I had not heard of the society."

"Oh yes," Lord Bertridge said, "disadvantaged girls and all that."

"Miss Wilcox's father, Baron Manley, is a cousin to my mother," Lord Langley said. "I am certain Miss Wilcox would have come to us regardless of any society the ladies have thrown together to amuse themselves."

Georgiana was grateful beyond measure at this rescue, and well aware that it hinted at a standing with the family that she certainly did not have. Her father was so distant a cousin to Lady Mendleton that he was not even sure of the connection—two grandmothers had been cousins, perhaps? She was further grateful that the conversation would not continue, as Lord Ryland stood at the top of the room and dinged his glass.

"Welcome, my esteemed guests," he said. "As my regulars are well aware, there is no getting out of this house without a mystery to solve. You will also know, there is always a unique prize given to the person who discovers the solution first. You will hear of it when and if you have won and I must say this year's reward is rather spectacular. Look under your plates and enjoy."

Georgiana had some trouble making sense of what Lord Ryland was attempting to get across, as she had been so sure the funny dinner that had discomposed Lady Redfield had involved food and not a mystery. As everybody else in the room was lifting their plates and removing a folded piece of paper, she did too. As she did so, she also noticed sticks of Barrowdale graphite, sharpened and wrapped with thin ribbon, laid by, she assumed for notetaking.

She was rather delighted with the scheme. Mrs. Arrowford of her own neighborhood had put on any number of mystery evenings. The lady spent months coming up with the clues and the solution always came together wonderfully at the end. So far, Georgiana had only been the first to solve a mystery once, but she had become accustomed to the way the thing was set up. Every statement had a meaning—either toward the solution or deliberately away from it.

Of course, Mrs. Arrowford did not attempt to do the thing at a dining table, so that certainly was an unusual aspect.

"Goodness," Lady Annabelle said, "I hope I am not overcome by this new report of a grisly circumstance. Last year, poor Lord Langley had to fetch a vinaigrette."

"You may depend upon me," Lord Bertridge said. "If it is needed, I will retrieve it at once. I believe Ryland keeps hartshorn handy by the doors for just such a circumstance."

Georgiana turned her attention to the paper, as she did not find Lady Annabelle's threatening to faint at all interesting.

The case of John Herbert

At 3 o'clock on the Sunday afternoon of August 12th 1810 in the neighborhood of St. Giles, John Herbert, 22, was found murdered by way of a stab wound to his back in his garret on the top floor of a rooming house. Other than the victim, nobody was discovered in the room and the door and only window were securely locked from the inside. Those were the only two ways into the room.

Herbert had only some months before been released from forced labor after being convicted of stealing hot buns from a shop. He had not been in any further trouble with the courts and was regular in leaving each afternoon for an apprenticeship of some sort. Little of his personal life is known, though he was said to have been seen at a tavern with tenant Janet King, and an argument a week prior had occurred between Herbert and tenant Merle Rider over noise.

On the day of the discovery, the landlady, Mrs. Alice Trembly, was informed by tenant Matthew Hillsbury that a red substance suspected to be blood was dripping through his rafters. Hillsbury lives directly below Herbert's garret. The constable was fetched soon after.

The list of tenants in the building were:

Occupying the garret: John Herbert.

Occupying the upper floor: Janet King, unknown age, heavy with child, no husband known of, claims John Herbert was a friend and appears distraught. Merle Rider, 34, butcher, with his wife Jemmy, 32, and two children under age 10. Rider is a burly man and known in the neighborhood as a hot temper when he drinks. Matthew Hillsbury, 29, hackney driver, bachelor, cleft lip, speaks with a lisp and is known to talk to horses more often than people.

Occupying the ground floor: Alice Trembly, 63, landlady, widow, rheumatism infirmity assisted by the use of a cane.

John Herbert was found slumped in a chair at a table facing the window. These various things were upon the table: a receipt for forward payment of rent for three months, a cheap silver-painted pendant of unknown origin with the initial J engraved, the key to the door, and a broken watch. The room was in disarray, there were three circular stains presumed to be dried blood on the floor, and a larger pool of blood beneath Herbert's chair that had subsequently leaked through the floorboards and into Hillsbury's room. No weapon was found.

When the constable arrived, he, with the assistance of Hillsbury, broke down the door, as no spare key was on hand. The landlady, upon leading them up to the garret, had explained that Herbert had taken the spare key a week ago, having lost his own, and had not yet made a copy.

Who killed John Herbert? How did they do it? And WHY did they do it?

Georgiana studied the facts as the white soup was brought round. It was unusual, awkward even, to attempt to eat soup while reading, but there it was.

"I am afraid this may well have been a crime of passion," Lord Bertridge said. "While *we* may not comprehend such things, I understand the lower classes are prone to fits of that unwelcome state. An unwed mother lives in the building? Her given name starts with a J and there is a pendant with a J engraved? I suspect he ruined her and made an attempt to buy her off with the pendant that was found on the table and she stabbed him in a fury. Do you see what I say?"

Whether Lady Annabelle understood what Lord Bertridge said, Georgiana could not guess. The lady was far too busy fanning herself and looking overcome while staring determinedly at Lord Langley to discover if he would notice.

"If it were Janet King and a fit of passion, as you speculate," Lord Langley said, "how did she do it?"

Lord Bertridge shrugged.

"I do not believe it to be her," Georgiana said. "It was noted that John Herbert was only released some months ago. Certainly, that would hint a shorter time than would be necessary for the lady to be heavily pregnant. And, if she were trying to hide her actions, she would not have claimed John Herbert as a friend. She would claim him only a distant acquaintance."

"Honestly," Lady Annabelle said, "while I enjoy Lord Ryland's balls exceedingly, I could do without this tawdry tale. I ought to visit the retiring room, I am sure my hair is a fright."

Lord Bertridge said something consoling about the lady's delicate sensibilities and her hair. Georgiana had no idea how a piece of paper would have done anything to the lady's hair but wished she *would* visit the retiring room. And stay there.

She went back to studying the facts.

"I suspect," Lord Langley said, "that the solution revolves around the missing key. John Herbert lost his key and had to take the spare. The murderer may have stolen the key and then used it to enter the room and then lock it again when he left."

Though Lord Langley's supposition had a deal more merit than Lord Bertridge's had, there was still something not quite right.

"John Herbert was sitting at his table facing the window," she said. "It was August, it would have been stifling hot in that garret and yet the window was closed. Surely, he had just entered the room. I think he was followed in and he was not worried about whoever it was."

"Janet King," Lord Bertridge said, as if this entirely proved his theory.

"But if so," Lord Langley said, "how does that person lock the door behind him when he left, if he did not have the key?"

"I'm not sure," Georgiana said, "though another thought occurs to me. How does an apprentice pay his rent for three months ahead of time?"

"He doesn't," Lord Langley said.

"And yet he did," Georgiana said.

Georgiana wondered if that were not the real crux of the matter. John Herbert had got a sizable amount of money from somewhere and at least one person would have known that he'd got it—the landlady.

But the landlady was infirm and used a cane. Further, she'd been well-paid, there was no reason she would wish to kill a tenant who paid ahead of time.

Unless he had something of far more value to take then three months' rent.

If that were so, might she have told somebody else of it? An accomplice? Or might she not be as infirm as she claimed? After all, she'd led the constable up all those stairs to the garret. And why did John Herbert have that pendant? It was described as cheap. Who was it for? Who was J? Was it for Janet King, after all? Or was it something entirely unrelated?

So often in these composed mysteries, there was something purposefully highlighted to lead one astray—could the pendant be that?

The soup had been cleared and footmen brought round platters. Georgiana nodded absent-mindedly at a platter of duck and Lord Langley placed some on her plate. She picked up one of the graphite sticks and began to circle each fact that might be a clue.

John Herbert had money that could not be explained. The landlady had been paid ahead of time. The window and door were locked. He had been sitting at his table, window shut and back toward the door. He'd lost his key. The pendant left on the table was engraved with a J.

She paused. The pendant was *cheap* and there was also a watch that was *broken*. Despite their worthlessness, they had come from somewhere. Somewhere most likely stolen, because what poor apprentice would waste his money on such things?

Might there not have been other more valuable things that had been stolen and those two valueless items left behind? Might that not account for John Herbert's mysterious funds? Had he been selling off goods he'd pilfered? He'd just been released for stealing, so he was likely not terribly opposed to the idea. Further, most apprenticeships began early in the morning, not the afternoon. Perhaps he was not an apprentice at all.

"I think the pendant and the broken watch were left behind because they were worthless," Georgiana said. "There would have been other more valuable things taken from the room, and that's where the money he could not have come by honestly originated from. He was robbing houses and somebody knew it."

Lady Annabelle and Lord Bertridge did not pay any mind to

her statement. Lord Bertridge had given up on the mystery, having convinced himself that it was Janet King, though he could not say how. Lady Annabelle was attempting all manner of gambits to attract Lord Langley's attention and had just flung her napkin at his feet though he had not noticed.

Lord Langley considered the idea that there had been things more valuable in the room. He said, "Possibly. But even if that was the case, we are still in the dark about who did it and how."

Georgiana went back to staring at the paper. And then, as if the clouds had parted to let in the sun, she saw the one thing her eyes had kept glossing over.

CHAPTER SIX

GEORGIANA CURSED HERSELF for not noticing it sooner. Tucked in among the other clues to Lord Ryland's mystery was the one that really mattered. It was the one bit of information that pointed in one direction, and one only. The round red spots of dried blood on the floor. Not a footprint, a round red spot.

"I think I know what happened," she said. "The missing key was never proved a fact, it was only what the landlady reported. *She* knew he had money and valuables as *she* had been paid."

"Do you suppose she told some younger accomplice to go get more, or hired somebody to do it? Then, the robbery somehow goes wrong and Herbert is killed," Lord Langley said, leaning forward over his own copy of the mystery.

"No, I think she did it herself," Georgiana said.

Lord Langley's brow creased. "An older and infirm lady?"

"How infirm, though?" Georgiana asked. "She led the constable up to the garret so she *was* able to get herself there. I do not believe she was as infirm as she made out."

"Possibly," Lord Langley said, though he looked dubious over the idea.

"He was followed in," Georgiana said, her ideas forming themselves as she spoke. "He was not worried, he would have had his back to whoever was in the room. He sat defenseless, probably paying out her extra rent, as she'd already written the receipt and brought it with her. She stabs him in the back with a dagger or sword hidden in her cane, pushes it back in to its case, searches the room for the jewelry he'd stolen, leaves the receipt as well as the two pieces of no value, and locks the door behind her with the spare key she had all along. She makes sure to leave the receipt, as who suspects an infirm landlady who has been paid? The only thing she didn't consider in her hurry was that the bottom of her cane had left three red circles of blood on the floor. You see? She did not clean the blade before she replaced it and it dripped out of the bottom."

"Good God, that is at least plausible," Lord Langley said. "Write it out and submit it, Miss Wilcox."

Amidst heavy sighs from Lady Annabelle, Georgiana did as she was bid and wrote out the sequence of events she speculated on the blank back side of the paper. When she was done, Lord Langley added her name to it, folded it, and held it up for a footman to take to Lord Ryland.

Georgiana doubted she'd have been the first to unravel the mystery as once she'd thought about the round red circles it seemed the most obvious thing in the world. They had been mentioned for a reason and they could have come from nothing but a cane tip. Still, she was very satisfied with herself and found her appetite back.

Somehow, while she'd been pondering the mystery, Lord Langley had filled her plate with all manner of things—thin slices of lamb, duck and ham, pickled asparagus, a tartlet of some sort, and a rather large helping of broiled fish.

Before she could get very far with it, Lord Ryland once again dinged his glass. "For those of you who are fed up with my mysteries," he said, "you will be relieved to know it has been solved. I will pin it up on the board just outside this door, but for your edification—the elderly landlady was the culprit. It was discovered that she had a dagger concealed in her cane that was found to be the murder weapon, she was in receipt of jewelry she could not account for, several of the pieces were engraved with a J just as the pendant that had been left behind, and she had the spare key to the garret door hidden in her rooms. John Herbert had stolen a respectable cache of jewelry, the nosy old gal knew it and was not as infirm as she looked. She'll hang in a month. Miss Wilcox is to be congratulated."

There was a polite applause heard round the room, though no such accolade came from Lady Annabelle who looked rather put out.

Lord Bertridge only said, "I am surprised it was not Janet King, I was quite convinced of it."

Lord Ryland approached the table and Georgiana was beginning to wish she'd not put so much effort into the matter. She rather felt like she was becoming a spectacle and doubted very much whether Lady Mendleton or the other ladies would like it.

"Miss Wilcox," he said, bowing. "Our good Queen Charlotte has shown some little amount of appreciation for my efforts to subdue the criminal element in this Town and graciously offered herself as this year's prize. You are to have tea with the great lady on Wednesday next. You may bring one guest with you."

As Lord Ryland strode off, Georgiana said, "Tea? With Queen Charlotte?"

"Quite the honor," Lord Bertridge said, looking a bit crestfallen that he'd not worked harder at it or bothered to submit his rather thin theory, though it was wrong.

Lady Annabelle only sniffed.

Lord Langley at first seemed pleased, but then suddenly his expression darkened.

"Is there something wrong in it, Lord Langley?" Georgiana asked.

"Wrong? No, not at all," Lord Langley said. His expression cleared just as fast as it had clouded.

"Now I suppose we may return to the more usual subjects of a supper?" Lady Annabelle asked peevishly.

AFTER THE MYSTERY was solved, the supper had seemed to drag on for Georgiana. Whatever subject was raised, Lady Annabelle somehow managed to steer it in her own direction. She was like a fisherman on the banks of the Thames, casting her line to reel in compliments.

A comment on how pleasant Hyde Park was in the afternoons made a sharp turn to Lady Annabelle's new riding habit, which was a very dark green. The lady was sure it would not compliment her complexion. Lord Bertridge claimed that it would, though Lord Langley only looked as if he wondered why she'd had it made in that color in the first place.

Lord Bertridge, who apparently was a keen reader, spoke of a new author he quite admired, a young man going only by PBS but who was discovered to be named Percy Shelley and currently studying at university. Lady Annabelle wondered if reading made her eyes squinty and claimed she must look frightful at the pastime.

Lord Bertridge, rather indefatigable in the face of these fishing expeditions, claimed her eyes could never look squinty, they simply wouldn't dare. Lord Langley, on the other hand, seemed out of patience with the sport and only said, "You might try better light."

Georgiana had not added much to the conversation, not yet having been to Hyde Park, not worried about the color of her own riding habit, not having read *Zastrozzi* by young Percy Shelley, and not having ever thought of squinty eyes.

She was not sorry to be so quiet, she thought she had put herself forward quite enough for one evening. As well, it gave her ample opportunity to observe Lord Langley, which was developing into a very enjoyable pastime. Though she could not look for anything serious there, it was pleasant to be seated close by and examine his rather wonderful hands and listen to the deep timbre of his voice and note the varying shades of his dusky hair in the candlelight.

WHEN THEY HAD departed, Lady Mendleton fussed with her cloak and her fan in the carriage and then said, "You know my dear, it's all well and good to be clever. But I do think triumphing at Lord Ryland's mystery may have been a bit...conspicuous. And of course, Lady Featherstone was a bit let down, she does try so hard at these things though she never seems to succeed. Well, there's nothing to be done about it, I only say for future..."

Georgiana had been afraid the lady might feel something like that, as she'd felt rather conspicuous herself. As for Lady Featherstone, Georgiana would not have had the first idea that the lady was keen on murder mysteries. She was rather sorry she did not know it, as she would have been happy to step aside and not have put so much thought into it.

"The prize," Lord Langley said, "is tea with Queen Charlotte. Miss Wilcox may bring a guest."

Lady Mendleton dropped her fan on the carriage floor. As her son retrieved it for her, she said, "Tea? The queen? Well, my goodness, that does put things in a different light!"

"I thought it might," Lord Langley said drily.

JASPER POURED HIMSELF a brandy and paced his bedchamber, having waved off Marcus for the night. Though it was near three, he doubted he would get much sleep.

He'd had the vague idea that it would be informative to view how Miss Wilcox approached Lord Ryland's mystery. Well, now he'd seen. He'd wondered if she would carry on like so many ladies before her, fanning herself and pretending at shock. She'd not appeared shocked at all, not at the mention of murder or a young woman heavy with child but with no husband.

She had not been shocked, but she *had* been exceedingly clever. He had watched her, head bent over the clues and circling them, a loose dark curl falling over her shoulder. He'd had both the urge to touch the curl but also ask her if she'd spoken to the newspapers. He'd both wished to lean toward her to pick up her scent but interrogate her on her purpose in his mother's house.

Could it be true, though? Could this alluring lady have been sent in to gather information about the king and his infirmities to relay to the newspapers? If it was, how was she supposed to do it? The encounter with the king on the road was pure happenstance. If she was sent here to gather information, how was she to go about it?

Pry information from himself, he supposed. There was every possibility that whoever the villains were, they knew or suspected that he was tasked with protecting the king's privacy. If there were spies about, and he was certain there were, they could not have missed his numerous visits to both Kew Palace and the queen at Buckingham.

Now Miss Wilcox was to have tea with the queen. Was that a lucky accident or had she somehow been tipped off beforehand that it would be Ryland's prize? She certainly had made every effort to win the prize, not at all like Lady Annabelle, who had no more insightfulness than a fish.

Jasper threw himself into a chair by the window. He very much wished Miss Wilcox was just another lady he met at a ball.

What if she had been? What if he'd turned up at Ryland's ball this evening and spotted her across the room?

He would have made straight for her and been delighted by her rather forthright manner. He would have wondered at a lady so beautiful that seemed to have not a care for her looks. He would have taken her into supper and marveled at her cleverness.

He might have...he might have pursued her. Despite his rather constant claim that he was too busy to think of marriage, he'd always known that if he saw *the* lady, he would not tarry. The seasons were filled with simpering females. Simpering, coquettish, short, and irritating. If one were lucky enough to happen upon quite a different sort of lady, one should not drag one's heels. There would be plenty of other fellows who wouldn't. While he could do little to imagine life as a female, he certainly understood they had a horror of being put on a shelf.

That horror caused decisions to be made with alacrity. Only last year, Miss Bernes had accepted Lord Gregory, to the woe of Lord James who'd taken his time. Too much time, as it turned out. No, if a gentleman had interest, he ought not twiddle his thumbs.

Good God. He could not allow himself to think of Miss Wilcox in that manner. He did not know what she was. Not yet, anyway.

He must somehow tell the queen of his suspicions to put her on her guard. Yet, he must be careful not to entirely condemn Miss Wilcox. He might be wrong.

As he thought of dancing with her, her light feet and graceful movements, her pretty face looking up at him, the surprising heat of her hand through her glove, he *hoped* he was wrong.

AS SHE CROSSED the garden with Jenny, Georgiana had decided to put all thought of Lord Ryland's ball from her head, as she had a far more important thing to think of. Lady Mendleton was determined to take her to Hyde Park to promenade and she had yet to even examine a sidesaddle closely. She had seen no end of ladies on them, but of course their skirts covered up the mechanics of the thing. She had a general idea that one of their legs wrapped round a large pommel, which seemed simple enough, but she had to be sure.

Her decision to stop thinking of the ball was not particularly successful, as there was the difficulty of not thinking about her time with Lord Langley. He was so handsome and full of sense and subtly urbane. He was manly, in a certain way that she had not encountered before. It was not blustery or forceful, it was as if he were confident of himself without having to shout it from the rooftops.

There was no doubt in her mind that whatever Lady Mendleton's hopes might be, Lord Langley was not enamored of Lady

Annabelle. Of course, that did not mean much. She was certain there must be a lady who *had* caught his eye. Lord Langley was a viscount and would eventually become an earl. The lady he would wed would be the daughter of some highly placed lord, perhaps the daughter of a duke, who could graciously step into the role of countess.

Georgiana supposed she had enjoyed a certain standing in her own little neighborhood as being the daughter of the local baron. But here! Here, she was only the daughter of some rustic lord, low on the ladder, and not something to look twice at. Worse, Lord Bertridge had referred to her as a *cause*.

She must stop thinking about Lord Langley! Or *Jasper*, as she sometimes thought of him.

She had managed to convince Lady Mendleton that it was imperative for her to meet her horse well ahead of mounting her. Georgiana claimed it was a notion strictly enforced by her father. Lady Mendleton had thought the idea eccentric, but had finally agreed to it.

Fortunately, it was no hard task to arrange. The mews sat directly behind the house with a small pass-through gate at the back of the garden. Jenny was just now escorting her to the stables and she went at a brisk pace as if she were no stranger to the trip. Carstares would be on hand there to show her her horse, as when the family stayed in Town, the fellow was both coachman and stablemaster. Of course, she would be delighted to have a look at Minerva, but what she *really* wished to see was her saddle.

"Here we are," Jenny said as they reached the gate. She unlocked the latch and they went through to a narrow alley that led to the front of the building.

Lord Mendleton's stables were commodious, and exceedingly clean. It had the subtle smell of hay and horse, but it was clear enough that the stalls were cleaned out regular and thorough. Georgiana thought that, for all Carstares' grumpiness, he ran what her father would call a neat-kept cupboard.

He tipped his cap and showed her the way to the stall.

Minerva was a large chestnut and Georgiana could see instantly that she was indeed as spirited as Lord Mendleton had claimed. One need not ride a horse to get such a clue—Minerva was nosy, peering out of her stall as they approached, she shook her head, snorted, and her eyes were wide and bright. Short of kicking the stall door, this horse spoke of energy and excitement.

"Mr. Perry said you was to meet the horse?" Carstares said, his dubiousness all too evident.

"Indeed," Georgiana said, rubbing Minerva's nose. "And if you would not mind, may I see the saddle you will employ?"

Carstares appeared even more dubious over *that* request, but he waved to a groom to fetch it.

Georgiana had brought an apple with her, knowing full well that there were two ways into a horse's heart—favored treats and a competent rider. As she did not know if she would fulfill the second criteria, she thought she ought to come prepared with the first.

The boy brought the sidesaddle forward and placed it on a nearby sawhorse while Georgiana examined it. As she looked at all its parts, having a general idea of how she was to seat herself on it, Carstares said, "Do somethin' seem unusual about it?"

"Not unusual precisely," Georgiana said. "It differs somewhat from what I'm used to, so of course if there were any tips? Any particular thing to ensure I kept my seat?"

"Now that gives me the shivers," Jenny said, "even thinking about falling down that great height. I wouldn't like to try it myself."

"What's different about it?" Carstares said, staring at the saddle as if the difference would spring at him.

"Not so much different as...not exactly the same."

A light seemed to come on in Carstares' eyes. "Is you in the habit of ridin' astride, then? My sister does favor it, though she's in a lonely corner of Cornwall and nobody blinks over it."

"Oh, does she?" Georgiana said, wondering how much she

ought to admit to Carstares. "Well, from time to time I might…"

"I see," Carstares said. "Well here it is—your knee goes round there," he said, pointing at the pommel. "Lean back a bit more than you're used to, use a cane like you would your right leg to direct your horse—lightly—Minerva knows what she's doing. That's about it, I think, though I never tried it myself."

"Oh yes, precisely as I do at home," Georgiana said, trying to imagine using the cane instead of her right leg. Of course she had seen ladies holding such an instrument but she'd paid so little attention to it that she supposed she'd assumed it was a decoration of some sort. It would take all her concentration—she hardly thought about what she was doing when she rode astride, she just did it. Now, her right leg was to be decommissioned.

Georgiana thanked Carstares and patted Minerva before leaving with Jenny. On the way through the back garden, she said, "Jenny, I do not suppose there would be any cause to mention the details of my trip to the stables?"

"Mention it?" Jenny said. "I don't see why I would. If a lady wants to ride astride she ought not be bothered 'bout it, even if she ain't in Cornwall like Mr. Carstares' sister. I never did know he had a sister, so that's interesting. I wonder what she's like. Anyhow, nobody likes a gossip."

"That's very true," Georgiana said. Though, she did have some doubts about Jenny's strict adherence to *not* being a gossip. The girl could be very voluble and had told her no end of tidbits about the other servants while she curled Georgiana's hair or helped her into a dress. Georgiana was certain it was not her business to know that one of the kitchen maids was in love with Mr. Brummel or that Perry was in the habit of a small glass of sherry before retiring or that the cook often swore in French thinking nobody understood him, or that the mysterious Mrs. Ripperton who had been left in the country slept more than she woke.

Georgiana decided not to dwell on it. If Jenny spoke of their odd visit to the stables, she did not suppose the other servants would find much interest in it. More importantly, sidesaddles worked just as she'd thought they did, she must just acclimate to it. And to Minerva.

JASPER HAD WATCHED out of a second floor window as Miss Wilcox had gone to the stables. His mother had told him she was adamant about *meeting her horse*. What was she really doing though? Why did she wish to get a look at the stables?

Was she planning on using it as a drop point for any reports she could gather? Did she look for some discreet hidey-hole she might slip a note into, to be retrieved by somebody casually making their way down the mews?

If she had been any other lady under usual circumstances, he might view her determination to say hello to her horse as a charming eccentricity. Very charming, actually. He could not imagine the likes of Lady Annabelle setting foot inside a stable. But she was not any other lady. She was Miss Wilcox, who'd failed to mention she'd met the King of England on the road…

Jasper had a rather sickening feeling when he thought about the possibilities. Watching her determined strides, her straw bonnet obscuring her wonderful hair…he had to know the truth!

Part of him did not wish to know the truth, as the truth might be awful. But what if it wasn't? What would he do then?

He could not know until he had found out one way or the other. First, he would warn the queen and gather her impressions upon meeting Miss Wilcox at their scheduled tea. Then, he would set a trap and see if she fell into it. He did not want to set a trap, but he must. It was his duty. And, he needed to know.

He was rather startled to notice that his shoulders had cramped up while he contemplated a trap.

CHAPTER SEVEN

T HOUGH GEORGIANA HAD thought that riding sidesaddle
would be the only challenge of visiting Hyde Park, she was
now not quite sure. It was almost incredible how much she did
not know about the habits of Town.

She had since discovered that nobody in the world called it
Hyde Park—it was just *the park*. She'd also found out that, though
taking a horse out in the cool of early morning would be sensible
and far better for the horse, nobody went to the park before two.
Lady Mendleton was set on going at five, which she felt was the
most fashionable of all the fashionable hours. Jenny told her that
there was a favored jaunt called Rotten Row. Lady Mendleton
instantly corrected this and informed her *they* referred to it as the
King's Old Road and, in any case, it was not suitable for a carriage
and they would sensibly take the carriage road.

Even her riding habit had been a bit of a mystery as she was
certain there was a loop somewhere that would hold her skirt up,
but it had been well-concealed. While a particular modiste named
Mrs. Lanchester had made the rest of her clothes, that lady would
not do for a habit. This was made by a certain Mr. Clark and was
a lovely dark blue with matching braiding down the front of the
jacket and around the cuffs. Lady Mendleton had explained that
some young ladies fancied gold braiding, but she would not have
her own girl riding around looking like a Hussar. The resulting
garment was well-cut and discreetly sophisticated. The whole was

topped off by a deceptively flimsy silk-covered bonnet that had firm padding in the crown, presumably to soften any blows to the head that might occur should one lose their seat.

Now, they had entered the park and Georgiana realized how much she had missed the countryside. Rather than cobblestones and bricks, she was surrounded by grass and trees. The very air seemed cleaner. It was extraordinary that such a place could exist in the heart of London.

As they rode in a barouche with the hood rolled down, it was unnecessary for Lady Mendleton to rap on the roof to stop the carriage. She simply said, "Carstares, there is a mounting block by that old oak. That will do very well."

As Carstares angled the carriage in that direction, Lady Mendleton patted Georgiana's hand. "You will be all elegance upon a horse, my dear girl."

Georgiana certainly hoped that was true, but did not give any promises to it.

Worse, she realized that she had not thought through how to mount. Usually, she would hitch her skirt, put her left foot in the stirrup, pull herself up and throw her right leg over the back of the horse. Somehow, she had to pull herself up and fold her right leg around the pommel. But how was that done? Her right leg was used to going over the back of the horse but now it must land at the front.

Well, it must be done somehow or other.

Carstares had come down from the box and taken Minerva's reins from the groom. He helpfully positioned Minerva close to the block. Georgiana stepped up and looked at the distance to the saddle. The block was shorter than the one outside of Manley Hall's stables, Minerva was taller than her father's sturdy hunter, and the stirrup was set higher than usual. How on earth would she get up there?

Georgiana took a deep breath and attempted to get her left foot high enough to place it in the stirrup. It was impossible, one would have to be a circus performer to manage it.

Carstares shook his head. "A moment, miss. Jimmy will give you a boost up."

Georgiana nodded, thinking how stupid she was. She was so used to doing everything on her own that she had presumed that all ladies must mount themselves. But of course, they did not. The distance was so great and the stirrup placed so high that it could not be done. Goodness, what a ninny—how many times had she seen Miss Webster mount with assistance? All along, she'd just thought the girl was only lazy.

At least now she understood how it *was* done. The groom's laced hands would act as a second, higher, mounting block. All she need do was push off and pull up, as hard as she possibly could.

The groom placed his locked palms between the block and the stirrup. Georgiana put her left foot upon them and said, "Ready?"

"Ready, miss," he said, "one, two, three."

Jimmy pushed up while Georgiana pushed down with her foot and pulled up with her hands, using every ounce of strength she could muster.

For a brief second, the scheme seemed to work exceptionally well. She traveled upward with remarkable speed.

After that brief and hopeful moment, it became apparent that the force of the groom and herself together was too much of a good thing.

Rather than landing gracefully in the saddle, Georgiana continued her upward ascent. She knew the exercise was an entirely lost cause when her hands lost touch with the pommel. A branch overhead stopped her progress, she grazed the far side of the saddle on her way down and hit the ground with a thud.

Amidst Lady Mendleton's shrieks, Georgiana heard a voice not far off say, "My dear Miss Wilcox, are you quite all right?"

Georgiana was just assessing that very thing as the groom helped her up. Jimmy's expression was at once horrified, and also relieved that she was not dead.

She could not yet see the speaker, he being on the other side of the disaster, though she recognized the voice well enough from Lord Ryland's ball. It was Lord Asturt—the great fan of Lord Langley and referrer of his new valet.

She brushed her skirts and became determined to make the best of it. "Quite all right, my lord," she called. "It is only that I have just discovered that my own groom at home is a rather weak cup of tea. I should have known I would not have to do so much work with Jimmy at the helm. Very foolish of me."

The groom appeared greatly relieved that he would not be blamed for throwing a lady over a horse and nodded vigorously. He pointed at her bonnet, which had gone askew, and tapped his finger to his cheek to indicate there was a smudge on her own.

Pulling herself together as best she could, Georgiana patted Minerva's neck, the horse rather wild-eyed at this unusual turn of events. Then she walked round the horse to face Lord Asturt.

It would have been trying enough to face down Lord Asturt and Lady Mendleton. In particular, Lady Mendleton, as the poor woman had pinned all her hopes on Georgiana's skill on a horse.

As it happened, things were a deal more trying than that. Lord Asturt escorted Lady Annabelle, who appeared vastly entertained, and an older woman presumed to be Lady Annabelle's mother. Behind them, two mounted grooms looked on in amusement.

"Goodness, Miss Wilcox," Lady Annabelle said, "you have given Lady Mendleton quite the fright."

Though Georgiana would like to claim that everything Lady Annabelle said was wrong, she was not wrong in *that*. Lady Mendleton leaned back, her eyes half closed, while Carstares rummaged through a trunk and brought out a vinaigrette. He waved it under her nose and brought her round.

"Dear Lady Mendleton," Georgiana said, rushing to her side. "There is no need for alarm. None at all."

"But I never saw such a thing," Lady Mendleton said weakly. "One moment you were there and the next you were...gone."

"Most common circumstance in the world," Lord Asturt said. "Does a day go by without some poor young lady being thrown entirely over her saddle? I rather doubt it."

Georgiana certainly *did* doubt it, but she was grateful for the lord's kindness. Lady Annabelle only looked at him in astonishment.

"Miss Wilcox," Lord Asturt went on, "allow me to introduce you to Lady Kerster, Lady Annabelle's mother."

Georgiana curtsied, though she had never involved herself in such an odd introduction in her life.

Lady Kerster only nodded coolly and said to Lady Mendleton, "How do you do, Louisa? I have not seen you since Newmarket last year."

Lady Mendleton, with the help of strong smells and vigorous fanning, had recovered enough to say, "Indeed, we have not met since then, Harriet. You look very well."

Georgiana thought this awkward conversation amidst a very awkward situation might go on for quite some time if she did not do something about it. She motioned for the groom to go back to the block. She would get on Minerva one way or the other.

Jimmy did as he was bid, though he did not appear to relish the idea. As Lady Kerster and Lady Mendleton exchanged vague pleasantries, Georgiana said softly, "Do it just as you ought, the fault was mine, but I shan't push so hard this time."

This seemed to give the groom some amount of courage and he nodded. Georgiana placed her foot in his palms and said, "Go."

By keeping her hands on the pommel and allowing the footman to do most of the work, Georgiana found herself quite easily in the saddle. She maneuvered her right leg into position, her left foot in the stirrup, and it was done. Now, she must just remember to lightly tap her cane instead of use her right leg when she wished to signal the horse.

Her managing to get on the horse also managed to stop the rather endless and pointless conversation between Lady Mendleton and Lady Kerster.

"Goodness," Lady Mendleton said to Georgiana, "You're on, I thought you might give it up."

"That is the grace of youth," Lord Asturt said, "no harm done in the end, eh? Though, I will say the horse is looking ready to get skittish. Best not keep her standing about."

Georgiana nodded gratefully. She was beginning to feel rather bad about her thoughts on Lord Asturt when she'd danced with him. He was turning out to be a very handy fellow. There was nothing more she'd wish to do at this moment than get away.

"Well, I suppose we might go forward," Lady Mendleton said, not sounding particularly confident about the idea.

"I will escort you myself," Lord Asturt said gallantly. "I only encountered Lady Annabelle and Lady Kerster quite by accident and am certain I have already overstayed my welcome."

Lord Asturt might be certain of it, but Lady Annabelle did not seem quite as certain. Georgiana doubted that the lady would find herself bereft upon losing Lord Asturt's company, but rather she was put out at being thrown over for another lady.

Lady Kerster did not seem to have the same qualms. In a rather imperious tone, she said, "Good day to you, Lord Asturt. Louisa. Miss Wilcox." She turned her horse and her daughter reluctantly followed.

TO GEORGIANA'S GREAT relief, the rest of their time in the park had passed by uneventful. Lord Asturt had gone back to asking questions about Lord Langley, who he really did seem to excessively admire, but Georgiana found she could not condemn him for it after his very recent rescue. They passed by any number of gentlemen who tipped their hat, and perhaps turned round in their saddles after she'd passed by. Lady Mendleton seemed to gain in equanimity and cheerfulness by every foot they traveled without incident.

The sidesaddle, once she became used to leaning a bit further back than was her habit and using the cane in place of her right leg, was a welcome surprise. It was a deal more comfortable than riding astride and most surprising, she felt confident in her seat. Though ladies always *appeared* in danger of sliding off their horse, in fact it felt very secure. Minerva had a few sidesteps and head shakes to perform, in order to point out that she had been recently alarmed, but it was no trouble to check her. Over time, the horse settled and was no doubt relieved that they had gone on to activities she understood, rather than having her rider unaccountably sailing over her back.

They ended with Lord Asturt assuring Lady Mendleton he would call at her next at-home day.

Georgiana felt she must be somewhat satisfied with the excursion. It had not gone perfectly, but she had survived and gone on to master the sidesaddle. She could only hope that Lady Annabelle would not spread the tale of her flying over her horse far and wide. She did have the hope, at least, as that lady would be far too taken up with how her hair must be a fright or her dress the wrong color for her complexion.

JASPER HAD SET off for Buckingham to see the queen, leaving in good time on horseback. Though it was not a great distance to travel, at this season the London streets were crowded. Worse, they were almost always crowded with at least one person he knew who would wish to blather on about something with no regard for how they blocked other people trying to reach a destination.

He was not at all surprised that he failed to get to the palace without one of these encounters, though he found himself annoyed that this time it was Lady Annabelle and her unpleasant mother, Lady Kerster, who were the culprits. They rode in a carriage as a bevy of grooms took care of their horses, having just come from the park.

Amidst the shouting of cart drivers for them to move on,

Lady Annabelle told the alarming story of Miss Wilcox somehow getting thrown clear over her horse. Jasper might have almost thought she invented the tale, as Lady Annabelle was no stranger to insulting other women, had it not been for Lady Kerster's grave nodding.

He was to know that Miss Wilcox stood and shook herself off as if this were an everyday occurrence for her. He was also to know that Lord Asturt had been so alarmed by the scene that he had insisted on escorting Miss Wilcox in case she were to throw herself to the ground again.

Jasper could, at least, confirm from this report that Miss Wilcox had not come to any serious injury. He was rather relieved to know it, though he found himself irritated by the idea of Asturt coming to the rescue.

Asturt was such an odd fellow! His accent was a mishmash of he knew not what. He had not been in Town for a season before this one, apparently squirreling himself away on some remote Irish estate, which was an exceedingly odd thing to do, as he was apparently not short of funds. He'd somehow got himself admitted to Brooks's and then when he'd overheard Jasper complain that his valet was packing off to America, he'd leapt into the conversation with a recommendation.

Marcus had worked for an old cousin of Asturt's who had spent his last remaining years on a property he owned in Germany. Because of his extensive travels, Marcus spoke a number of languages—French, German, and even some Russian and Italian. Jasper had thought it might come in handy some day and so had hired him. That was all well and good. But Asturt could not seem to let the thing go—he was forever inquiring about Marcus as if Jasper had forgotten to pay him a finder's fee for the valet. It was all very ridiculous.

As he entered the palace, he determined to put the matter aside. There was nothing to be done about it and he had far more serious matters at hand than a fall in the park.

QUEEN CHARLOTTE RECEIVED Jasper in their usual room. It was not by any means the largest receiving room in the palace, but it had the advantage of only one set of doors on the far side and no connecting rooms. This prevented anybody nosy enough to wish to overhear from listening at keyholes or through walls.

The room was sumptuously decorated in all manner of fine furniture and expensive fabrics, but the decorations paled in comparison to her two ever-present companions—a pair of very unpleasant Pomeranians. The dogs were odd-looking piles of fur who were surprisingly vicious, given their laughable stature. They had no hope of overcoming anybody, unless a person could be killed via ankle nip, but they considered themselves exceedingly ferocious.

They both growled and eyed Jasper with some mixture of suspicion and contempt after the queen had invited him to sit.

"I have had a report," Queen Charlotte said, shaking an indulgent finger at her bad-tempered dogs, "a most alarming report."

Jasper waited to hear what it was, though his trepidation led him to think all manner of things.

"The Stuart has fled Russia and may well be in our own neighborhood. Scotland, perhaps, or even closer."

In that brief moment before she had spoken, a hundred thoughts had crossed his mind. That had not been one of them. Of all the concerns he'd had, the Stuart had been perhaps the most farfetched, and by far the most serious. He waited for the queen to go on.

"It seems," she said, pouring tea, "that the Tsarina found something worthy in the man and contracted him to marry an heiress. The fool then proceeded to proclaim his love for the lady's sister who was contracted to another. At the same time as he was causing that scandal, his banker failed. All but penniless and having caused outrage, he fled. He has always seemed a far-off danger, but now he seems rather closer."

Jasper nodded. "Because he has nothing to lose," he said.

"Precisely," the queen said. "I was confident that you would grasp the situation instantly. If he had weighed his chances over the years, he would have considered it not a gambit likely to run in his favor and with much to lose. Now it is still not in his favor, but nothing in particular holds him back."

Jasper thought the timing could not be worse. That the Stuart might be convinced to make some sort of bold move just when it appeared the king was incapacitated for good and the regent was less than regal. The prince was so disliked—so flagrant in all his habits—spending, consuming, and conjugating. The Stuarts still held a place of fondness in some people's hearts, whether or not it was earned. Distance always did wonders for reputation. Even Henry the VIII, an absolute despot-murderer, was looked upon far kindlier than he ought to be or than he ever was in his time.

Further, every monarch throughout history was ruled by the will, or at least the apathy, of the people. Were the people to turn away from the Hanovers in a decisive wave, they might turn toward the Stuarts of old. The House of Lords might be convinced to do something, as they had no love for or faith in the current regent. The armies might throw in with a scheme. The generals might love their king, but they were hardened men that had an abiding distaste for the regent's foppishness. All those parties might point to inherited madness to excuse whatever they would do.

He had vaguely wondered if the reports about the king were somehow connected to the Stuarts, but it had seemed such a far-off possibility. Now it was a deal more credible a threat.

"There is nothing to be done at this moment," Queen Charlotte said. "We must bide our time until the Stuart resurfaces somewhere. If he dares make a move, though, he will be dealt with speedily."

Jasper only nodded, but his mind raced. Where would the Stuart go? Who would be his allies? Scotland, of course, would still house those who'd never really given up on a Stuart claim. But he would need more support than that. France, perhaps?

France had just broken with Russia and the Stuart had just caused a ruckus in St. Petersburg. It seemed a flimsy argument, but he could not know what else went on behind the scenes. Deals may have been struck.

"Now tell me of this Miss Wilcox I must have for tea," Queen Charlotte said. "Lord Ryland tells me she is exceptionally clever and is one of your mother's latest projects."

"Yes," Jasper said slowly, "you will find Miss Wilcox charming and direct. I would only caution you to pay close attention to what she inquires about. As you know, she encountered the king on the road during that unfortunate incident, but when asked about her travels she said nothing about it."

"I see," Queen Charlotte said thoughtfully, "so she is either a marionette of one of my enemies or a young lady with particularly fine sensibilities."

"Precisely," Jasper said.

"And which do you think it is?"

"I do not yet know, I only know which I *hope* it is."

"And how do you plan to discover which it is?" the queen said, looking sympathetically at her dogs as they yawned with boredom.

"I am going to plant an innocuous but false report on my desk in the library. I will leave it there for days to give her every opportunity to finding it. If she has been spying, the report will surface in the newspapers."

"Make it both innocuous and in our favor. As you know, the poor king is subsisting on broths and soups and refuses anything else. Let the report say that he has developed a voracious appetite for lamb and venison and becomes agitated if beef or chicken is placed on the table. It is eccentric enough to grab a newspaper's interest, but not damning, and it will obscure the real case of things."

Jasper nodded, as always appreciating the queen's cunning. He also noted that the dogs certainly understood some words, as the mention of lamb, venison, beef and chicken had awoken them from their ill-tempered stupor, and they looked hopefully around the room.

"Capital idea—it points directly away from the truth."

"Just so," the queen said.

>>>><<<<

GEORGIANA'S DAYS HAD been filled with calls and dinners and routs. The routs she found particularly exhausting. Such a crush of people meandering about! For all that, though, her circle of acquaintance was expanding rapidly and that was why she had come to London. So far, no gentleman had sent her aflutter, except of course for Lord Langley who she had firmly ruled out. But she might meet someone at any moment at any place.

At Lady Mendleton's at-home day, there had been a stream of people coming in. Based on their rather ill-disguised curiosity, Georgiana presumed they had come to get a look at Lady Mendleton's latest project, which was her.

Her dear sponsor had taken the precaution of roping the pianoforte shut and claiming it needed repair so there could not be any uncomfortable requests for Georgiana to play it. The duchess had stopped by and nodded approvingly at the scheme, Lady Heathway had only looked nonplussed and grilled Lady Mendleton on who she'd hired to do the repairs.

Lord Asturt had been as good as his word and come. He was odd as ever, seeming delighted to encounter Marcus in the hall and staying out there to converse with him for some time. Still, he was charming in his odd way. He made no mention at all that he'd seen her ungraciously sail over her horse in the park and Georgiana was grateful for it. In truth, it seemed he was beginning to grow on her. After all, he was rather good-looking, seemed to be eminently suitable, and based on his rather laissez-faire comments in the park he was not easily shocked. Perhaps that was what she liked best about him. She was beginning to find that the pretty ways of Town were perhaps *too* pretty. There was something to be said for a man who did not take it all too seriously.

Georgiana thought she must have made a credible showing to Lady Mendleton's callers, as there had been numerous invitations extended and the lady herself had seemed well-pleased by the end of it.

Today, she had been left to her own devices. Lady Mendleton had gone to the duchess for a tête-à-tête and Georgiana was not needed. Her tea with the queen was on the morrow and she decided the best way to avoid thinking about it overmuch was to immerse herself in a book. In fact it was the only way, as she could not practice on the roped-shut pianoforte, sewing would only aggravate her and fail to produce anything useful, and unlike the country, she could not saunter out alone. For all the things she *couldn't* do, reading at least was one she was well-versed in and very proper. She made her way to the library, encountering nobody in the hall, and slipped in.

Georgiana had thought she would have the library to herself. It was Lord Langley who most often occupied it, but he'd left the house hours ago. She was, therefore, surprised to encounter Marcus at Lord Langley's desk.

He held a sheet of paper which he put down quickly upon noting her. "Ah, Miss Wilcox," he said, "I was just straightening. I will get out of your way."

Georgiana nodded and watched him hurriedly put the paper into a drawer in the desk and hurry out, seeming a bit red-faced.

It was very odd. She had not understood that a valet would act as a secretary too. But perhaps it was so. After all, how much did she really know about a valet's duties anyway? Her father's valet was more like his friend, which she was certain was not usual. And certainly, a man as busy with the queen as Lord Langley seemed to be probably required a secretary and she had not seen one about the place.

Georgiana scanned the shelves of old books full of dusty

reading until she spotted the far side of the lowest shelf that seemed to be given over to newer novels. There, she was surprised to come upon *Zastrozzi*, the book Lord Bertridge had spoken of at Lord Ryland's dinner. As she read the description and thumbed through it, she decided it was suitably gothic and probably very terrible. Precisely what she looked for.

She had almost decided to leave and take the book to the drawing room, but something about the valet's demeanor kept tugging at her. He had seemed embarrassed to be caught holding that paper. Why should he look as if he'd been caught out if he only acted in a proper role as secretary? Had whatever he'd been reading *really* been meant for his eyes, or had Marcus been snooping?

Georgiana had a great inclination to go to the desk and see for herself. But of course, that would make *her* a snooper. On the other hand, if her suspicions about Marcus were right and it were something of vital national interest, or even worse, a private missive from the queen, Lord Langley ought to be told to lock his desk.

She really was of two minds over it, though she noticed her feet were carrying her slowly toward the desk.

CHAPTER EIGHT

G EORGIANA STOOD OVER Lord Langley's desk and sighed over her own curiosity. Or nosiness as some might call it. Nevertheless, she would snoop on the valet's snooping. Just to check if any great secrets had been uncovered by Lord Langley's valet.

She listened for sounds in the hall. Hearing none, she pulled the desk drawer open and slipped the paper out.

As she read it, she felt a vast relief. She quickly replaced it and shut the drawer. It was only some report from a senior servant of the king, explaining that the king was growing particular in his meals. Lamb and venison were in, while chicken and beef were out. There was no mention of fish, so she did not know how the king got on with that. The most outrageous thing noted was that the king became agitated if beef or chicken were placed on the table. Odd, but hardly a great sin.

Did not her own father become agitated when a dish was too liberal with garlic or onion? If Marcus had been snooping, he had not been well-paid for his trouble. She would say nothing of it to Lord Langley and began to view herself a ninny. Certainly, such an astute gentleman must be clever enough to keep all important correspondence suitably locked up. She really ought to have thought of that notion first.

And she would not like to be known as a snooper. Though she had snooped.

As she crossed the hall from the library to the drawing room, she encountered Perry. She smiled at him and held the book up, as if to account for her foray into the library.

Now that she was convinced that she'd done wrong, she only hoped she did not look as guilty as she felt.

PERRY, PRIDING HIMSELF that his eyes were sharp as a hawk, his hearing as good as a fox, and his guiding instincts rivaling a cloud of barn bats, was often listening to and observing his staff while they were quite unaware of it. Having started his career as a junior footman, he well knew the gossip and hijinks that might remain hidden from an incurious butler.

For some days, there had been a private joke passing between the footmen. Some story that amused them. As he had viewed Thomas and one of the stable's grooms with their heads together in the back garden at the beginning of it all, he suspected the story had originated in that hay-strewn locale. He also surmised the tale would be some low account of a loose woman, gambling, boxing, excessive drink, or all of those together—those subjects always intriguing youths who were full of their oats.

Now, as the servants had their tea, he was determined to bring the merriment to a close. He would inquire into it, their faces would turn red, and they would deny discussing anything. The fear of God, or he should say, the fear of the *butler*, would be put into them. The fear would not last forever, but it would last long enough to be done with this current nonsense.

"Boys," he said in a low tone that stopped all other conversation at the table, "I insist you regale all of us with whatever amuses you these days."

Perry leaned back, satisfied that he was shortly to see the red faces he had so anticipated.

Oddly, he did not.

"Oh, Mr. Perry," Thomas said, "we was just laughin' over the story Jimmy told us 'bout Miss Wilcox on Minerva." Thomas hesitated, then said, "*Kindly* laughing in good fun, a course."

"That's right," William said, "we don't mean no disrespect to the lady. Only, it was so very funny a picture Jimmy did paint."

Perry had not heard anything of Miss Wilcox on Minerva and could not imagine what could be funny about it. However, he abhorred finding himself in a situation where he was very much in the dark.

He cleared his throat. "I am, naturally, aware of the matter. Though, I would ask you to repeat it. I do not favor how stories are embellished as they travel from person to person and would confirm for myself that the unfortunate habit has not occurred under my watch."

Thomas appeared rather enthusiastic about being given leave to tell his tale, and he did tell it, though Perry grew more incredulous with every moment.

"So you see," Thomas said, "she don't know that Jimmy's gonna give her a good lift up and she adds in her own lift up and goes sailing right over poor Minerva. 'Parently, her own groom at home is as weak as a baby so she never did see it coming."

There were titters and giggles up and down the table, though all who did so also looked to Perry to see if he would confirm the veracity of the story.

"*Sailing* over Minerva sounds excessive to my ears," he said, having no idea what else to say.

"Flyin' then," William said, appearing perfectly agreeable to amend the description.

"Must have been a sight, however she got from one side to the other," Thomas said.

Jenny gave three sharp raps on the table with the salt cellar. "Stop your amusement, you beggars," she said. "Poor Miss Wilcox ain't never been on a sidesaddle before as she's used to ridin' astride. Nobody gets things perfect on their first go."

A lady riding astride? This idea seemed even more outlandish to Perry.

"That's right," Jenny said. "She's used to ridin' astride like what Carstares' sister does in Cornwall. *That's* why she encountered the difficulty and the hands in the stable ought to keep their ideas to themselves."

All eyes once more turned to Perry. "Our Jenny," he said, in his best butler tone, "has managed to home in on a most salient point. The grooms *should* keep their ideas to themselves. I am not entirely sure they should even have ideas. Further, it is not for us to stand by and act as magistrate, judging what is before us, and you'd best all remember it. I will hear no more talk about Lady Mendleton's protégé, or I will take steps."

Perry then very determinedly turned his attention to the buttered bread on his plate, knowing full well that once he'd mentioned taking steps, that would be the end of it. Though he had never fully defined for himself what *taking steps* would entail, exactly, none of these rascals had ever dared find out.

Though it would appear as if the bread and tea in front of him was all-engrossing, he was rather stunned by what he had heard. Miss Wilcox was quickly verging on the bizarre.

First, she attacked the pianoforte as if she was an assassin attempting to murder it, now he was to understand that she'd never been on a sidesaddle? Was she some sort of daughter of Charlemagne, riding *astride* through her neighborhood? And, had he not just seen for himself that of all the worthy books she might have chosen from the family's library, she had somehow taken out a low gothic tale? Did her parents, whoever they were, sanction these activities?

He had of course known that bringing a girl in from nowhere was a terrible idea. But was it more than ill-judged? Were the family somehow at risk of censure over this girl? Where had she come from? What life had she lived before arriving?

Certainly not a life he would call usual.

A sudden and very alarming thought occurred to him. What if the girl was some sort of imposter? What if that were why she did not seem to possess any of the typical talents a young lady of rank was imbued with? What if she had weaseled her way into Lady Mendleton's good graces so that she might...what might she do?

He set his teacup down with a clatter. She might seduce the eldest son. She might have her sights set on Lord Langley. Good God, did the lord know what risks he ran? A climbing sort of girl might dare anything to catch a man who would make her a countess someday. It would be a disaster!

Perry suddenly clutched at his chest, the full enormity of this idea coming down upon him.

"Mr. Perry," Jenny said loudly, "are you quite all right? I don't like to see a gentleman of your years grabbing at his heart like that."

⟫⟫⟨⟨

When Jasper returned to the house, he asked Perry to send coffee into the library. He intended to write various of his far-flung contacts in some vague and questioning way to discover any news of the Stuart. He thought it might be safe enough to send a general letter with news, and in the middle of it casually insert the story of the Stuart, the Tsarina, the scandal, the failed banker and the fact that the Stuart had fled Russia. He would then end the tale with a humorous warning along the lines of: *He could be anywhere, lock your daughters up and let me know if you spot him!*

After all, it was the sort of gossip one *would* pass on. He hoped he might hear something back about it, or even some mention of a gentleman new to a neighborhood that nobody seemed to know anything about. If there was one thing a person could count on when receiving a letter from the countryside, it was that it would document the smallest change in it. Whether it be that one of the gentry had daringly gone from cows to sheep, or that the quality of a certain farmer's eggs was on the decline, or that a neighboring estate had been newly rented by an as yet

100

unknown occupant. Were that mysterious occupant discovered to be a single gentleman, and Jasper did think the Stuart would travel alone, the news would be the constant topic of every dinner table in the neighborhood that happened to have an unmarried daughter on hand.

As he approached his desk, he stopped in his tracks. The letter he'd left as a ruse to determine if Miss Wilcox was some sort of infiltrator was gone. Good God, had she had the nerve to take it? Would it be printed in the newspaper verbatim?

He hurried to the desk and opened it. No, she had not taken it. It had been put in the drawer. She'd forgotten where she'd discovered it in the first place. That, though, was extremely clumsy. It certainly did not speak of a seasoned spy. Anybody wishing to rifle through another's belongings, be they spy or otherwise, would take careful note of where the item was placed to begin.

Jasper paused. He had not yet any direct evidence that Miss Wilcox was the culprit. Perry might have put it away for some reason. Or a new maid who did not understand not to go near his desk—his mother was forever hiring new maids who had not the first idea of their duties. She often explained that everybody had to start somewhere, though his father did not understand why the somewhere was always their own house.

Perry came in with the coffee tray and set it down on the desk.

"Perry," Jasper said casually, "did you happen to move a paper from my desk to a drawer?"

Perry seemed rather astounded by the question. "Certainly not, my lord. I would never touch one of your papers."

Jasper nodded. "Did you happen to notice anybody in the library this morning?"

"Only Miss Wilcox coming out of it with a book," he said in a disdainful tone. "A rather lurid tome, if I saw the title rightly. Very strange choice, I thought."

Jasper did not know if it would be a strange choice or not. As far as he could tell, young ladies adored lurid tales that kept them up at night. But then, Perry was a traditional stickler and probably would not have been satisfied with anything more daring than an insipid book of poetry. "Thank you," he said with a sigh, "that is all."

That would have been Perry's cue to make his exit from the room, but the butler hesitated, staring down at the coffee tray.

Jasper looked at it too and said, "Have you forgotten something?"

"No, my lord," Perry said. "I only hope nobody in this house forgets who they are!"

With that, he practically fled, slamming the door behind him.

Jasper might have wondered if Perry were in the midst of some mental crisis, had he not more pressing things to consider. It had been Miss Wilcox who had moved the paper. Who had *read* the paper before she moved it. Now, all he had to do was wait. Would it show up in the newspaper or not? If it did, he had his answer and he would tell his mother that Miss Wilcox must depart the house. If it did not, then he supposed it would give him a different answer—Miss Wilcox was only a rather nosy meddler.

He dearly hoped she was only a nosy meddler. Based on his experiences with his mother, he did not think it an uncommon trait in women. While he was waiting for his answer as to who Miss Wilcox really was, he thought he might as well discover what Perry considered to be a lurid tome. While he was doing that, he might press the lady into revealing something.

He certainly had reasons to seek her out that had nothing to do with admiring her hair or enjoying any conversation they might have. *That* would not drive him thither. It was only duty that called him.

Satisfied that he had entirely rational reasons for going, Jasper took his cup of coffee and headed to the drawing room.

G<small>EORGIANA WAS SURPRISED</small> to see Lord Langley come into the drawing room; she had not heard him come into the house. A rather jittery surprise, she noted. She was always struck by the look of him, and now she was also shaken. If he'd come in a half hour sooner, she might have been caught rifling his desk.

Now, Lord Langley left the doors to the drawing room open for propriety's sake and made his way to a nearby chair.

Perry had brought in a tea tray some minutes ago and she thought she would offer it to him, but he already carried a cup of coffee in his hand.

"Lord Langley," she said.

"Miss Wilcox, how do you get on?"

"Very well," she said, "Lady Mendleton has been most kind."

She noticed he was eyeing her book and she said, "It is *Zastrozzi*, the book Lord Bertridge recommended at Lord Ryland's ball."

"I see," he said, still seeming intent on the book. "I would ask how you find it but based on the bookmark I presume you have just recently begun it."

"Yes," Georgiana said, not preferring to mention she had been in the library not very long ago.

"I assume it is from our own collection? I did not purchase it, but my mother often orders a thing somebody has mentioned. I would not like to think you bought it based only on Bertridge's recommendation."

"No, indeed, I did not buy it," Georgiana said, wishing to get off the subject. "But why should you wonder about Lord Bertridge's recommendations? Do you find his judgement unreliable?"

"Bertridge? Oh, I suppose he's a fine enough fellow. Rather stiff like his aunt, though. Frowns on...well I sometimes wonder what he *doesn't* frown upon."

Georgiana nodded, as she had thought the same herself— Lord Bertridge was rather a stick. "It was an amusing dinner, at Lord Ryland's house," she said. "We have had similar mystery nights held in my own neighborhood, though not on as grand a scale. Though, I did not think either Lady Annabelle or Lord Bertridge saw much in it."

"No," Lord Langley said. "Speaking of Lady Annabelle, I happened to see her on the street some days ago. She mentioned you had taken a fall in the park."

Georgiana felt her face grow hot, and probably an unflattering shade of red. "Did she?" she asked.

"She did. She said there was some difficulty in mounting Minerva."

Georgiana should have known Lady Annabelle would not keep such a thing to herself. Well, she would own what occurred and anybody could think what they liked about it.

"As it happens," she said defiantly, "I discovered that your groom is far stronger than my own at home. I had been quite used to doing at least half the work myself to mount my father's horses. So, you can imagine that my efforts combined with Jimmy's were rather more powerful than necessary. Resulting in a fall."

"But you were not hurt?"

"Not in the least," Georgiana said, jutting her chin out to make her point.

Lord Langley had apparently decided to drop the subject as he said, "Your appointment for tea with the queen is on the morrow."

Mention of tea with the queen stole the wind from Georgiana's well-filled sails. She set her cup down. "Indeed it is. I will not prevaricate—I am rather quaking over it and have had thoughts of wishing I had not worked quite so hard on Lord Ryland's mystery."

"Why should you quake over it?" Lord Langley asked, his brow wrinkling. "She is elevated, to be sure, but she is still a person and it is only tea, not an inquisition."

Georgiana twisted her hands together. "I am worried that I will somehow put out a wrong foot. I am not afraid of what the queen will think of me, as whatever it is she is unlikely to ever think of me again. But, I *am* afraid of what Lady Mendleton will think about what the queen thinks of me. I would not wish to in any way embarrass that kind lady."

Lord Langley looked at her seemingly critically and Georgiana looked away and fussed with the teapot. She always found herself a little shivery when he regarded her so plainly.

"I shouldn't worry over it," Lord Langley said. "She is a perfectly agreeable person. Just be yourself, as she does not like airs or pretension or false modesty and simpering. Also, she has two rather awful Pomeranian dogs, do your best to pretend you admire them."

Georgiana nodded, grateful for the hints. The dogs might be her best chance with the queen—she got on with dogs of all sorts and did not suppose regal dogs were so very different from any other dog.

"I do like dogs," she said hopefully.

"Well, these are less dogs and more spoiled attendants who believe they hold a rank of the highest importance."

"They cannot be so very bad…"

Lord Langley rose and said, "You shall judge for yourself. Enjoy your book. When did you say you found it in the library?"

Georgiana had not said and was rather taken aback by the question. "Just a while ago," she said.

"I see. Well, let us hope Bertridge has steered you in the right direction."

With that, he made a short bow and left the room.

Georgiana contemplated the door as it shut behind Lord Langley. It had been a strange conversation. So many questions. First about the book, and then when she thought he'd done with it, he came back around to it and inquired when she'd got it.

It was impossible that anybody had seen her snooping. The door had been shut.

She wished she hadn't done it. She should have left well enough alone. It had seemed, at the time, that she ought to determine that Marcus had not been spying on some sort of sensitive correspondence. But it had not be any of her affair!

Well, what was done was done. Were she ever pressed about it, she would tell the truth. She just hoped she would never be pressed about it.

Thinking of the visit to the queen, Georgiana had a great wish to go back to the library to see if there might not be a book that contained something about Pomeranians.

She did not dare do it, though. She was not certain she would ever set foot in that room again.

＊＊＊＊＊＊

JASPER WENT BACK to the library to contemplate his conversation with Miss Wilcox. As Perry had claimed, she had been in the library earlier, giving her every chance to read the letter. She had also seemed rather cagey about the whole thing, changing the subject to his opinion of Lord Bertridge. All of that was not in her favor.

What had possibly been in her favor though, was the mention of having previously attended mystery nights in her own neighborhood. Could that account for how skilled she'd turned out to be at the activity? Or was it a clever ruse?

Her mention of her trepidation over visiting the queen had surprised him—it hardly represented the temperament of a hardened spy. He had, for a moment, thought that might be just a ruse too. Until she mentioned that it was not fear of the *queen's* opinion but of his mother's that worried her. His instincts told him she had been genuine in that expression.

And then, she had not prevaricated about *when* she had been in the library. A person guilty often sought to put distance between themselves and the crime.

It seemed as much of a muddle as ever and he would not know anything for certain until he determined if the report made its way into the newspapers.

For now, he must be careful and not be swayed by how beguiling she could be. She had been so prettily charming upon hearing that Lady Annabelle had told of her fall from a horse. Her rosy cheeks became even rosier and she faced down the whole thing with aplomb. She'd defended herself without voicing any low opinions of Lady Annabelle. Though, he was certain she held them. It was far more grace than could ever be expected from Lady Annabelle herself.

He did not often wish that he was found to be wrong in some matter. But if it pleased God, he would be wrong in his suspicions. Let there be no report of the king's sudden preference for lamb and venison in the newspapers. It was altogether possible that the evidence he'd gathered was just coincidence and even if she had read the letter, she might only be nosy. If she were only a meddler, that he could accept.

CHAPTER NINE

A S THE CARRIAGE made its way to Buckingham Palace for tea with the queen, Lady Mendleton had directed Georgiana on everything that lay ahead. The lady had met the queen on many different occasions, though she did not hold herself out to be as favored or as intimate with the royal as her son was. Still, she thought the queen's fondness for Jasper certainly did her no harm.

The key to royalty, according to Lady Mendleton, was to afford them far more courtesy than one might otherwise do. Or as she termed it: *When in doubt, inflate, elevate, overstate, exaggerate—what is good becomes superb and what is fine becomes sublime.*

They would arrive exceedingly early, as it would be their pleasure to wait upon the queen's convenience. Their curtsies would be very low with an extended pause at the drop down. They would not dare touch the tray of edibles until the queen had urged them to it and informed them of what she thought was best. This was likely to be the rather noxious sandwiches of butter and dill. One must suppress any expression not hinting at delight when consuming them. Most importantly, Lady Mendleton would allow the queen to direct the conversation. She was a terrific gossip and was likely to convey her opinions on any number of people. Georgiana, herself, was not to have opinions on anybody.

The queen was to be addressed as Your Majesty, and then

ma'am. For heaven's sake, *don't* say Your Royal Highness. Some European dunderhead did just that a few years prior and had been unceremoniously marched out of the queen's presence and put on a boat back to wherever he'd come from.

If there was to be any taking a turn round the room for exercise, never discover yourself in front of the queen, no matter how slow she goes or how many times she stops.

The tea would likely be short, for after all it was only a favor to Lord Ryland the lady was doing. The queen would indicate the visit was over in some subtle manner. Lady Mendleton had often seen her simply turn her teacup so the handle pointed to her butler. He then swooped in and cleared the tea things, she rose, and everyone in attendance understood the queen was done with them. They would leap to their feet, curtsy again, and remain in the room until she departed. Finally, servants would whisk them out.

Georgiana thought she might easily follow the rules by simply following Lady Mendleton's lead. She planned to say as little as possible. Therefore, simply remembering Your Majesty and ma'am, doing as Lady Mendleton did, and answering anything she was asked ought to do it.

She had, though, brought one advantage with her. Sometimes, the knowledge gathered from country life was found to come in handy. Knowing that the queen doted on her Pomeranians made Georgiana certain that the lady would look kindly upon anybody the dogs took a liking to. To ensure that they would take a liking to *her*, at breakfast she had very carefully dabbed the smallest bit of grease from a mutton chop onto a handkerchief and carefully folded it. It was just now tucked into her bodice. The two very reliable things about dogs of all sorts were that they could smell subtle scents that people could not, and they adored the smell of meat. There was a reason a stray dog would follow a butcher down the lane, though the man did not carry any meat with him.

"Well, my dear," Lady Mendleton said, patting her hand,

"here we are."

They had come through the gates and driven up the drive, all the while Carstares taking the horses at a dignified walk to suit a royal approach. The coachman had been to the palace many times and knew he was not to descend, nor had there been any footman brought in past the gates. Finely-dressed queen's guards approached and opened the door.

They were then handed over to another servant who led them through one fine room after the next. They finally arrived in a room smaller than the others, but exceedingly charmingly done. It was light and airy and done mostly in cream—cream satin on the furniture, cream silk curtains, and a pale patterned carpet of light blue on cream.

As Georgiana gazed round it, Lady Mendleton said softly, "The color is to match the dog's, I think. The shedding won't show."

This nearly made Georgiana giggle, as it was so unexpected. Being surrounded in splendor, it had not occurred to her that a queen might face very usual practical household problems.

As they had planned on arriving exceedingly early, they waited for some time. They dared not sit before the queen arrived, and Lady Mendleton took to shifting from foot to foot. The poor dear lady was used to sitting everywhere, only moving from one seat to the next, and the prolonged standing was beginning to wear.

Just when Georgiana began to fear that the lady must sit or fall over, the doors were thrown open.

A stern-faced and exceedingly tall and dignified butler came through, followed by the queen. She was dressed rather old-fashioned with ribbons and bows sprouting up everywhere, and wore a heavy necklace of rubies and diamonds. Two fat Pomeranians trotted at her heels and a bevy of footmen brought up the rear.

"Your Majesty," he intoned, "The Countess of Mendleton and Miss Georgiana Wilcox, daughter of Baron Manley."

Both Georgiana and Lady Mendleton swept down in low curtsies.

"Lady Mendleton, charmed to see you. Miss Wilcox, I bid you welcome," the queen said. "Please do sit yourself."

Lady Mendleton appeared vastly relieved and sank into a chair. Georgiana sat on the settee on the other side of her, while the queen took a chair at the head of the small table made of fine-veined pale marble and mahogany wood.

Four footmen who had come in now lined the far wall as if it needed holding up. More footmen filed in with a tea tray, cakes, tarts, carefully peeled and cut fruit, and the dreaded butter and dill sandwiches. Meanwhile, both dogs' ears perked up, they sniffed the air, and they slowly turned toward Georgiana.

The queen seemed to notice the interest and said, "Do you like dogs, Miss Wilcox? I hope you do, as I cannot abide those that don't. Particularly women who pretend to be afraid of them. I have just got one of my ladies over the fault as I was quite determined in it. How she imagined she would serve me and at the same time shriek at my dear little ones, I know not."

"I adore dogs, Your Majesty," Georgiana said.

The Pomeranians had been slowly making their way round the table and toward Georgiana. As she watched them, she thought they seemed rather cautious—curious, an occasional nervous wag of the tail, but not the unbridled enthusiasm of her father's hunting dogs.

The queen poured the tea, and Georgiana took that fact in with interest. She had not been sure if a queen would pour her own tea and had rather expected some servant to do it. A servant *was* on hand to take the cups from her and deliver them to Lady Mendleton and herself, so that at least was a slightly different operation.

"Do choose something," the queen said, waving her hands in the direction of the trays on the table. "I recommend the butter and dill sandwiches. I, personally, cannot abide them, but all my guests seem to adore them."

Both Georgiana and Lady Mendleton dutifully put one on their small china plates.

"Lady Mendleton," the queen said, "I have heard of your latest project—The Society of Sponsoring Ladies, I believe it's called?"

"Yes, Your Majesty," Lady Mendleton said.

"Very interesting," the queen said. "I have always thought that lack of coin ought not hold back a suitable young woman from taking her rightful place, so I deem it a fine notion. Though, I do pity the girl who is thrust into Lady Heathway's clutches."

Both Lady Mendleton and Georgiana were startled by the comment and Georgiana had to suppress her urge to laugh. It was all too true—whoever landed in Lady Heathway's house would likely have a time of it, though she had not expected anybody to ever make the comment. She supposed that was one of the privileges of being the queen, one need not even be afraid of Lady Heathway.

"She can be a trying woman," the queen said. "Though, I expect she will do her best, in the end. She always does, I think."

Georgiana only nodded at the statement, as she would not know what to say to it and, in any case, her entire plan revolved around saying as little as possible. Having taken a bite of the sandwich, she was not certain she could have said anything if she wished to. The butter was unbelievably thick and the dill…well, it was dill. Quite a lot of dill. She swallowed the wretched thing as soon as she was able and took a sip of tea to attempt to obliterate its memory. She quietly placed her plate on the table, strategically behind a vase of flowers, and hoped it would not be noticed.

The Pomeranians had made their way around the table and were now at Georgiana's feet. She thought she might dare scratch their ears and casually reached down. They did not flinch, nor bite, but rather leaned into her hands.

Once they had consented to be scratched, it seemed the ice was broken between them. They hopped on the settee and settled themselves as best they could on her lap, occasionally quietly sniffing at the greased napkin in her bodice.

"Miss Wilcox!" the queen exclaimed. "You have the gift, I see. So very rarely do my dogs take to anybody so quickly. Lord Langley quite despairs of them, or so he tells me. It is not his fault that they do not warm to him though, they don't like men."

Georgiana only smiled down at her two new friends, thinking that ought to be sufficient.

"Alas," the queen said, "they will have you quite cornered and immobile now that they have settled themselves. I am afraid you will not be able to eat further sandwiches as that would unsettle them. It will be Lady Mendleton's good luck to have them all to herself."

"I had much rather have the company of dogs than food, ma'am," Georgiana said. While that would not always be the truth, it certainly was the truth in the face of *those* particular sandwiches.

Lady Mendleton, looking down at the butter and dill sandwiches with some hint of sadness, said, "Georgiana is so charming, ma'am, certainly the dogs must sense it."

"Nonsense," the queen said dismissively, "they care nothing for charm, I can assure you. But they have a remarkable ability to sense who they can trust, and that is what they have done here."

"You're very kind, ma'am," Georgiana said, having taken to petting heads, one on either side of her. She had debated the greased handkerchief gambit before she'd left the house, but now she was very glad she had done it. She had made two new friends, and they were friends the queen liked very much. As she had told Lord Langley, the importance of the visit was not so much to impress the queen, but to impress Lady Mendleton and assure her that her choice to sponsor Georgiana had been correct.

That, she was certain she had done. Though poor Lady Mendleton had been left with the dreaded sandwiches.

Georgiana hoped the visit might in some little way make up for her lack of accomplishments and recent disaster on Minerva in the park.

The queen and Lady Mendleton then took to discussing different acquaintances, and Georgiana was grateful for it. She would not be expected to comment on the Duchess of Stanbury's new habit of wearing brocade, which the queen thought was ludicrous and Lady Mendleton thought not to mention she'd had some like dresses made herself. Georgiana was fairly certain that after hearing that pronouncement, the lady's newly-made brocades would find themselves given to Jenny and never thought of again.

They traded opinions on Lord Alvanley's latest witticisms, and both ladies were agreed that he *was* the wit of the day. Some, according to the ladies, thought Mr. Brummel might challenge Lord Alvanley as the wittiest, but the queen was of the opinion that Brummel was often too cutting and it would ruin him some day. Let a lord find himself the butt of a joke from a mere mister once too often and he would weary of it. She also thought that while it was a fine thing for a man to take pride in his appearance and dress carefully, Brummel took it to such an extreme as to strike her as rather feminine about it. One should, Queen Charlotte said, aspire more to Lord Langley's style of dress—exceedingly well done but not looking as if half the day was spent on it.

This, naturally, pleased Lady Mendleton beyond anything. Of course it would, a way into any mother's heart must be hearing of some approbation of her children.

And so they went on. Georgiana nodded when it seemed right, but otherwise employed herself in gently stroking the Pomeranians' heads as they gently snored on her lap.

They discussed Lord Ryland's unusual dining room and Georgiana discovered she had been correct in speculating that he had indeed knocked some walls down to transform it to its current enormous dimensions.

Suddenly, the queen said, "Miss Wilcox, do tell me how you were clever enough to unravel Lord Ryland's mystery presented at his ball."

This, Georgiana felt, put her in a bit of a quandary. Would it be right to discuss a murder with the queen?

But then, if she did not wish to hear of it, she would not have asked. She decided she'd just better tell the story as it was.

After she'd ended, the queen said, "I see, so it was the three round circles of blood that gave it away as they could not have been made by anything else but the bottom of a cane."

"Yes, ma'am," Georgiana said.

"Very clever," the queen said. "Well, Lady Mendleton, it appears you have chosen well as the first out of the gate with this new society of yours. I will be interested to hear of what match is made as a result of it."

The queen then turned her teacup with the handle facing the waiting butler and rose.

Georgiana gently roused the dogs and placed their sleepy heads on the settee so she might rise herself. Their visit was over and it had gone better than she had even dared to hope.

JASPER HAD BEEN diligent in reading all the newspapers each morning and so far there was no mention of the king's alleged obsession with lamb and venison and abhorrence of beef and chicken. This came as a great relief and he began to think himself a bit nonsensical in imagining Miss Wilcox to be a spy of some sort. Or more outrageous, a spy for the Stuarts. It began to seem ludicrous, really. She was just a young lady recently come to Town from the countryside.

He especially began to be convinced of it after seeing the queen. Queen Charlotte was utterly confident of Miss Wilcox being an innocent, as proven by her dear dogs' trust in the lady. Some might have thought that a silly notion, but Jasper did not. He *did* think dogs had rather good instincts. They did not become influenced by pretty speeches, but they paid close attention with other senses.

Years ago, at the estate, he had noticed his father's hunting dogs shying away from one of their handlers. The dogs never did seem to get used to him. Some time later, the fellow was found to be on the run from a heinous crime—he had poisoned his wife and fled his village. He had managed to take on a new identity and brought with him forged references. The dogs had understood that there was something to fear in him all along, though the fellow came off as extremely mild mannered.

He also knew the queen's two Pomeranians well enough. They were highly unpleasant personalities, and so Miss Wilcox having found a way to befriend them certainly said something.

Having put aside his suspicions, he began to allow some other feelings to grow. She really was quite marvelous. Did she think *him* marvelous, though? That he could not tell. There seemed to be something between them, some spark, but he could not be absolutely certain. And then, if he were to begin to court her, it was rather awkward that they lived in the same house. He had always presumed that when he'd decided to go forward with such a procedure, he'd begin by calling on the lady.

Though, as she *did* live in the house, he'd found he enjoyed their nights in and had begun to give up going to his club so much. Their small family dinners seemed to please everybody and there had grown an ease between them all. Though she was only recently known to the family, it seemed as if she had always belonged there. Miss Wilcox was exceedingly kind and respectful of his mother and she expertly entertained his father by asking him questions about his horses. And, well, when she looked at him directly or laughed at something he said...it was all rather wonderful.

He also found that he began accepting invitations that he normally would not, after hearing that his mother had accepted them on Miss Wilcox's behalf.

But now, those interesting family dinners were becoming far less regular than they had been. The queen had told several people of a gossiping nature that Miss Wilcox was found to be charming and had been well-received. This had made the lady suddenly very popular and everybody wished to see her.

He found he could not like this development. He also found himself wondering if he were going to do something firm about Miss Wilcox. If he were, might he not have to do it soon? How long would it be, now that she had found such favor, before some other gentleman would swoop in?

He realized he had counted on her rather uninspired background to put off a horde of admirers. But he also realized that had been a mistake. Even without the queen's approval, who could ignore the lady? She was so beautiful and clever and unburdened with pretense!

He had also begun to notice that Lord Asturt was becoming a regular visitor to the house and could not like it at all. That fellow was no match for the lady! Asturt was extremely presumptuous if he'd got that notion in his head.

This evening, Lady Featherstone hosted a ball. Jasper was at once determined to secure Miss Wilcox for supper, and wondering if people would note it as saying something. Would *she* note it as saying something? If she did, what would be her view of it? Then, of course, there was his mother who was still firmly set on Lady Annabelle. It was one thing to escort Miss Wilcox into supper at Ryland's ball. Lady Mendleton had been approving of that, as it had been Miss Wilcox's first outing. But how would she view it this time?

He wished to declare some sort of intention, and at the same time declare nothing. He well knew he was being rather a dunderhead about it, but then he had never found himself so affected by a lady. He supposed all men were dunderheads in similar circumstances.

FAR MORE HAD been made of Georgiana's triumph over the queen than she would ever have thought possible. She had, of course, expected Lady Mendleton to be pleased, as that had been her primary goal. But then it seemed that the meeting had been made public, as the queen herself put it about that she highly approved of the ladies' new society upon meeting the clever Miss Wilcox.

This had caused an avalanche of invitations to arrive at the door, as Georgiana discovered that whoever the queen even slightly favored was favored by all. She could not help feeling rather a fraud about it, as all she'd really done was put a handkerchief dabbed in mutton grease in her bodice.

As for Lady Mendleton, the development was both thrilling and fraught with difficulties. There was no possible way to accept all the invitations, as so many conflicted with one another. She did not wish to insult anybody, but decisions had to be made. She comforted herself with assuaging anybody's hurt feelings with an invitation to the ball she would host herself some weeks forward. As far as Georgiana understood it, this had grown the guest list to rather enormous proportions and there were many on it that Lady Mendleton would not have initially considered, and some she did not even particularly care for.

This evening, though, it had been no great matter to decide where they would go. Lady Featherstone, one of the ladies of the society and a dear friend to Lady Mendleton, hosted a ball.

Georgiana had been gratified that Lord Langley would come to it, though he went on horseback and not in their carriage. She did not know why he should do so, but perhaps it was for the best. Though she had worked very hard to put the gentleman from her mind, she had not been all that successful.

Their quiet dinners in, though not as often as they had been, were such a delight! Something was growing between them, she was certain of it. And, while it was wonderful, it was also terrible.

It could not be!

Lord Langley would never marry a lady with her middling background. Lady Mendleton would never approve of it. Not just on account of Lady Annabelle, though that particular lady still seemed highly favored, but on account of her having much grander plans for her eldest son. Georgiana might be many things, but she was not grand. Not even Queen Charlotte's approval could make her so.

She suspected that Lord Langley might enjoy her company, and even find her pleasant to look at, but he would not be so foolish as to forget his duty. She, herself, would not forget her duty. That duty was to Lady Mendleton.

Even so, she could not help wishing that he would put his name down on her card.

CHAPTER TEN

GEORGIANA AND LADY Mendleton had set off in the carriage, on their way to Lady Featherstone's ball. Lord Mendleton had managed to wiggle out once more, though according to his lady the gout had changed feet again. Lord Langley was to go on horseback.

They arrived at Grosvenor Square in minutes as it was not more than a quarter mile from the house. Though they got there soon enough, the line of carriages was long and they spent some time slowly making their way forward.

Lady Mendleton filled the time, as she was quite enamored of the queen's approval of Georgiana. Each moment seemed to suggest a new individual who might consider the news. Lady Heathway was bound to be approving. Lady Annabelle's mother could have nothing to say against it, though the woman *could* be implacable. Though Georgiana herself knew very well she'd done nothing remarkable, she was ever so grateful that she had pleased Lady Mendleton and not particularly anxious to know what anybody else thought of it, especially not Lady Kerster.

Finally, their carriage door was opened and they went inside.

Lady Featherstone's house was finely apportioned and the lady herself gracious. Of all Lady Mendleton's friends, she certainly was one of the least prepossessing and she did not make Georgiana quake as the duchess and Lady Heathway did.

Georgiana's cloak had been taken and she had received her

card. As Lady Mendleton led her toward the ballroom, Georgiana saw a rather alarming sight.

The ladies of the society, sans Lady Featherstone who remained at the door greeting her guests, approached en masse like a bank of determined swans. The duchess led the way, flanked by Lady Heathway, Lady Easton, and Lady Redfield.

"Louisa," the duchess said, grasping Lady Mendleton's hands in her own. "We have of course heard of your triumph at the palace."

Lady Heathway, looking the slightest bit friendly which was exceedingly friendly for herself, said, "Well done, Miss Wilcox."

"Goodness, yes," Lady Redfield said, "absolutely everybody is talking of it. Anybody who has been to see the queen knows what those two dogs are like."

"Indeed," Lady Easton said. "Lord Granger was even bit on the ankle a few weeks back."

"But *our* girl brought them to heel," the duchess said proudly.

Lady Mendleton was almost overcome by the approval surrounding her. Though, she managed to recover herself enough to speak. "I knew how it would be," she said softly. "The queen was quite taken with Georgiana, just as I knew she would be."

Georgiana did not think Lady Mendleton had ever really had hopes in that direction and had rather satisfied herself with praying they'd get through the meeting without a terrible gaffe. Still, it pleased her that Lady Mendleton was so delighted and that she had given the lady reason to crow to her friends. Even if the reason was only a bit of mutton grease on a napkin. It was certainly superior to anybody wondering why they had not yet heard her play the pianoforte or hearing how she had sailed over her horse in the park.

"Let us proceed in together," the duchess said. "Miss Wilcox will be much in demand and we must see that she is not approached by anybody we do not find suitable."

"I quite agree," a deep voice said behind her. Georgiana of course knew the voice, it was a voice she sometimes heard when the person owning it was not even near. It was unmistakably Lord Langley.

"I feel I ought to step in and take Miss Wilcox's supper," Lord Langley went on. "We should not like the lady to have any extended conversations with a gentleman who has not been thoroughly vetted. The queen's approval may bring in a less savory, grasping, individual."

"Well said!" the duchess said. "We cannot be too careful."

"Very astute to the ways of the world," Lady Redfield said.

Lady Heathway nodded in acquiescence.

Lady Mendleton appeared a bit unsure of this plan until Lady Easton spoke.

"Louisa, it is to be commended that your son supports our society and our efforts with such vigor! I am sure I could not prevail upon my own to carry the standard so willingly. Well done!"

Lady Mendleton, helpless against any sort of approbation, began to see the charm of the scheme.

As for Georgiana, she stood silent, rather thankful that nobody had thought to ask her what her own opinion of it was. She was gratified beyond measure, but felt a bit wobbly. She was also certain it was not a sensible idea and wondered why Lord Langley had suggested it. The speech he'd given did not precisely sound like him. It sounded invented, though none of the ladies seemed to think so. Grasping individuals? What could they hope to grasp, exactly? She was no heiress, after all.

Dining with Lord Langley would be wonderful and yet dangerous. She was already having a hard enough time suppressing whatever feelings she was developing for the lord.

Lord Langley put his name down and strode off, suddenly seeming a bit gruff for all that it had been his own idea.

The duchess imperiously pointed toward the ballroom and said, "We proceed."

Georgiana found herself surrounded by the ladies as they made their way in, feeling very like a princess who must be guarded against rogues. She smiled to herself and did not let it go to her head—she was favored *now*, but always cognizant of the idea that what went up eventually would come down again.

Still, as she gazed at all these ladies, she could not forget what efforts had been made on her behalf. She had been nobody with no means, living quietly in the country, and there she would be still if not for their care. Whatever her attraction might be to Lord Langley, she could not let them down. She would not allow herself to go too far.

Georgiana scolded herself for her own ridiculous pride. Why was she worried about going too far? It was not as if Lord Langley had any ideas in that direction. At least, she did not think so. He was a kind and affectionate son and had taken her supper to please his mother and her friends. That was all, and she'd better remember it.

THE FOLLOWING HALF hour was extraordinary. It would even have been comical, had Georgiana been able to view it from afar, rather than find herself in the middle of it. The ladies of the society, all powerful in their own right, were an unstoppable force when they came together. They seemed to gather courage from one another, though no courage had been lacking in the first place, and became an insurmountable obstacle to any gentleman not deemed up to snuff.

Lord Bertridge, as Lady Easton's nephew, handily gained access to Georgiana's card. Mr. Vance and Lord Asturt, both of whom she liked very much, did not. Those two gentlemen, and some others, were turned round firmly. She assumed Mr. Vance's family was not long enough in history, as it was Georgiana's understanding that his grandfather had been a gun maker. Lord Asturt must be considered odd from his long residence in Ireland and mishmash of an accent.

The strategies the ladies used were amusing and forthright, generally consisting of the duchess leading the way with: "Miss Wilcox is fully engaged, but see here, it appears Miss So and So across the ballroom seeks your attention. Do be a dear and see what she wants."

Georgiana felt very managed but there was nothing to do about it, so she resolved to remain unbothered. There was, in any case, a certain charm to it. It was as if she were a lone cygnet guided by five terrifying swans.

The first dance had been taken by Lord Bertridge and Georgiana found she liked him better on further acquaintance. He seemed to have thrown over some of his stiffness and was rather approving of her for befriending the queen's dogs. He was very fond of his own dogs, particularly a bull mastiff that had the run of his house, and he had a respect for their instincts. It appeared that a couple of Pomeranians had vouchsafed for her far better than her ability to solve Lord Ryland's mystery.

The second set ended up taken by Lord Asturt, though the society of ladies had initially chased him off. It ought to have been Mr. Damian, son of a baron and exceedingly rich, but he had been called away unexpectedly. Lord Asturt claimed that Mr. Damian had an old aunt staying in his house who had suddenly taken a bad turn and the gentleman had asked him to step in while he left to attend to her.

Georgiana was not sorry for it, though she wished the best for the gentleman's sick aunt. Mr. Damian had seemed exceedingly serious and Lord Asturt was generally not. As they moved through the changes, they had talked of this or that and Georgiana had launched one of her very reliable questions—did the gentleman have any hobbies?

She favored the question, as it invariably went in one of two directions. Most usually, she would hear of horses, or hunting, or some other common pastime. But every so often she would be told of something delightfully odd.

In her old neighborhood, she'd discovered that Mr. Brent was in the habit of going out in the rain to collect earthworms who'd stranded themselves on gravel. It seemed they could get themselves on it but not off again. He would carefully collect them and relocate the creatures to his garden. He was convinced that his large population of worms accounted for his superior roses. He also named the creatures and gave most of the credit for his roses to Reginald, a very large specimen he'd found one rainy afternoon, moments before it was to be obliterated by a peddler's wagon wheel.

Then, of course, there had been Lord Frederick, an aging viscount who had spent his entire adult life experimenting with different materials for their ability to retain heat. This had, at first, sounded dreadfully scientific and scholarly. That was, until she was informed that all this effort was to accomplish keeping his tea warm in a jar in his coat when he rode into the village. His current solution was a glass jar wrapped in fashioned tin and then wrapped again in wool. He was still working on the problem, though.

Lord Asturt's response to her question about hobbies was not precisely usual, but it was not odd either. It was altogether interesting.

"I have, for some years, been researching and writing a tome on English kings—the twists and turns of history and how each came to ascendency," he said. "I find the past fascinating, 1066 and all that, you know. Though, it really is only to amuse myself and I very much doubt anybody will ever read my scribblings."

"I must think you are wrong about that," Georgiana said. "Certainly, if you have been researching for years, you must have come upon a thousand interesting facts."

"Ah, yes, indeed I have…"

Lord Asturt had trailed off and Georgiana got the distinct impression that he'd be delighted to share some of his discoveries. If only he were pressed.

They had returned to their beginning place as another couple took their turn. "Do tell, Lord Asturt," she said, hoping to nudge him on.

The lord seemed pensive. Then he said, "I am not certain I should, actually. The information I came upon recently is of such a nature as to…well, as to perhaps create instability."

"Certainly not," Georgiana said playfully, "but now that you have so intrigued me, you cannot deny me the story no matter how outrageous."

"Very well," Lord Asturt said in a low voice. "It seems that the current king's grandfather was once whisked away to Hanover and stayed there for some months."

"As would be usual, as they are Hanoverians," Georgiana said.

"Yes, that is indeed why the destination was chosen, but not why a destination was needed in the first place. It appears that the fellow suffered a bout of madness and his courtiers sought to hide the condition. Fortunately, it did not last and it did not come again."

Lord Asturt looked at her intently, as if to divine what she would make of the story. She could not say she was overly shocked. If one were to look back on the history of English kings, what was widely known was shocking enough. She supposed they had all sorts of secrets. After all, what excuse could Henry VIII have for killing off wives, or King John managing things so badly that he found himself signing the Magna Carta? Were they not all a bit mad in their way?

"Do you see what I hint at, Miss Wilcox?" Lord Asturt said, with a note of urgency in his voice. "The madness is in the Hanoverian blood; it has been inherited and passed down. Naturally, some have always suspected it, but if the British public were to know it as a fact, well…I do not see how the Hanovers would carry on."

"Goodness, Lord Asturt," Georgiana whispered, "do not say such things! It borders on…treasonous."

"Though it is the truth," Lord Asturt said. "I suspect Lord Langley knows it well enough, being privy to the queen and involved in the king's care."

"I would not know what Lord Langley may be privy to," Georgiana said.

"Certainly, he must drop hints here and there?" Lord Asturt asked.

"He does not," Georgiana said, uncomfortable with the direction of the conversation.

It was their turn once again and the lord led her out on the floor. "Never mind me, Miss Wilcox. I do sometimes go twisting and turning through rabbit's warrens in my research—perhaps it is nothing, only a coincidence or aberration. Perhaps the regent will prove me wrong, after all."

Georgiana wished that was the case, but who really knew? The regent was known to be excessive in everything. She just hoped that was not a harbinger of some malady to come.

The dance ended and Georgiana was not sorry for it. She really would prefer not to engage in discussions of royal madness.

A succession of other gentlemen, most of them very forgettable, took the next dances. They were, perhaps, only particularly forgettable because Georgiana could not help thinking of the supper to come. She could not help thinking of Lord Langley.

JASPER CURSED HIMSELF. He'd gone back and forth over the idea of taking Miss Wilcox's supper and then determined he would not. He was not in the habit of fooling himself and he knew he had been doing just that over the past few days.

While he did not *think* Miss Wilcox had been sent to spy in the house, he had in no way proved it as fact. However, because of his own personal inclinations, he had persuaded himself that he had somehow proved it. A careful reckoning earlier in the day had presented him with that unfortunate conclusion.

He'd decided that he must step back and bide his time, whatever his personal feelings might be. He'd gone so far as to inform his mother that he would not escort them in the carriage but would take his horse instead.

It had been such a firm resolution! It had been grounded in facts and sense. And yet, as soon as he'd seen her, he'd marched over to the old cabal of his mother's friends and insisted on putting himself down for her supper.

And what reasons he gave! She was not to have extended conversation with anybody who had not been thoroughly vetted? It was absurd. She might have conversation with anybody she liked and of course everybody attending Lady Featherstone's ball was perfectly respectable.

They were all to worry over *grasping* individuals? Grasping of what? The two thousand pounds of dowry his father had laid out? A truly grasping gentleman had need of rescuing his estates and two thousand would not turn his head.

Upon hearing the scheme, his mother had almost hesitated in the matter, and would have, had not Lady Easton ridiculously commended him for his support of their society.

Support, indeed. He was weak, that was all that it was. He was becoming irrational. It was his job to protect the king from ruthless reports and he was still in the midst of trying to capture the culprits. The primary culprit might even be the Stuart. It was no time to allow his personal feelings to sway his opinions. He ought to only follow facts, and there were not enough facts to follow at the moment.

Then, he had been so distracted by the whole matter that he'd not spied Lady Annabelle stealthily making her way to his side. He had been determined to avoid her this evening, making like a fox into the brush if she were in the vicinity. He had no patience for whatever she had to say to him, particularly not after he'd seen her on the street and she'd rushed to tell him of Miss Wilcox's fall in the park—a story she had no doubt advertised far and wide.

By the time he'd spotted her it had been too late. He knew he would have to offer a dance and he knew she would accept. A gentleman did not have much choice in such matters when a lady was determined. It had been an added irritation that the only dance left open was her first. Certainly, she had held it open. Certainly, she wished him taking her first would say something to the company present.

Though she was exceedingly short, he at that moment did rather feel like a fox looking for escape from a ruthless hunter. A pale and irritating ruthless hunter.

The ball had begun, and with it had come Lady Annabelle's usual chatter. He answered her almost mechanically, saying the things that were expected of him. The London air having done something to her hair again was of no surprise, nor was his denial that it could be so. The color of her dress, which was a pale yellow, was claimed to do nothing for her complexion. Jasper dearly wished to tell her that she was right, but only said something nonsensical about the shade being cheerful.

After she had thoroughly examined her person, found it wanting, and then was assured why she was wrong in every instance, Lady Annabelle said, "I do hope Miss Wilcox has recovered from her tumble in the park."

"It was nothing," Jasper said curtly.

"It did not seem as nothing, Lord Langley," Lady Annabelle said, gazing up with her insipid pale eyes. "It seemed almost as if the lady were not familiar with the operation of mounting a horse."

Jasper did not answer and hoped she would go back to examining her own person and leave Miss Wilcox out of it.

"Well," Lady Annabelle said, "I suppose when one has been locked away in some little backwater in the countryside...one cannot wonder...I did hear, I think, that her grandfather on her mother's side was in trade...I suppose some things cannot be taught..."

The music had blessedly come to an end. Unfortunately, Jasper's patience had come to an end with it. He really could not control himself longer. "Apparently, Lady Annabelle," he said, "manners and good grace are also things that cannot be taught to everyone. Not even, on occasion, to a marquess' daughter," he said stiffly. He bowed and left her standing alone.

He should not have said it, though it had felt rather glorious. In one moment, he had conveyed to Lady Annabelle everything he thought of her. It may have been ungentlemanly, but then she had been exceedingly unladylike in her talk about Miss Wilcox. Further, he was confident that Lady Annabelle would have no further use for him after *that* conversation. His mother would be disappointed, but that was unavoidable and would have happened sooner or later.

He had a sudden vision of his fishing expedition the summer before off the coast of Ramsgate. He'd reeled in a cod and found it riddled with sea lampreys. Their horrifying round mouths full of teeth had attached themselves to the poor fish and were draining it of its life-giving fluids.

That was precisely what he thought of Lady Annabelle—a vampiric lamprey that he'd finally shaken loose and watched drift to the sea floor.

⋙⋘

GEORGIANA HAD EXCUSED herself to the retiring room before being led into supper. Her dance with Lord Langley had felt fraught with tension, though neither said anything about it.

In fact, neither said much at all. It was their eyes that had talked. Every time their eyes met they conversed. She was attracted to him, he was attracted to her. At least it seemed so. It *felt* so. She'd worked not to feel anything, but she'd not at all succeeded.

He was as graceful and assured as ever, and she supposed she'd appeared composed enough. But she was not!

Being so close to him made her feel a bit woozy and she'd worried she would do something ridiculous like faint in his arms. What would she say then? What would she say to dear Lady Mendleton? *Terribly sorry to make a scene, it is just that I was overcome by your son. Yes, that son that you are determined to marry off to Lady Annabelle. As I said, my apologies.*

Worse, a rather terrible idea had stolen over her as they danced. All along, she had thought she might direct her feelings. Her head would decide what was right, and her heart would follow suit, even if only reluctantly. She had imagined she'd been in control.

As it turned out, her feelings had run on ahead of her with nary a glance back. They refused to be turned. They couldn't care less what she thought about it.

What now?

She had indicated she would go to the retiring room not because she had any real need of it, but because she wished for a moment alone. A moment away from his presence. A moment to attempt to marshal her scattered thoughts into some semblance of order.

The room, as she entered, clearly spoke of having been designed by a woman. It was not a single room, nor small, but a cavernously long corridor of small private apartments. The carpets were deep and the door leading in was thick and solid—there was a quiet that seemed diametrically opposed to the noisy ballroom. A middle-aged female attendant stood near the door and behind her was a shelf housing an array of handy items, such as handkerchiefs, hairpins, needle and thread, and powders and scents of all sorts. Pots of hyacinths sat outside of each apartment door along the corridor to overpower any unwanted scent that might have the audacity to make an appearance in a ladies' retiring room.

Each private apartment was large enough to hold a lady and three of her friends should they only be looking for a moment of privacy to exchange gossip. It was set up for everything necessary—a bourdaloue and a chamber pot being the most practical—and a few things unnecessary but welcome, including a table, chair and looking glass, an elegant hairbrush with a cherry wood handle, a stack of handkerchiefs embroidered with Lady Featherstone's initials, and a velvet settee where a lady might comfortably faint while being ministered to by her friends.

Georgiana had taken herself to the last apartment but one, closed the door and sank down, wishing only for a few minutes of silence.

Even that appeared to be too much to ask for. She heard a loud sob in the next apartment and, as it came through rather sturdy walls, it must have been loud indeed.

The sob was followed by a series of snorts, chokings and further sobs. Georgiana recognized the sounds well enough—a lady was quite hysterical.

It appeared the lady was alone, as she did not hear any other sounds. Why did not the attendant see to it? The matron had placed herself near the front at the doors leading in, but surely she could hear what was emanating from behind that far door.

Georgiana sighed and rose. It was likely a matter of a lover's quarrel or a girl having to sit out or some such nonsense.

On the other hand, the sobs were rather violent for something of that nature. Perhaps it was a lady who was not squired into supper? The hostess should have done something to rectify the matter but sometimes a thing might be missed. That particular dreadful circumstance might indeed cause such howls.

Somebody was going to have to see if the lady were becoming ill and required assistance.

She left her own apartment and gently knocked on the other door. No answer was given but the sobs had instantly stopped as if they did not like to be caught out.

"Madam," Georgiana said, "may I help you in any way? Are you in distress? Might I find one of your friends and bring them to you?"

The door suddenly flung open. Much to Georgiana's surprise, it was Lady Annabelle making all the racket.

The lady pointed at Georgiana and said, "You!"

CHAPTER ELEVEN

L ADY ANNABELLE HAD flung open the door to her apartment in
the retiring room and cried, "You!" Georgiana though it
might not have been a particularly alarming thing to say had it
not been said in an accusing tone. A condemning tone, really.

"Lady Annabelle?" Georgiana said, for lack of anything more
intelligent to say at the sight of the disheveled young lady with
very red eyes.

Lady Annabelle staggered back and collapsed on the settee.
She heaved sobs.

Whatever Georgiana's prior feelings had been for the lady,
she could not ignore that she was in a dire state. She hurried in
and sat next to her, handing her a handkerchief from the neatly
piled stack on the side table.

"Whatever has happened," Georgiana said, "please do allow
me to assist you."

"You cannot help me," Lady Annabelle said, "nobody can. He
despises me!"

"I cannot believe that," Georgiana said. "Whoever you think
of, I am certain it was only a misunderstanding."

Georgiana might have wished she had not posited that idea.
Lady Annabelle, determined to prove Georgiana wrong and show
her that there had been no misunderstanding whatsoever, poured
out the story of Lord Langley's insult. She, a marquess' daughter,
had no manners, according to him.

It seemed incredible. Of course, Georgiana had speculated that Lord Langley was not overcome by the lady, but he would never be cruel.

"But why should he say that you had no manners?" Georgiana asked. "That does not sound very like him. What on earth could you have said to cause such a grievous insult?"

Lady Annabelle seemed rather uncomfortable with that particular line of questioning, twisting her handkerchief into a small knot. "Well, I only said, oh I don't know exactly. You know, you *did* fall off your horse and I *did* hear your grandfather was in trade and I suppose I said...something about that."

Georgiana was rather taken aback, though she supposed she ought not be surprised. What did cause surprise, though, was that Lord Langley would have put up a spirited enough defense of her to cause Lady Annabelle to collapse in a heap.

"Oh, Miss Wilcox, you do not know what a terrible person I am!" Lady Annabelle said. "I am really the worst person on earth and deserve no consideration at all!"

Georgiana had often thought so herself, though she knew very well that might be taking things a bit far. The lady was irritating, but hardly grand enough to be the *very* worst person on earth. She patted Lady Annabelle's hand and said, "If you really were, you would hardly claim it. I am certain that the very worst person on earth, whoever they are, has engaged in far darker deeds and keeps them a closely guarded secret."

"So I've got that wrong too," Lady Annabelle said. "You see, I am very stupid and have nothing but my looks and mama says I have to make the most of them. I cannot make enough of them, though. No matter how many times I point them out or point out a wrong done by another lady so I might look better, it matters not. Nobody loves me, nobody declares themself for me. *You* might fall off your horse a thousand times and it makes no difference, it does not put me in a better light at all! I shall be an old maid and a disappointment to my parents. Lord Langley does not love me, though they so hoped that he would!"

"Do you love *him*, Lady Annabelle?" Georgiana said cautiously.

"Him? No, of course not. He is so…serious and ill-humored. He does not dote on me. I believe he knows I am stupid. But what matter? I was determined to do my duty, even if I had rather not. It's all for nothing, though. Nobody in this Town will love me and I will be shamed. Nobody dotes, though I was quite sure that they would."

Georgiana was rather touched by this. She had not realized that Lady Annabelle was under such pressure. Or that she did not even like Lord Langley. Or that she was longing to be doted on. A sudden idea occurred to her.

"Was there ever somebody who *did* dote on you, then? Somebody not currently in Town?"

Lady Annabelle sniffled into her handkerchief. "Mr. Pottsgrove dotes, though he is only the son of a baron and my mother does not think his prospects good enough. He is a neighbor and I see him often when we are at home, but he does not come to Town."

As the idea of Mr. Pottsgrove presented itself, Lady Annabelle seemed to cheer. "He's ever so genial. He talks a great deal, it is really very pleasant as I do not have to fill the silences with anything stupid. I need say nothing about my person or anybody else because he just rambles on about how pretty I am and how sweet I am. He does not give a fig that I don't read much or care what's in the newspapers or know so little about anything, he says I am perfect just as myself. I told him I must go to Town and get married and he swore his life was over and he would die a despondent bachelor. That was nice, I thought."

"Rather more than nice, *I* think," Georgiana said, suppressing her humor over the situation. "Goodness, Lady Annabelle, rather than fuss over what Lord Langley thinks, I feel you ought to have a frank conversation with your mother. Mr. Pottsgrove has been left bereft and so have you."

Lady Annabelle gently sighed. "Did I say he has red hair? Not dark red, but very light, almost blond. And freckles that come out in the summer, right across his nose. He's very tall and he can give me a lift up to my saddle with only one hand. Can you imagine, I step on his outstretched palm and up I go. He swears we would have the most charming children in the world, and I would have to do nothing but be a hostess at parties, which I should like very much. He says I am his perfect person."

"I am certain he is right. Now dry your tears and resolve to put your foot down with your mama. He will be a baron, after all, not a grocer. He is perfectly eligible."

"He will, will he not? And I do get on smashing with his father, after all. He's a jolly old fellow and calls me *my pet*. Just think, I might be myself all the time and still be admired. I ought to do it! I ought to put my foot down with Mama."

"Indeed," Georgiana said, "though please do me the courtesy of leaving me out of the tale. This has to be your idea and yours alone."

Lady Annabelle nodded and said, "Mr. Pottsgrove, Frederick, he once told me, Annie, you can be the queen of my house and eat marzipan all the day long with a small white dog on your lap. That was nice, I thought."

That *was* rather nice of Mr. Pottsgrove. Georgiana dearly hoped Lady Annabelle would find the fortitude to insist on the gentleman, as she did not see that any other gentleman would find his genial ideas at all practical.

"Now, dry your eyes and blow your nose. Let us go into supper or we will be missed." Georgiana looked over Lady Annabelle's person. Her red eyes and red nose would not go unnoticed. "We will powder your nose and it will be perfectly reasonable for you to claim an allergy from one of Lady Featherstone' flower arrangements. Claim it is the hyacinths, the retiring room is overflowing with them."

Lady Annabelle dried her eyes, and then blew her nose with a force more suited to Mr. Pottsgrove himself. As she did so, Georgiana reflected on what she had discovered. There was to be no match between Lord Langley and Lady Annabelle. Even had Mr. Pottsgrove not been in the picture, they'd had a falling out from what had never been a particularly genial acquaintance. A falling out on her own account, it seemed.

That, of course, was gratifying.

And yet, it must not be gratifying! As soon as Lady Mendleton was apprised that her scheme was doomed, she'd search out another eligible lady for her son. That favored lady would never be the penniless daughter of a baron who had married a trades-man's daughter. It would never be her.

She must get all thought of that out of her mind at once!

GEORGIANA HAD FINALLY convinced Lady Annabelle to depart the retiring room after straightening her gown, powdering her red nose, fixing the ribbons in her hair and assuring her that, aside from red eyes which would resolve shortly, she looked exceeding-ly well.

Most ladies might believe what they saw in a looking glass over what they were told, but Lady Annabelle was perfectly amenable to putting great stock in Georgiana's opinion. She also apologized for telling almost everybody she knew about the fall in the park. Or, as she said, "Everybody gossips and it was all I had, but I shan't say another word about it."

In the end, Georgiana found she could not dislike Lady Anna-belle as much as she had done. The girl was silly, exceedingly so, but Mr. Pottsgrove did not seem to mind it and so neither would she.

When they emerged, she realized they had been closeted away for quite some time as it was only Lord Langley and Mr. Avendale who waited, everybody else having proceeded into the dining room.

Both men appeared uncomfortable, though Lord Langley far more than Mr. Avendale. Lady Annabelle threw her chin up rather decidedly as she passed by Lord Langley, having grown courage over the idea of Mr. Pottsgrove and his outlandish promises.

As nobody seemed to have anything to say, they walked to the dining room with only a small sniffle from Lady Annabelle accompanying them.

They were so late to the supper as to be the last in and footmen led the couples in different directions to pairs of open seats. Georgiana thought that was well—poor Lady Annabelle could not be expected to keep herself composed in the face of the man who had so insulted her. Not even with Mr. Pottsgrove to think about.

After they were seated, Lord Langley said, "I had almost resolved to send in a search party, did you and Lady Annabelle run into trouble?"

Georgiana was fairly surprised at the question, as it was not usual that a man would comment on a lady having been to a retiring room at all, much less how long they spent there. Feminine creatures were not to have any bodily functions, at least none that would be acknowledged.

But then, he'd seen her exit with Lady Annabelle, and he knew very well that he'd insulted her. This line of inquiry was a fishing expedition to discover what she knew about it.

"As you can imagine," Georgiana said, "Lady Annabelle was quite distraught over...recent events."

Lord Langley nodded and was silent for some time. To his credit, he did not pretend he did not understand her meaning. He said, "Whatever I said, it was well-earned."

"I imagine so, but she is not what you think," Georgiana said. "Or rather, her situation is not what you think."

"Her situation?" Lord Langley asked, looking surprised.

"She is not in love with you," Georgiana said. For some reason, she felt the need to somehow vindicate Lady Annabelle. It was the silliest thing in the world—the lady had gossiped about her all over Town. Still, she had not meant much by it, in the end.

"I...never said she was!" Lord Langley said. He said it rather vehemently and Georgiana could see perfectly well that he'd been under the impression that the lady had set her cap on him.

"She finds you far too serious, ill-humored, and you do not dote on her," Georgiana said. "It will not do."

"I am glad it will not do," Lord Langley said. "Though ill-humored..." He looked into her eyes. "My interests lie in an entirely different direction."

Georgiana turned away and stared at her plate, though there was nothing yet on it. Why was there nothing on it? If there were, she might use her fork to push things around.

What did he mean by his interests lay in another direction? Was there another lady who he'd been in love with all along? But then, why did he look at her so? Was he hinting that she...

He cleared his throat and said, "I must ask, though—"

Ask? What? What would he ask her?

"Why did you fail to mention that you'd seen the king on the road when you journeyed to London?"

Georgiana felt as if someone had thrown cold water on her to wake her. Why did he ask her that? That was not what she'd hoped, or feared, or imagined...

"I only wonder," Lord Langley went on, "as it was so extraordinary an encounter and you *were* asked about the journey."

"I did not realize the news would travel further than those who were present," Georgiana said. "I suppose Jenny?"

"The report of what occurred was in the newspapers," Lord Langley said.

The newspapers? How could that be?

"No, that is impossible," Georgiana said, her mind racing. "I do not believe anybody there would have..."

"But why did you not say anything about it?" Lord Langley said, his voice low and insistent.

"Because it was private!" Georgiana whispered. "We should not have seen it. It was very like we had crept up to a house and peeked through its windows to view an intimate moment."

"And the public need not know of it," Lord Langley said.

"*Nobody* need know of it," Georgiana said. "Goodness, what

would you have thought of me, had I regaled the dinner table with the tale on that first night? What would you have thought if I posed it as an amusing story? The man is suffering!"

"I would have thought you were very like Lady Annabelle," Lord Langley admitted.

"Well I am not," Georgiana said, "I do not have a Mr. Pottsgrove waiting at home who dotes on me."

"Mr. who?" Lord Langley asked.

"Oh never mind, I should not have said."

A footman appeared at Lord Langley's side, offering a large platter of beef. As the lord dished it out for her, it seemed to break the current of their conversation.

Georgiana stayed silent, hoping he would continue. He did not and they moved on to more usual things. Georgiana was forced to turn from time to time to converse with Lord Matthew, a rather genial older fellow with a love of lawn bowling.

Her thoughts, though, were not at all about bowling. The more she considered it, the more questions surfaced. Where did his interest lie? Who had told the newspapers? Had Lord Langley really thought *she'd* done it? It seemed so, he did wonder why she had not revealed that she'd seen the king on the road.

Could he really have thought so ill of her right from the start? But then, he did not really think ill of her. No, she could tell he did not.

As she mulled it over, she could not believe Jenny or Carstares or the footmen would have told the tale. At least, not to the newspapers. It was far too likely that Jenny had told quite a lot of people, and one of them had done it. It would be impossible to identify the tattler.

Still, she did not like this vague suspicion hanging over her head. Especially not in Lord Langley's mind. Especially not when it seemed to stop him from saying something else. If there were some way to discover who the culprit was, she would very much like to do it.

What *did* Lord Langley think to say before he found he must ask her about the king? It had sounded somehow momentous, but then it had come to nothing.

Georgiana knew very well that she should be grateful that he had not said anything momentous. She also knew very well that she was as ungrateful as an unruly child. She would very much like to stamp her foot just now.

JASPER WAS GLAD he'd ridden his horse to the ball, rather than go in the carriage with his mother and Miss Wilcox. It afforded him time to think and he found he had so much to think about that he passed by the house and kept on going. A light fog hushed the road, dampened the sound of his horse's hooves, and made soft halos round the streetlamps.

Making his way through the neighborhood of Mayfair, he began to check off the list of things that must be considered, beginning with the easiest of them.

He was well and truly done with Lady Annabelle. He always had been done, but now they were of the same mind. Though, according to Miss Wilcox, they had *always* been of the same mind. He was too serious and ill-humored? It was outrageous! It simply was not true.

Well, perhaps it was more true lately, and especially true when he found himself in the presence of that lady. It was also mentioned that he did not dote on her, and that most assuredly *was* true.

But who exactly was Mr. Pottsgrove? If Lady Annabelle had left some paramour behind in the countryside, why did she not simply get on with it, rather than torturing people here? Well, he'd better not wonder over it—it was, happily, no longer any of his affair.

Though he was not sorry that he'd been direct with Lady Annabelle, rude even, he was uncomfortable with the idea that she and Miss Wilcox had some tête-à-tête in the ladies' retiring room. They'd been in there for ages!

He supposed Lady Annabelle had told Miss Wilcox what he'd said and she thought him rather a brute for it. What had she said about it? Lady Annabelle was distraught.

For all that, it was rather marvelous that Miss Wilcox was to be found at Lady Annabelle's side. He was certain she had no love for the lady, though she was too good to say so.

Too good to say so...and too good to say other things as well.

When he asked Miss Wilcox why she had not revealed seeing the king on the road, she had said it was because it was a private moment.

His instincts told him she had not prevaricated on the subject. There had been too genuine a surprise to discover the tale had made its way into the newspapers. There was also every reason to believe she'd not seen the newspapers—they were all delivered to *him*, while his mother only received Ackerman's and various other publications full of gossip and fashion. Miss Wilcox's reasoning for staying silent had been full of kindness and good grace. Noble, even.

The queen had commented that Miss Wilcox was either a marionette in the employ of her enemies or a lady with very fine sensibilities. It had been her fine sensibilities that had kept her quiet. Nobody, not even a spy, could have invented her defense. In fact, a spy would have had all sorts of flimsy excuses lined up and at the ready—she had been sworn to secrecy by one of the king's guards who had fetched the king, or she had not realized it was the king, or she had been asleep the whole journey and missed the encounter.

She was everything she represented herself to be. He knew that now. All his worry over what she was had burned off, just as the fog that surrounded him would burn off by morning.

It was rather glorious to think about!

Though, thinking was all well and good. The question was, what would he *do* about it?

He would ask for her hand. That's what he would do. In fact, that was what he must do, for if he did not some other fellow, Asturt perhaps, would swoop in ahead of him. That could not be stood for.

As the idea drifted through his mind, another idea came too. He was not just considering Miss Wilcox as a genial partner. He was in love with the lady. He had been for some time. He'd known that, somewhere in his heart. He'd just not allowed himself to *really* know it. Now, he rather had the inclination to shout it at the dark windows that loomed over him so all in the neighborhood, asleep or not, might know it.

When had it happened to him, exactly? He did not know. What he did know was that for quite some time he had been trying to convince himself of her innocence because of it.

He no longer need try—he was certain.

There were new questions, though. Did she love him, or even like him enough? That was the big question. The smaller question, though an equally high fence to be jumped, was how his mother would take the news. His father would be no trouble, the old man seemed fond of Miss Wilcox and the estate had no need of a large dowry. As far as his mother was concerned, though, he was on his way to being engaged to Lady Annabelle. She must be turned round on that idea.

"None of it is insurmountable!" he said loudly into the silent night.

His horse sidestepped and danced in surprise, not at all used to his master having such an outburst.

Jasper laughed and turned him round. It was time to go home.

CHAPTER TWELVE

T HOUGH GEORGIANA HAD told Jenny she had no need of her coming to her after the ball—the dress she wore was easy enough to get out of—the maid had bustled into her bedchamber nonetheless.

As she helped Georgiana out of her clothes, she said, "As it was Lady Featherstone's ball, I suppose it was fancy as anything? How did you get on?"

"Everything was lovely," Georgiana said.

"Aye, it would be," Jenny said wistfully. "My own evening should'a been lovely too, what with them all out of the house."

"Was it not, then?" Georgiana asked, by now having come to know Jenny well enough to know there was a story she was itching to tell.

"Well, you see," Jenny said confidentially, "when they all go out and it's just us servants in the house, we're used to having a merry time of it round the dining table in the servants' quarters. We play cards and such and Mr. Perry allows us an extra glass of ale or wine, assuming we done our work. We might laugh as loud as we like, as there ain't nobody to disturb."

This all sounded quite reasonable to Georgiana, though she was certain she was meant to understand that this particular evening had not gone as planned. She did not know if the extra glass of spirits had not been forthcoming or the laughter not quite as liberal it could have been, but something had been amiss.

"It would'a come off just like that, if Marcus had only kept his lips from flapping."

Georgiana could not fathom what on earth the valet had said via flapping lips to upset what seemed to be a regular and pleasant routine.

"Mr. Perry done told him a dozen times," Jenny said, "that he's a valet and his business is Lord Langley's person, not Lord Langley's affairs. But Marcus would go on and on about the king and how poorly it seemed he was getting on and how none of us knew what we were to hear next and did anybody overhear Lord Langley talkin' about what we could expect comin' down the road at us."

Georgiana did not think Jenny would have helped this problem very much by telling them all about her encounter with the king, which she was fairly sure the girl had done. How else would it end up in the newspapers? Marcus had likely told everybody he encountered of the tale, since it was of such interest to him.

"Well," Jenny said, "Mr. Perry did finally run through all his patience and said: *If I hear mention of the king at this table one more time, steps will be taken!*"

"What sort of steps?" Georgiana asked, thinking it would not be so easy for a butler to get a valet dismissed if *that* were the step threatened.

"That's the question," Jenny said. "Whenever Mr. Perry gets in a lather over something, he says he'll take steps. Nobody has ever gone on to cross him further so none of us know what the steps are. We reckon they're terrifying though."

"Jenny," Georgiana said, "I believe *you* also mentioned the king at the servants' table on some earlier day? Did you know that what we observed on our journey somehow made it into the newspapers?"

Georgiana peeked at the maid to see how she would take this particular line of questioning. The girl had the good grace to blush furiously.

"Now, I admit that I did tell of it," Jenny said. "I know I said I wouldn't, but then it just came out of me like a faucet! Things do sometimes. And Marcus is so encouraging too—he always asks if I remember anything else. Well, I reckon one person tells another and they tell another and I shouldn't be surprised if it were a butcher or baker clear across Town what heard it and put it in the papers. People *will* gossip, you know."

"Yes, I do know," Georgiana said, pressing her lips together so she would not laugh over Jenny's complete lack of guile and nonexistent awareness of her own habit.

"I'm truly sorry for it and I vowed to myself that if I ever see the king again, I won't say a word about it. I'll take it to my grave and not even tell the vicar of it as I lay on my deathbed." Jenny paused, the comb in her hand in mid-air. "Only God will know of it and who would he tell?"

"That's all suitably dramatic, Jenny," Georgiana said, biting her lip, "but as it is unlikely you will encounter the king again, perhaps vow not to spread any other tale of something you might witness."

Jenny considered this. "I can try, miss. Though interesting things do come out of me like a faucet!"

As Georgiana had no advice on how Jenny might shut off her faucet, Jenny finished combing and braiding her hair and bid her goodnight.

Left alone, Georgiana was satisfied that Jenny had been correct in her theory. She'd told the servants in the house about their encounter with the king, and then they'd proceeded to tell all and sundry. One of those people had seen an opportunity and gone to the newspapers with the story, and they were most likely well-paid for their trouble. Surely, Lord Langley had figured that out? Why should he have questioned *her*?

But then, he did work for the queen and Georgiana had been asked about her journey and she had said nothing of it. Perhaps he only wondered about it.

What was he going to say to her, though? Before he asked about that? It seemed as if he needed to assure himself on that point so he might move on to something more important.

Georgiana sighed. Never in her life had she been so torn. She at once wished to always be loyal to Lady Mendleton and whatever the lady's plans were, and at the same time go in the complete opposite direction.

As she had noticed earlier in the evening, her heart had plowed on ahead of her. She well knew now that she loved Lord Langley. She loved Jasper Stapleton, Viscount Langley. That first night, that first cozy dinner with the family, she'd felt the thrill of it. She'd attempted to brush it off and had gone forward looking at other gentlemen and waiting for the same thrill that never arrived. There was a flatness to those encounters, as if an old friend had arrived for a quiet tea. There was nothing thrilling, there was nothing like Lord Langley.

If only he were to stay a viscount! If only he was of some middling estate nobody expected great things from. If only he were not Lady Mendleton's son.

He was as he was, though, and could there be anybody more wonderful than he was? She thought not.

Then, this evening, she'd begun to get the idea that he might also feel…

But it was wrong! How could it be anything but wrong? If Lord Langley did have some feeling for her, were they to only make themselves happy while disappointing absolutely everybody else?

That's what it would be—nobody would look upon the match as brilliant, everybody would think the lord had wasted his prospects. Worse, Georgiana would be hailed as a schemer. A schemer who'd wormed her way into the house and somehow seduced the lord. A schemer who had betrayed the kindness and good faith of her benefactress. What was she, anyway? Only a charity case, sponsored by a group of ladies who wished to amuse themselves. A charity case who took advantage.

And that would be a fair assessment, she was afraid. What a poor choice of a sponsored daughter they had made.

Still, though there were so many reasons against it, if he asked, would she not say yes?

She knew very well that she would. She was a weak and craven person who would chase her happiness despite what anybody else thought of it.

"I was always so sensible," Georgiana said softly. "What has happened to me?"

PERRY SETTLED INTO his chair in front of the fire. It was not a large fire as the season was warm, but some sort of flames were always necessary to beat back the cold and damp of the basement's thick stone walls. As the butler, he had been granted an apartment down the corridor from the kitchens that consisted of a bed-chamber, sitting room, and even a small dressing room. Gone were the days of sharing a single cramped room with some other person. Gone were the days of being allocated a single candle. Gone were the days of sweltering in the attics.

He had even made a careful purchase of a finely carved cherry wood table. Upon it sat a polished silverplate tray and a glass decanter Lord Mendleton had given him for his own personal use, the decanter filled with Perry's preferred brand of port. Sometimes, there was another tray filled with leftover cakes and biscuits. Of an evening, once the house had gone quiet, he quite enjoyed his London accommodations. But for the cook, he had the downstairs to himself. As the Frenchman slept like the dead in a room just off his kitchens, Perry was free to stroll un-harassed into that domain and help himself to a plate of cold ham or a chicken leg whenever he liked.

This particular evening should have been quite genial. The staff's work had been light, as the family had gone out and had not required a sit-down dinner before going. Just a light repast set up on the sideboard and then off they went. All would have been well, had not Marcus insisted on aggravating him yet again!

In truth, it had gone beyond aggravation and proceeded into suspicion. There was something unnatural about Marcus' obsession over the king's condition. How many times would he question Jenny to discover if she had more to say about her encounter? The whole world must be able to divine that anything that went into that maid's eyes came out of her mouth just as fast. There were no hidden recesses in Jenny's mind, there were no hidden depths of cunning that might hold back any details. Still, the valet would go on with it.

But then, perhaps he was too suspicious these days. Perhaps considering what Miss Wilcox's real purpose might be had awakened a natural distrust in everything he viewed. He still could not work out whether she was just a naturally un-talented young lady who was inept on a musical instrument, had a lowbrow reading habit, and was prone to flinging herself off horses, or whether her lack of accomplishments hinted at something more sinister. His conviction of her evil intentions had been a bit shaken when it appeared the queen herself was approving of Miss Wilcox. As an upright Englishman, he trusted the queen's judgment in all things. Still, he must keep his eyes wide open when it came to that particular miss. Even a queen might be mistaken here and there, as anybody who'd had the bad judgment to marry Henry VIII had found out.

Now, on top of wondering about Miss Wilcox, Marcus struck him as suspicious. He was new, for one, and had been working in Germany of all places. Perry had oft indicated his disfavor regarding the valet's ongoing speculations and questions about the king's condition, so why did the fellow go on with it? Was he stupid, or was he up to something?

Perry took a long draught of his port. Only six months ago, his life had been very simple. His largest difficulties were managing the new chef's outlandish French ideas, waking Mrs. Ripperton from her endless drunken naps, and hiding his despondency when yet another stray dog turned up at the door.

Now, it seemed there were all sorts of other complications, and he did not know what he was to do about any of them.

JASPER SAT IN the library, waiting for Perry to bring in coffee and rolls and the newspapers. It seemed as any other day, it was what he did on any other day, but it was *not* any other day.

The problem was, how to proceed? He must somehow encounter Miss Wilcox alone. But that done, what was he to say? It was his understanding that in these matters a gentleman must be prepared. He must say something monumentally flattering if he was to get anywhere at all.

Jasper sat back, having a sudden recollection. When Renninger had proposed to Miss Saviston, he'd even gone so far as to write a bit of poetry for the lady. The fellow had read it aloud at the club and been roundly mocked, though all in attendance were perfectly amenable to believing that Miss Saviston had adored it.

No, he could not write a poem, that was out of the question and would only end absurd. He'd best stick to straightforward flattery.

Of course, there was no end of flattering things to say about Miss Wilcox, but which would she prefer? Which would sway her to decide that he must be the right choice? If it had been another lady, he might have thought that becoming a countess someday might be seen in a positive light, but he did not think Miss Wilcox would be influenced by it. She had not seemed at all impressed with titles and had even handled herself with confidence in front of the queen. No, she would not be overawed by a title.

Perhaps he might indicate his lack of interest in musical ability? No, that was probably not right—she might not like to be reminded that she was in the habit of thrashing the pianoforte rather than playing it.

His thoughts felt very muddled and he supposed that was

quite the usual condition. Once a gentleman had made up his mind, it seemed that happiness was within grasp. And yet, the lady knew nothing about it! In fact, the lady might have different ideas altogether. It was a very odd thing. In every other part of life, when he sought something, he simply took the necessary steps and it was done. None of those other steps filled him with this strange combination of anticipation and dread.

Still, it must be achievable. After all, how had all these people throughout time managed to get married? His own father had managed it, and so must he too.

Should he talk to his mother and father ahead of it? No, he thought not. Let it be a fait accompli and they would resign themselves to it. Miss Wilcox would not be his mother's first choice, but then she *was* very fond of her charge. They had no need of a large dowry and they would not get one, but they would get a daughter-in-law filled with grace and intelligence, not to mention stunning looks. They could not be against it, once they got used to the idea.

There was a soft knock on the door and Perry came through. As he laid out the coffee tray and a footman came in behind with a pile of newspapers, Jasper resolved that he'd carry on as if it were any other morning. Then, he'd lurk round the house, waiting for an opportunity.

As he did so, he heard bustling in the hall and the front door open and close. He drifted to the window in time to see Miss Wilcox, dressed in her riding habit, get into the carriage. Carstares was on the coachman's box, and two grooms rode the back. Another groom sat atop Minerva behind and yet another rode his mother's horse, Biscuit. That was almost all the grooms they employed.

He had no idea what she was doing, but my God, she looked rather marvelous doing it.

"Miss Wilcox goes for a ride?" he said to Perry. "So early?"

"Indeed," Perry said, practically with a sniff. "Apparently, though it is odd, Miss Wilcox was able to prevail upon Lady

Mendleton that horses ought to be ridden early, and not at the fashionable hours. The entire stable has been sent out to accompany her."

It *was* odd. For Town, it was bordering on the eccentric. But it was also right. Miss Wilcox was correct in her opinion. In the country, he would never think of taking his own horse out in the late afternoon if there were even a hint of heat in the air. Further, after a night in the stables, horses were generally ready to get out for a gallop. Just now, Minerva pawed the cobblestones as if to confirm this idea. Of course, there were occasionally some horses who did not have the same willing spirit—Biscuit only looked behind herself as if she hoped they would all turn around and give up this mad scheme.

As Jasper watched the train of carriage and horses depart, Perry dismissed the footman and closed the door. He said, "My lord, if I am not being presumptuous, may I ask how you get on with the new valet?"

"Marcus?" Jasper said, entirely distracted by Miss Wilcox's departure and wondering if he ought not ride after her. "Well enough, I suppose. He's bound to get the hang of my neckcloth sooner or later."

Should he ride after her? No, that would look ridiculous and she would not be alone. She would be surrounded by grooms. And worse, the brooding Carstares. Jasper could not imagine anything more painful than exposing his feelings in front of Carstares.

Jasper finally noticed Perry standing there staring at him. "Was there anything else?"

"No, my lord," Perry said in a regretful tone.

The butler left the room and Jasper thought the fellow was in a dour mood this morning. No doubt he was dealing with some contretemps below stairs and perhaps even involving his valet, since he'd asked about him.

Well, Perry had better handle it on his own. Jasper had far more important things to think about. He would do his work, and then when Miss Wilcox returned to the house, he would lie in wait. No, *lie in wait* sounded threatening, as if he were planning a murder. He would hang about. Yes, that was what he would do, hang about and wait for his opportunity.

He poured his coffee and opened the first newspaper in the pile.

LADY MENDLETON NEVER descended before ten, at the earliest. It was not that she would not have liked to be up earlier in the day, but it was simply impossible. She did not wake before half past eight, then there was breakfast to be brought in, and then a leisurely dressing where Jenny would amuse her with some tale or other.

Louisa had, when dear Georgiana came to her, arranged for the girl to breakfast in her own room too. After all, who would even be in the breakfast room? Her lord could not be bothered with it, and Jasper was always closeted in the library. As well, she liked to think that her staff was very lucky that they did not have to prepare an elaborate set-up every morning. Only in the country must they get up a full sideboard of rashers of bacon and platters of hot eggs and fried kidneys. They must all be grateful for the courtesy, and she simply adored anybody being grateful to her—it felt as if she were really accomplishing something.

Georgiana, according to Jenny, had her breakfast sent up at eight and was downstairs before nine. Well, that was the energy of youth, was it not? But this morning, the girl had been very intent on riding out early, with some notion that the horse preferred it. It was peculiar, and yet it was also endearing. She was such a caring girl, was she not? To even take Minerva's feelings into consideration.

Louisa had not seen the harm in it, as long as she was well-protected by a bevy of grooms. After all, what could she deny the girl? She was so very fond of her.

Yes, there had been a few hiccups at first, not the least of which were her frightening lack of skill on the pianoforte and her alarming way of mounting a horse, but the charming girl had overcome the queen and did not everything else pale in comparison? Further, was not her card filled up ever so quickly at Anne's ball the night before? Georgiana was admired! Her girl was sought after. Certainly, some suitable gentleman would ask for her hand. Though not so soon, Louisa hoped, as she liked the way they went on at the moment. Perhaps there might even be a second season? And then, could not Georgiana come to them in the country between this season and the next? And then, after all those pleasant months, a proposal would be made and she would crow to Lady Heathway over it.

All in all, the situation was very satisfying to think about.

A soft knock on the door brought Jenny, though her breakfast had not even arrived yet.

The maid hurried in and Louisa at once spotted that she carried a letter. A letter that must have come private messenger, as the post did not arrive so early.

Louisa's heart sank. The only missives to arrive so early were invariably from Lady Heathway. Everybody she knew was afraid of these arrivals, they were like disconcerting birds who had suddenly dropped out of the sky and landed on one's tray. If Lady Heathway had roused herself early and wrote, Lady Heathway was unhappy about something.

Jenny hurried to the bedside and said, "This was just delivered, the fellow was in Lady Heathway's livery, as you might expect."

Louisa took the folded letter and said, "Oh, dear."

"I'll go below stairs and tell them to hurry your breakfast," Jenny said. "I expect you'll need a fortifying tea after...whatever that is."

"You are a dear, Jenny," Louisa said distractedly, "excellent notion."

Louisa slowly opened the letter, completely perplexed over what Penelope could have written. She'd been in such good spirits the night before. Or, as good spirits as she ever was. What had gone wrong?

Louisa steeled herself and perused its contents.

My dear Louisa,

As you know, when a notion presents itself to my mind, I do not allow the moss to grow under my slippers before I put pen to paper.

I thought it only right to inform you immediately of something I observed last evening at our dear Anne's ball. It was quite chivalrous for Lord Langley to offer to take Miss Wilcox into supper, nobody can deny it. However, my eyes are like any falcon's, always searching out the truth.

My dear Louisa, there were looks. Looks between Lord Langley and Miss Wilcox. Looks that ought not to be ignored, lest you find the lady a permanent fixture in your household—a permanently related sort of a fixture.

Further, as my instincts were telling me to pay close attention, my eyes were upon her last evening relentlessly. Miss Wilcox spent some amount of time in the ladies' retiring room and what do you suppose was the end of it? I must tell you that I resolved to view it and so placed myself behind some well-positioned drapery. Miss Wilcox departed the retiring room with Lady Annabelle, WHO HAD CLEARLY BEEN CRYING!

What could Miss Wilcox have said to make Lady Annabelle cry? That I cannot be sure of, but certainly it was to do with Lord Langley. At least, that is what I suspect and my suspicions are always correct.

I write this to put you on your guard. Nobody can take away Miss Wilcox's triumph over the queen, which I fairly give her credit for. But be aware of what is under your nose, Louisa.

Kindest Regards,
Penelope

Louisa dropped the paper. Looks? Between Jasper and Georgiana? She had not noted anything like that. Though, she did not herself have Lady Heathway's falcon eyes. Or think to hide herself behind drapery at a ball, for that matter.

Perhaps it was only Penelope going too far, as she was sometimes wont to do. She was so confident of her instincts and her eyes, but there had been times where she *had* gone too far. Had she not been convinced, only last season, that Jasper was in danger from Miss Agatha Willoughby? Louisa had not been convinced of it; it was too nonsensical. The girl was a rich American who did uncomfortable things like ask how much something cost and then if that were not bad enough, comment on where it could be had cheaper. She laughed too loud, she flirted with abandon, and she pronounced no end of things old-fashioned. What on earth would they have done with such a person?

It had all come out well, in the end. Miss Willoughby had married ancient Lord Gaston which probably suited them both. He'd rescued his estates with her money and he'd probably not be walking around those estates all that long to bother Miss Willoughby. She'd had a son already and could rest easy now that her place was secure, whether Lord Gaston was walking around or resting peacefully underground. Penelope still would not own that she'd been wrong with a capital W.

Certainly, this was a like circumstance.

But why had Lady Annabelle cried after encountering Georgiana in the retiring room. That was the one point that Louisa could not reconcile. Why would Georgiana not mention the circumstance on the carriage ride home?

If it were true, if Penelope's instincts were correct, what then? Georgiana was a dear girl, that was undeniable, but Louisa did have her heart set on Lady Annabelle! She and Jasper seemed so well-suited and it would be a brilliant match. It was the sort of match one's mama might be congratulated upon.

No, she must dismiss this letter from her mind at once. It

simply could not be.

Jenny hurried in with the breakfast tray. She set it down and said, "Is all well, my lady?"

"Oh yes, I think so. I am sure of it. Lady Heathway has only allowed her imagination to run away from her."

Jenny nodded and said, "Well you ought to have some tea straight away to fortify yourself after such a fright so early in the day."

Louisa patted Jenny's hand. "What would I do without you? You do understand me so well, Jenny."

CHAPTER THIRTEEN

GEORGIANA HAD PREVAILED upon Lady Mendleton to allow her an early morning ride. She'd wished to clear her head and thought the only thing that would do it would be to find herself on a horse in the fresh air. Had she not done just the same at home?

The dear lady had allowed it, but insisted that a parade of grooms accompany her. She thought she must look quite ridiculous, leading such a procession through the park, had there been anybody to note it. As it was, the grounds were delightfully quiet—those multitudes who would turn up later were still abed or lazily having their breakfast.

Though she would have wished to, she could not advance down Rotten Row—the carriage would not do well and Lady Mendleton would not like her to leave Carstares behind. She resigned herself to the carriage road and took in the greenery and fresh air with relish.

She did find that the air and the rhythmic trot of the horse settled her mind. If Lord Langley were to ask for her hand, she would accept. Despite who else might be made unhappy by it. After all, Lady Annabelle would not be unhappy and she hoped Lady Mendleton would come round on the idea. As for wider society, was she to throw over her happiness for the sake of those she did not care about?

She would not.

Perhaps it was selfish. No, not perhaps. It was entirely selfish. She supposed she had discovered something about herself—she was not a tragic heroine from a novel willing to sacrifice her life's happiness as some sort of do-gooder martyr. She might have imagined herself capable of it before this, but now she understood it was not so.

Of course, this was all supposing he would ask. He had not firmly indicated any such thing. And yet, she did have the distinct feeling he admired her and he had been fairly persistent about taking her into suppers. And then, last evening, he had wanted to say *something*.

Oh, what it was to be a man! To make every decision on when and how to move forward. If she were a man, she would march into his library and demand an answer.

But she was not and must wait and hope. That was a woman's lot, it seemed—waiting and hoping. She was very much against it!

Minerva had just turned a bend in the lane and Georgiana was struck to see Lord Asturt. He had dismounted his horse by an old oak and stood talking to Lord Langley's valet, Marcus.

She found she must do her very best not to laugh. It was too ridiculous. Lord Asturt seemed nearly obsessed about how his recommendation of a valet was turning out. He seemed nearly obsessed with Lord Langley's approval.

But then, she must take pity. It was the way society worked that a young gentleman must find his set and that the young gentleman would always aim as high as possible and seek to impress. The success or failure of such a venture must weigh heavily upon them.

Seeing he'd been spotted, Lord Asturt waved. Marcus, himself, hurried off, pulling his hat down as he went.

Lord Asturt mounted his horse and trotted over to her. "Miss Wilcox," he said in a jolly tone. "I often come out at this hour and find myself quite alone, but here I've just run into Marcus, and now you. Very charming circumstance."

"Lord Asturt," Georgiana said, smiling.

"May I accompany you?" he asked. "We go in the same direction."

Georgiana nodded, and did her best to ignore the smirks on the grooms' faces. Only Carstares retained his grim visage.

"Marcus tells me he has become quite determined to stretch his legs after he completes his morning duties, he believes it staves off colds. Have you made a similar resolution to exercise that brings you out so early?"

"I am afraid I am not particularly resolute," Georgiana said. "It was a bit of a whim."

"I see Lady Mendleton has indulged that whim by sending you out with a full retinue," Lord Asturt said.

"Yes, she is very kind and thoughtful."

"Indeed, and sensible too. These are rather unsettled times."

"Are they?" Georgiana asked.

"It seems so," Lord Asturt said. "Marcus tells me there is another report in the papers this morning about our poor king. Things do not appear to go well for him."

Georgiana only nodded, not caring to comment on the king. For one, she did not much care, as she had her own affairs on her mind. For another, the subject of the king was an uncomfortable one, having been so recently questioned by Lord Langley about her encounter of him and having been graced with favor by the queen. And for another, Lord Asturt took these developments for more seriously that he probably should on account of his research. The king was no longer directing anything other than his disordered thoughts and they should all leave him to it and hope the regent would pull himself together.

"Well, whatever is to be the end of it," Lord Asturt said, "it is an uncommonly lovely morning."

Relieved he'd decided to take himself off the subject of the king, Georgiana nodded. They proceeded down the lane and the rest of their conversation was quite ordinary. She bid him goodbye at the gate.

As she dismounted and entered the carriage, she could not help think that Lord Asturt was such a funny gentleman. At once charming and not taking a mistake very seriously, but also fretting about royal inherited madness. What could it matter to him, in the end?

Well, some gentlemen did get excessively enthusiastic in their intellectual pursuits. Her father's friend, Mr. Handleton, had been trying to convince everybody for years that with the advent of the steam engine they would soon see a carriage with no horses that was propelled forward by such means. All that had to be worked out was how to carry enough coal, steer the thing, and ensure its passengers were not burned to death with hot steam. The very idea that horses would be put out to pasture and people would all race around in carriages without them…it was delightfully absurd.

Lord Asturt would do very well to avoid following Mr. Handleton's peculiar example.

As the house came into view, all thought of Lord Asturt flew from her. Jasper Stapleton was in there somewhere.

JASPER READ THROUGH one newspaper after the next. It never ceased to amaze him how many there were to get through, who was reading them all? Aside from himself, as he did not have a choice.

He began with the broadsheets of smaller circulation. It was doubtful that he'd find much of concern in them, but if he did it would only be a matter of time before the bigger concerns circled the story like sharks to a sinking ship so it would be well to know of it.

There was nothing of note this day, and he moved on to the more established papers.

The Star and the Chronicle generally supported the king and

so it was unlikely there would be any unfavorable report, and indeed there was not. He left the last of the pile for the ones that always concerned him the most—The Post, The Morning Herald, and The Courier.

He'd made his way through the Herald and the Courier with nothing of alarm and slowly turned the pages of the Post.

On the third turning of pages, he dropped the paper as if he'd been burned by it. He slowly picked it up again. There, right on the page in front of him. What he had feared most.

This paper has it on good authority that the King's condition continues to deteriorate. It has been told us from a reliable source that the king has become fixated on lamb and venison to the point that he has an unhinged fit if he sees any other meat served. We are most disturbed, as it is said that the REGENT is also strangely particular in his food. Are the two eccentricities connected? Like father like son? One wonders…

Good God, it was not just the report he'd planted, but the suggestion that the king's malady had been *inherited* by the regent. That meant that whoever had reported the story was determined to undermine the monarchy by proving a succession of family madness. That person could only be the Stuart. And yet, the only person who could have repeated the story of lamb and venison was Miss Wilcox.

How could that be true? Miss Wilcox was in league with the Stuart? She would be guilty of…treason. How would she have even become involved in such a scheme?

His heart railed against the notion, and yet his head could not dismiss the evidence in front of him. He had planted a trap, and she had fallen into it.

To be involved in such a plot could not have been her idea. Certainly not. She was only a pawn, being used by more powerful people. But who? And how?

Her father. It must be so. Who else could prevail upon a young lady to carry out such a dangerous scheme? Who else would have the means and the leverage to do it?

Jasper did not know Baron Manley and put little stock in the recommendation that he was a distant cousin. Every villain was a distant cousin to plenty of other reasonable people. Still, it was unlikely that an obscure baron had been drawn into such a conspiracy unless he had no choice. And under what circumstances did a gentleman find he had no choice? Either blackmail over an embarrassment or a gambling debt that could not be met. Though, if either of those possibilities were at play, the baron should have taken the honorable route and blown his brains out.

Unless, perhaps, it *had* been gambling and Manley had been presented with an opportunity to save his estate. After all, Lady Mendleton had taken on Miss Wilcox because her father had not the means to launch her or provide a dowry. Add to that a gambling debt and, well, it might have been more honorable for the gentleman to do a violence to himself but that honor would do nothing for the prospects of his family. They would find themselves on the street either by debt, mortgage, or entail.

Further, a clever person wishing to put another under his power looked for those who were already weakened and preyed upon them—the perpetrator might act the rube at a tavern and lose a few hands of cards, then when the victim had plenty to drink, up the stakes and take everything he had. Perhaps that was what had happened to Manley. Then, the proposal, the lifeline was thrown to pull the old man out of his sea of calamitous debt.

How had his mother come upon Miss Wilcox anyway? Had the Stuart got wind of that society the ladies had put together and maneuvered it somehow? Or more likely, the scheme had been enacted after it was known that Miss Wilcox would come?

What was he to do? He could not bear to imagine Miss Wilcox convicted of treason. Though, when the queen became aware of the report, she would know from where it sprang.

Jasper's mind worked at a furious pace, looking for some way out for Miss Wilcox, and he supposed, her unfortunate father too. If the father were convicted of high treason, the daughter would be just as finished as if she herself had been. He also held out hope that Manley had never been told the extent of the plot. It was likely he had not, being only one cog in the wheel. He might have just understood that a political faction wished to poke at the monarchy with a little bit of gossip. It would have seemed simple enough, as all answers to prayers tended to do.

As the minutes ticked by, and then an hour, and then more, Jasper could only see one slim path that might be threaded to pull Miss Wilcox out of the mire she'd got herself into. He must convince the queen that the most effective way to defeat the Stuart was to quietly unravel his operation. There should be no public reports, no debates amongst politicians, no accusations thrown nor charges entered, no opinions voiced in public houses, and no speeches on street corners. Miss Wilcox would be sent home, a letter from the palace would be delivered to Manley that he was to remain within the confines of his estate, and a watch would be set on his house. All communication with the Stuart would be cut off.

That done, Jasper would arrange an interview with Manley to determine if he knew who else was involved, though he thought it unlikely Manley would have come into contact with the Stuart. Those that operated in the shadows kept their minions far away from one another on the off chance that somebody was caught out. Manley would know some other man, and that man was unlikely to have used his real name.

As he thought through the steps of everything that must be done, and done perfectly if it were to work, the clatter of the carriage brought the arrival of Miss Wilcox from her ride in the park.

Good God, the eccentric notion of riding out early took on another meaning now. Had she met someone there? If he had seen the report earlier, he might have followed her and put eyes on one of her contacts.

For all that, was she not lovely, descending from the carriage? Her looks were blooming from the exercise and she appeared as if she did not have a care in the world.

Jasper let the drapery fall closed again. He must put all that out of his mind now. He was ashamed to admit it, but whatever feelings he'd thought, or hoped, Miss Wilcox might have for him might be just part of the game. How could he have been such a fool?

He went back to his desk and put his mind to the plan. First, he would inform his mother that Miss Wilcox must leave the house before the sun had set. Then, he would see the queen. No. He would see the queen first. There was the remotest chance that she would not agree to his plan and he could not be seen abetting the departure of a lady who the queen had decided ought to be questioned—as much as he'd *like* to abet the lady. If she were to be questioned, it would be far better to quietly leave this house than to be collected from the countryside. London could be an anonymous sort of place—in her home county, everybody who laid eyes on her would know who she was, and wonder where she was going with an escort from the queen's guards.

Further, his mother could be obstinate and would be loath to part with Miss Wilcox, especially since Jasper would not tell her the real reason the lady must go. He could not, or it would only be a matter of time before she told somebody else and it would spread like a forest fire.

However, Lady Mendleton would not defy her own queen no matter how much she disagreed with an opinion. He would propose to the queen that he simply tell his mother that the queen had revised her opinion and wished Miss Wilcox to depart the Town. There would be no reason given, and that just might work, as the queen could be capricious with her favor and irritated for often mysterious reasons. It would be a blow, but he was certain his mother would never, in a thousand years, tell her friends of the queen's disfavor. She would find it a personal humiliation. Rather, she would tell them that Miss Wilcox's father had been taken ill, or some other likely excuse.

Perry knocked and came in to clear the coffee tray. Jasper stood up. "Perry, never mind the trays. Tell Carstares I need my horse this instant. I know he's busy unhitching the carriage and stabling the horses that have just been out, but I require *my* horse this instant!"

Perry came forward, his eyes on the tray, then retreated in confusion, seeming thrown off by this interruption of the usual morning routine.

"Yes, my lord," he said, "at once."

The butler turned on his heel and hurried out.

Jasper paced the room, waiting for his horse to be brought round. He felt an anger begin to burn in him. If only she had confided in him! If only she was not what she was!

Miss Wilcox might never know it, but she ought to be exceedingly grateful that he was in love with her. Her very neck ought to be grateful for it.

⇒⇒⇒⟨⟨⟨⟨

GEORGIANA HAD CHANGED out of her riding habit and into a day dress without the help of Jenny. She did not want to wait until Jenny turned up and so asked one of the housemaids to come in and do the buttons she could not reach herself.

The poor girl seemed both surprised and nervous but did as she was bid. Georgiana was well-aware it was an unusual thing to do in such a house, but she did not want to waste a minute above stairs. The air in the park had cheered her no end and perhaps infused her with more bravery than she'd begun the day with. She was determined to be in the drawing room in case Lord Langley wished to discover her. And say something to her.

Now, she sat with a book in hand, pretending to read. *Zastrozzi* was as dreadful as she had imagined it would be, but it was a useful prop to pretend she was doing something other than wondering if Lord Langley might make an appearance.

She knew very well he was in the library just now. The door was closed, and in any case, that's where he was every morning with his pile of newspapers.

She wished the two rooms were not separated by the great hall. If they had been side by side, she might hear him moving around.

As it was, she stayed very still and quiet, listening for whatever she might be able to hear.

A door suddenly banged open, sounding as if enough force was used to crash it into the wall. The book tumbled from Georgiana's hands.

At that same moment, she heard the front door flung open. Certainly, a footman was not causing all that racket.

She hurried to the window and saw Lord Langley charging out of the house. He flew down the stairs, grabbed the reins of his horse from a wary-looking groom, and leapt upon him.

In a moment, he was off down the street at a gallop.

Goodness, where could he have gone in such a hurry?

She had no more time to speculate, as Lady Mendleton came in and said, "Was that Jasper banging out of the house like that?"

"Indeed, it was," Georgiana said.

"I always tell him, a footman or Perry will get the door for him, but when he wants to be off, he's off."

Georgiana supposed so, but she had not before observed this rather frantic mode of departure.

"So tell me, dear," Lady Mendleton said, settling herself next to Georgiana on the sofa, "are you enjoying your time here?"

"Oh, very much," Georgiana said.

"I'm so glad of it. Now, I did wonder about something. Lady Heathway mentioned that poor Lady Annabelle had been in the retiring room crying last evening."

Georgiana only nodded, though she thought it not very kind of Lady Heathway to share whatever she had seen. And so quickly too! She must have told Lady Mendleton before they'd even departed Lady Featherstone's house.

"She did mention that you escorted the poor lady out," Lady Mendleton said. "I presume you were comforting her over some matter?"

"Yes, indeed I was," Georgiana said, very much hoping she would not be asked the details.

"What was the dear girl so upset by?" Lady Mendleton asked, twisting her skirt in her hands.

"I would not wish to deny you anything," Georgiana said. "Of course I would not, you have been so generous in every conceivable way. But I do not think it is my tale to tell. Perhaps you might ask Lady Annabelle directly?"

"I am not certain I could," Lady Mendleton said. "I admire her, of course, but I would not want to press her on something that might make her uncomfortable."

Georgiana nodded. "You are right, it probably would put her ill at ease. I will just say that Lady Annabelle was overcome by something said to her, but in the end it will all turn out right, I am sure of it. When it does, the matter will come to light both publicly and happily."

"I see," Lady Mendleton said, smiling and smoothing her skirt. "The course of love never does run smooth, does it? But then, Jasper always does get there in the end."

Though Georgiana thought she was suitably ambiguous, Lady Mendleton seemed to read a good deal into it. A good deal not at all in the right direction.

Georgiana was well aware that she carried a rather vague smile on her face. Somehow, Lady Mendleton had concluded that...what? That Jasper had said something definite to Lady Annabelle and the delicate lady had been overcome? But that it would all come out right, meaning Lady Annabelle looked favorably upon what was said?

Georgiana should not have said anything about the matter becoming public. Or happily. Of course, she had been thinking of the eventual banns read regarding Lady Annabelle and Mr. Pottsgrove. But Lady Mendleton had removed the unnamed Mr. Pottsgrove from the equation and inserted her son.

Once again, she felt the guilt of loving Lord Langley. As she looked upon dear Lady Mendleton's unsuspecting smile...how could she do it? But then, how could she not do it?

If only Lady Mendleton did not have her heart set on Lady Annabelle! If she had only carried the idea that her son must marry well, she might be brought round to accept a less lofty match. But she was so set on Lady Annabelle very specifically!

But then, Lord Langley must be well aware of his mother's proclivities. If he were to ask her the momentous question, would he not have already laid the groundwork with his mother and father? Certainly he would.

Goodness, she had been such a ninny to imagine this situation rested on her shoulders. Of course it did not, it was up to Lord Langley to manage. She supposed he would manage very well, for what could he not achieve if he wished to?

"You seem very distracted, my dear," Lady Mendleton said, bringing Georgiana's thoughts back to the drawing room.

"Do I?" Georgiana asked. "I do not mean to. I was just thinking of how pleasant the park was this morning."

"I cannot quite picture it," Lady Mendleton said. "I suppose there was not a soul to be seen?"

"Oh, on the contrary," Georgiana said. "Lord Asturt was there and accompanied me to the gate."

Of course, Lord Langley's valet, Marcus, had been there too, but she did not like to mention it in case he had slipped out of the house with nobody the wiser.

"Lord Asturt...hmm...he is a bit, I do not know, really. I'd thought I had met his father some years ago, I very specifically remember there was an estate in Ireland. Though, I also seem to remember that the name was Astur, not Asturt. Perhaps it is not the same or perhaps my memory betrays. In any case, it is said the gentleman has ample means and he *is* a lord, perhaps you might do worse."

"Oh! No, indeed!" Georgiana said, wishing to disabuse Lady Mendleton from that idea.

Lady Mendleton patted her hand. "I am glad you say so, at

least for now. I would not wish to part with you so soon."

"Nor I you," Georgiana said, repressing the urge to inform the lady that she wished never to be parted from her, by way of marriage to her son.

"Well, shall we proceed out into the day?" Lady Mendleton asked. "I have a great mind to paper Bond Street with bills to be paid by my husband. We shall choose out all sorts of pretty things—bonnets, gloves, perhaps order you some new ballroom slippers? Oh, and I must be fitted for a number of new gowns, you do recall what the queen said about brocade? Those outré dresses are on their way to being made into new draperies for the servant's quarters, though don't tell the duchess!"

CHAPTER FOURTEEN

J ASPER HAD BEEN admitted to Buckingham and led to the usual room. Arriving unexpected, he noticed the lack of regularity in the activity around him and once again thought it was a mistake to leave the office of Lord Chamberlain vacant for so long. As he *had* turned up unexpected and had no idea what the queen was engaged in at the moment, he directed the senior footman who led him in to tell the queen the word "meddle."

The footman, as was to be expected, could not make hide nor hair of it and Jasper had been forced to repeat it to make certain the fellow understood. It had long been the word used between himself and the queen to indicate that something of importance had arisen and she should leave her ladies behind. The queen herself had designated the word *meddle*, it amusing her to do so. When she had arrived to England as a young woman to marry the king, one of the first things he'd said of any import during those early days was that she was not to meddle in politics.

Of course, she had meddled, and quite often. Particularly when it had pertained to German affairs. The king had discovered he did not mind her good counsel, he had only been afraid of having a wife who stirred whatever pots were on the boil among his own countrymen. As it happened, Queen Charlotte had never been drawn to court skullduggery or parliamentary intrigue, other than the amusing gossip those boiling pots might provide. Society might shudder to think what tidbits she'd heard, commented upon, added to, and passed on, but the debates in Parliament or power maneuvers at court rarely captured her attention. The safety of the monarchy at home and abroad was her first concern. Who was in power in Parliament was of no importance—they were rather like reeds in the wind, they might bend one way today, but the wind direction would change on the morrow. The rest of her concerns tended toward who wore what and who said what and who had triumphed in a battle of witticisms.

The doors were thrown open and a bevy of footman preceded the queen and her blasted Pomeranians. The dogs, in particular, appeared irritated to find their routine disrupted on Jasper's account.

After the doors were shut, the dogs settled themselves to softly growl under the table and the queen bid him to sit. She said, "Must I hear of something terrible so early in the day?"

"I am afraid so, Your Majesty," Jasper said. He laid out the newspaper to the article and allowed her to peruse it.

"The lamb and the venison," she said with a sigh. "The trap you set in your own house."

"Yes," Jasper admitted. "I am afraid my fears regarding Miss Wilcox have been realized, though I wish they had not. I do not believe she acts alone, though. I think she is only a pawn in a larger game."

The queen's brow wrinkled. "Clever Miss Wilcox? A pawn?"

As the queen did not seem to think the idea likely, Jasper hurried on with all of his reasons for thinking so. Baron Manley likely having got himself into some difficulty, the proposal to spy, and no doubt the idea that it was all only a harmless poking at the monarchy. Neither Manley nor his daughter were likely to understand it was any more than that.

The queen laid down the paper. "So you believe that Miss Wilcox's only motivation has been to save her father from ruin?"

"I cannot know it absolutely, but I expect so. What other motivation could she have?" Jasper asked. "I really do not think either of them understand what sort of plot they are involved in. Whoever Miss Wilcox repeated the story of venison and lamb to quite deliberately added mention of the *regent's* particularities regarding food to establish a connection. They seek to prove that the king's malady has been passed down to the son."

"The Stuart, of course. Who else would wish to prove it? And then, I suppose a loyal daughter might well do anything to save a father."

"Ma'am, might I suggest a way to proceed in this matter?"

"Please do, as I have no firm ideas myself at this very moment. I am very vexed, indeed."

A soft knock on the door brought in a tea service and they were silent while it was laid out, the only sounds in the room the clinking of porcelain and the occasional growl of a Pomeranian.

After the doors shut, Jasper said, "I believe we should attempt a quiet unraveling. It does not appear that the Stuart has raised any troops or at all attempts to go about things as the Jacobites have done in the past. He does not seek to overpower, but to turn public opinion by means of reports in the newspapers. Were we to respond publicly, we would play into the Stuart's hands by making it a matter of debate in the taverns, in the papers, or even in Parliament. If the Stuart *is* in league with France or Russia, they have clearly taken a wait and see approach. After all, the Stuarts do not have a record of success in this matter. Miss Wilcox will only be one of the outermost strands of the web, but if we set a watch on Baron Manley's house, someone might arrive, providing a strand closer, and so on."

"And so on and so on. Then, if we were lucky, we might follow enough strands right to the heart of it and to the Stuart himself. Wherever he has hidden himself."

"Precisely," Jasper said.

The queen sighed and said, "I find myself nostalgic for the old days when one only needed to locate an enemy army and settle on a plan of attack. This feels like walking with one's hands in front of one through a dark expanse and hoping to run into somebody."

Jasper had not thought of it that way, but he supposed the queen was right—bold incursions were easily seen, but this sort of operation was cloaked in shadows. However, that did not mean one could not shed light on it.

"We must light the lamps along the strands, to better see where we are going," Jasper said. "As for Miss Wilcox, she must be sent away. However, I cannot divulge to my mother the real reason. I was hoping I might say you had changed your mind about the lady and wished her to leave Town. A sudden turn of opinion, I grant, but my mother would not disobey. Nor would she tell anybody of it. She would be too ashamed and would invent a likely excuse."

"Certainly not," the queen said firmly. "I will not have any-body think me so capricious, for one. I greatly admired Miss Wilcox and as much as she has inconvenienced me, I cannot say I positively dislike her now. After all, what might I do for my dear family at that age? Absolutely anything, is the answer. Did I not board a ship and sail through three storms to marry the King of England? Do you suppose I had not learned the history of Henry VIII and his queen-murdering habits as a part of my early education? I can assure you that I did. Oh, nobody would mention it to me, of course, but I wondered about it. A king had murdered one queen through exile and inattention and two by an executioner's blade. His daughter, Bloody Mary, murdered Lady Jane Grey, then his other daughter murdered Mary, Queen of the Scots. Then it was Charles I's turn to step up to the scaffold as if the English people had not had enough blood. What sort of barbaric land was this that welcomed regicide? I thought I risked my very neck to board that ship, but that is what one does for family."

Jasper had not had any idea that the queen, as a young girl, had thought herself contracted on her way to treachery and murder. How brave she'd always been, even then!

"Further," the queen said, "I think we may use Miss Wilcox's unfortunate circumstance to advantage. She has been sent to spy, and so let her. But from now on, she will only discover flattering reports about the king and my son."

"What do you think of?" Jasper asked, not certain what at all flattering could be said about either of them at this moment in time.

The queen pressed her forefinger to her lips, as she did when she was thinking. Suddenly, she smiled. "You shall set the following trap. A report that claims the king was attacked in the garden at Kew by an unknown assassin and fought back bravely, wounding the villain. The intruder escaped but was badly hurt. We now make valiant attempts to search the area for likely suspects."

The queen leaned back in her chair. "Let us see if *that* gets printed in the newspapers. I rather think not. However, it will put a bee in the Stuart's bonnet to think it so. After all, if someone attempted regicide, he must wonder who it was and what they were after. Such a thing would interfere mightily in his plans. My son would become king and, indolent and self-indulgent as he may be, there is not a hint of madness about him. The Stuart might even worry that he'd be blamed, once his residence in the country was unmasked."

"Clever," Jasper said quietly. "Yes, exceedingly so. It may press the Stuart to become more bold as he may think there is a clock ticking somewhere. Bold often leads to mistakes."

Though Jasper did indeed think the queen's plan clever, he found he failed to mention his thoughts on Miss Wilcox remaining in the house. How could he? What was he to say? *Your majesty, the only fly in the ointment is that I find myself besotted with Miss Wilcox and it will take all my strength to stay away from the lady.* No, that would not do at all. Yet, he must stay away. He must find a means of staying away.

"I find myself disappointed in Miss Wilcox," the queen said sadly. "She really did seem a cut above the other young ladies one encounters these days. I wish she had confided in me, but that would have put her father in danger and I suppose no dutiful daughter would do it. Not even for a queen."

Jasper only nodded. He supposed he must just be grateful that the queen was who she was. Another sort of lady might have Miss Wilcox in the tower before dinner. Of course, to do such a thing, she would have been forced to bring the regent into the matter. That was something neither of them wished for—Prinny's ability to keep a secret was in direct correlation to how much wine was served him, and too much wine was *always* served him.

The queen rose and said, "Do what must be done, Langley."

He bowed and she sailed from the room, the doors swinging open on her approach. The dogs made one last threatening snap at him and trotted after her.

GEORGIANA SPENT THE next days in a constant state of both anticipation and perplexity. She made it a point to be in the drawing room as early as possible and to be there alone as often as possible. Just in case Lord Langley should wish to say something to her.

He did not. In fact, if she saw him at all, it was only the back of his coat as he left the house. He was like a thief in the night, silently slipping out and not seen for the rest of the day.

It was strange, even when she'd been sure she would see him she did not. On one of their few nights in, Lady Mendleton had been certain her son was to dine with them. But then, he'd sent a note claiming he was tied up at his club. What could tie one up at a gentlemen's club? A card game?

After a certain amount of days, Georgiana could not bear to sit in the drawing room longer. The room itself almost began to take on a despised aspect, so little did it bring her any happiness.

She took to walking in the small back garden for some relief from it. She could not quite give up all hope and made certain that Perry knew her location out of doors, in case someone looked for her. As she paced the small paths and sat on various stone benches and stared unseeing at the shrubbery, she took to explaining to herself the likely causes of Lord Langley's absence. He worked for the queen, after all. His time was not his own. He might be knee-deep in some great mission for the lady.

Of course, he might not. He might just choose not to be in her vicinity. Perhaps she had misread him all along, but then he had *not* misread her. Her cheeks flamed to consider the idea that he was never in the least interested, but that he had sensed her own interest. How that would seem to him! His mother's latest project, a silly girl from the countryside without a farthing in her pocket, swooning over the great lord and he must now keep himself away to avoid an embarrassing situation.

"That cannot be so," Georgiana said to Lady Mendleton's prized China roses. The roses listened implacable, though she knew if she dared touch them they would retaliate by way of thorns.

She did not know what the truth was and supposed she would not until something positively happened. Jasper could not stay away forever.

Perhaps he would attend Lady Tredwell's ball? Yes, of course, he must attend. Lady Tredwell was sister to Lord Mendleton, it would be a familial duty to go. It was to be a masque and had not Lady Mendleton said she'd made all the arrangements for it?

Georgiana had not the first idea of what particular arrangements had been made, as Lady Mendleton had only said she would be dressed perfectly for a lady of her age and innocence.

However she was dressed, she did not much care. She would get her answer there. Would he take her into supper, as he had done before? Or, would he not?

JASPER HAD RESOLVED to interview the stable staff regarding Miss Wilcox's early morning jaunt in the park to determine if he might glean any information about her possible conspirators from it. Had she met with anybody there? Had she stopped anywhere and retrieved something—a note perhaps?

He'd gone back and forth on the idea, as it would be helpful to know, but might also tip off Miss Wilcox and whoever she was working for. The servants, though they would deny it under torture, were irredeemable gossips. It would not be a day before his questioning was known by all of them. It was not Carstares or Perry that would talk, but rather the junior servants. Both the stablemaster and the butler kept their own counsel as a matter of habit. Whether the news would cross out of the servant's quarters and into the family realms he did not know. If it did, Jenny was the most likely vehicle to carry the information to Miss Wilcox. If Perry were to be believed, Jenny's tongue was in constant motion regurgitating anything and everything that passed through her mind. Still, he had decided he must go forward, it might be the key to unraveling this mess.

He'd spent the past few days hardly living in his own house. He left early and returned late, spending most of the time at his club. While there, he did much as he would have done at home, scanning the newspapers, writing to the king's staff and some men he employed to search out information, and attempting to think up ideas to expose the Stuart's plot. The only difference was he was far less efficient in his work. For one, there seemed to be always some fellow about who attempted to drag him into a game of cards, or cajole him into wagering on something ridiculous like which hole an ant was likely to enter, or talk endlessly about a horse. For another, his own thoughts caused just as much distraction. Miss Wilcox seemed always to be before him, drifting in his mind like a dream he could not wake from.

Just an hour ago, before he'd left his house, she really *was* before him. He'd glanced out a window from the second-floor corridor before making his way down the stairs to cross the garden to the stables. It was lucky he looked, as Miss Wilcox was out there, determinedly pacing the garden paths. She was positively lovely in her lawn dress and straw bonnet, marching around as if she hardly knew she was meant to be admiring the shrubbery. Though she did not pause to retrieve anything, he supposed he'd have to search the bushes at some point to ensure there was no hidey-hole for messages.

As she *was* out there, he was forced to slip out the front doors and make his way round the block and into the mews to get to the stable that way. He knew from the look on Carstares' face that they would all consider it exceedingly odd—why had he gone for a walk round the block when he never went for a walk? It would be one more thing for them to talk about, he supposed.

He had pulled the stablemaster aside, hoping he would not have to interview any of the grooms, but that was not to be. Carstares could not confirm that he'd had Miss Wilcox in view at all times, as he had been much engaged with the carriage. Carstares had told him he'd seen both Lord Asturt and his own valet in the park, and Lord Asturt had proceeded to accompany Miss Wilcox to the gate. What they'd talked about, he could not say.

Was that a coincidence? And what in God's name was his valet doing in the park at that early hour?

Jasper remembered that when he'd seen the grooms depart with Miss Wilcox, it had been Thomas riding his mother's horse, Biscuit. Thomas would have remained within earshot of Miss Wilcox and so it had been Thomas he'd asked to see.

Carstares had given over the small room he used to keep his various records. It was a tidy place, considering it was in a stable, consisting of a desk, two chairs, shelves with a book for each horse, and a place for a teapot and cups. The lone window looked out upon the mews, and the dust from the hay drifted in motes through the feeble light.

Thomas, a rather eager-looking fellow on most days, now appeared as if he stood before a magistrate. He glanced nervously round the little room and twisted his hands together.

"Good God, fellow," Jasper said, "I only wish to ask you a few questions, not hang you."

Jasper thought he might not have selected the precise right phrasing, as poor Thomas had nearly jumped out of his skin at the mention of hanging.

"I only wish to know about your excursion to the park with Miss Wilcox early in the morning the other day. Of course I know she was quite safe in our servants' care, but as she is our responsibility, it is necessary that I have reports. As a usual and commonplace matter. Very usual."

Thomas nodded eagerly.

"I understand Marcus was there, and Lord Asturt, too."

Thomas nodded eagerly again and Jasper was beginning to fear that was all he would get.

"Yes, well," he said, "can you elaborate? Tell me what you saw and heard."

"Everything?" Thomas asked.

Jasper did not know why he should pose such a question. "Of course, everything."

Thomas began a slow pacing back and forth in front of the desk as if he were winding up to make an argument in Parliament. "Well, first, Carstares did scold me about how Biscuit handles. She's a bit of a layabout if you don't drive her forward. She's one of them what prefers stopping and eating grass, if you know what I mean."

Jasper did, exasperatingly, know what Thomas meant. He simply did not know why he was meant to care. Still, he knew from past interrogations that people often needed to get to the point in their own time and on their own winding path. He nodded encouragingly.

"So I got Biscuit going respectable-like, though she ain't happy about it, and Miss Wilcox was got on Minerva in the park and we went along very pleasant. Then we sees Lord Asturt and Marcus, though Marcus just hurries off like he don't know us. I reckon your average valet has got loads of free time 'cause how long can it take to put clothes on a person anyway, but they don't want *us* to know it. When I seen him strollin' in the park in the morning, he knowed I know it."

Jasper was not at all certain that hiding one's free time would account for his valet's appearance in the park.

"So then Lord Asturt joins Miss Wilcox and he says Marcus is determined to stretch his legs every morning after his duties as it keeps away colds. P'raps that's right, us grooms is stretching our legs every minute of the day and we never get colds."

"Excellent," Jasper said, hoping to move on from preventing colds, "so Marcus left. What did Lord Asturt have to say for himself?"

Thomas snorted and said, "Us fellas think the lord is sweet on Miss Wilcox, 'cept he don't know how to go about the thing. William says you got to say somethin' nice about a lady's dress, or if you're a darin' individual, you might even say a nice thing about the hair on her head."

Jasper folded his arms, beyond aggravated that the grooms were speculating on such a matter. Asturt sweet on Miss Wilcox, indeed!

"I presume, then," Jasper said, "that Lord Asturt made no such remarks?"

"No, he says it's nice that Lady Mendleton sent the whole stable with her as these is *unsettled times*. He says it all dark-like, as if a war's upon us. We reckon he was tryin' to scare her into affection and William says it won't work 'cause you can't keep a lady scared all the time. Either she gets unscared or she drops dead from exhaustion."

"What did he mean by unsettled times?" Though he asked, Jasper was certain he already knew—many a gentleman had employed Napoleon as a dark figure who might turn up in a lady's neighborhood at some future date and need to be defeated. He found he was rather in agreement with William on the ultimate inefficacy of such a gambit.

"I don't rightly know what he meant by unsettled," Thomas said. "He mumbled something I didn't catch, but Miss Wilcox turned her head away like she don't want to hear it. She was probably expectin' a compliment to herself and didn't much care whatever kind of times the fellow was blathering about. I reckon William is right about the romancing aspect of it all."

"And then what?" Jasper asked.

"Oh then he just babbles his way to the gate," Thomas said. "You know, the sort of thing a gent will talk about when he don't know what to talk about. He ought to been praising her hair to the skies but he was just ramblin' on about his horse and another gent's horse and another horse a fellow he knew might buy. It was embarrassin'—the fellow don't know horses like he thinks he does. Even Biscuit was shakin' her head over it. Then, runnin' out of road on that subject, he tells her all about his dog."

Jasper felt himself faintly color, as he could not entirely forget that he had, only a few years ago, blathered on about horses and dogs himself when no other subject presented itself to his mind.

He shook it off and sorted through Thomas' pointless information to distill it to what he must consider. Marcus had been in the park to stretch his legs. On closer consideration, that was not all that unusual, the fellow could walk there from the house in a matter of minutes. Further, Thomas' suspicions were correct—a valet did have a good amount of free time. Perhaps not as much as Thomas assumed, but a good amount all the same. That particular morning, Jasper had been dressed and down to the library a full hour before Miss Wilcox departed the house. And then, it would not be so unusual for his valet to stop and speak to Asturt, as the lord was forever wanting to know how the fellow was doing.

As for Asturt, himself, could he have meant something significant by unsettled times? Most likely not. It was bound to be something he said just to say something, very like his blathering about horses and dogs. If the man really thought he lived in unsettled times, he would hardly go announcing it in the park.

Especially not to a lady.

"Did Miss Wilcox ever dismount, or pause at a tree, or perhaps slip something into a pocket?" he asked.

Thomas seemed more than a little perplexed over the question. He shook his head no.

"And I do not suppose Lord Asturt handed her anything?"

Thomas smirked and said, "He handed her a lot a nonsense, I thought."

Jasper nodded and sent Thomas on his way, the fellow still smirking over his joke. There was no doubt he would repeat the entirety of the interview to his fellow grooms, as a boy like that would never fail to repeat a joke he'd made to good effect. He could only hope that Thomas had believed that requesting a report on a single young lady in their charge was indeed usual and commonplace among the *ton*.

As it seemed he would not gain anything useful from the interview, he called for his horse. He might as well go to his club to think.

There did not seem to be anything unusual in Miss Wilcox's visit to the park, strangely early though it might have been. She'd encountered Asturt and his valet, but she had been closely accompanied by a groom the entire time.

What to do next?

He very much wished he might simply ask the lady what she was up to and who employed her, but he did not think he'd accomplish anything more than putting the whole operation, whatever it consisted of, on alert. It was one thing for Miss Wilcox to hear some garbled story from Jenny that he'd interviewed a groom about her excursion. It would be another to confront her directly. She might panic and write her father, thereby raising the alarm.

He wished the Stuart to become careless, not more careful. In any case, if the villain thought Miss Wilcox was compromised, he might order her out of the way in some violent manner. After all, he wished to be king, and therefore felt he deserved to be king.

No, in fact he saw himself as already king, with only a kingdom to claw back from a pretender. A man willing to risk as much as he did would not allow an insignificant lady to stand in his way. If Miss Wilcox proved to be too much trouble, he might well decide to get rid of her via that oft used method called the Thames.

No, speaking directly to Miss Wilcox was far too risky.

What then?

His aunt, Lady Tredwell, was hosting a masque ball and his mother would be frantic if he claimed he would not attend. In fact, she'd already said she had a costume ready for him.

What if he could somehow work that to his advantage? What if he arranged his own costume so that absolutely nobody, including Miss Wilcox, could divine who he was. He might get close to her and listen in on her conversations. He might spy her leaving a note on a balcony, or picking one up. He might spot whoever it was she was contacting.

Using such a venue as a large ball to communicate was ideal and there might very well be a plan to exchange information there. As for himself, he might go as a servant and who would notice one more servant among the many? His aunt held the masque every year and the servants would be dressed in dominos, only their telltale stockings and footwear giving them away. He might easily copy a costume and move about freely. It was the perfect opportunity for him to slip around in the shadows unrecognized.

The sooner he could unravel the Stuart's plot, the sooner Miss Wilcox would be out of whatever danger she was now in. Sooner was far better than later. The lady had not crossed the queen so far as to get herself condemned, but the longer this went on, the higher the chances that she would. Even if nothing else occurred, the queen might change her view of Miss Wilcox. Queen Charlotte had sworn she would not tell Lady Mendleton that she had changed her mind regarding Miss Wilcox as she would never present herself as so capricious. But, the fact was, Her Majesty could be exceedingly capricious, whether or not she recognized it in herself.

Then, Miss Wilcox and her father were dealing with dangerous people. Far more dangerous than they likely knew. Something downright lethal might happen to her.

That, he could not bear to think of. Whatever Miss Wilcox had done, he could not condemn her. Not in his heart, anyway. He could only try to save her from herself.

Meanwhile, the queen had asked him to compose a list of gentlemen who ought to be investigated. She had become convinced that the Stuart was either on his way to London or already here and that he must have at least one well-placed sympathizer, perhaps more than one. There might even be some kind of organized faction.

Jasper did not know what she planned on doing with the list, though he suspected it would be turned over to Lord Ryland to investigate for some invented reason. She wished to have it no later than Monday next and he was just waiting to receive some answers to inquiries he'd made before delivering it.

Jasper sighed. He supposed he'd better add Asturt to the list— his background was relatively cloudy, having only recently arrived from Ireland. There was always the remote chance that he'd suddenly come to London in support of the Stuart. And, considering how much he'd taken to hanging about Miss Wilcox, Jasper would not mind knowing more about him.

Poor Ryland would be running himself in circles to no purpose. The gentlemen included on his list so far were all unusual in their own way, but he doubted any of them had dealings with the Stuart. It had been his experience that when one unraveled a deep plot, those involved were not the ones who drew attention to themselves. They were not odd, they were not obvious.

The question was, who *did* have dealings with the Stuart?

CHAPTER FIFTEEN

GEORGIANA HAD COME in from the garden, finally becoming tired of staring at Lady Mendleton's China roses. It was the lady's at-home day and so a stream of people would, in the next hours, make their way in and out of the drawing room.

The room's door stood open, as it always did when people would be traipsing in and out, and Georgiana paused to straighten her skirts and ensure she had not brought in any leaves or bits of grass from the shrubbery.

As it was early yet, she thought Lady Mendleton would be in the room alone. Then she heard her say," I must tell you that you were mistaken, Penelope. You may put to rest your fears."

"Louisa," Lady Heathway said in the condescending tone she was so practiced at, "I saw what I saw, there were looks between them and then there was a weeping Lady Annabelle. You cannot tell me I did not observe it!"

"Well, yes, part of it, you did!" Lady Mendleton said. "It is only that you did not know the cause. You see, Jasper *spoke* to Lady Annabelle. She became flustered, and why should she not, the poor innocent girl. She was quite overcome, but as it happens she looks favorably upon what was said. *That* was what was discussed in the retiring room. You see? It is to be a match!"

"I am not convinced of it," Lady Heathway said. "I still say, be on your guard about Miss Wilcox. She's a fine enough girl, but Lord Langley must reach a deal higher!"

"Oh Penelope, Jasper is never even here," Lady Mendleton said. "Does that not speak volumes?"

"Never, you say?" Lady Heathway asked skeptically.

"Really never," Lady Mendleton said. "He practically lives at his club these days."

"Well, that is something, I suppose."

Georgiana hardly knew what to do in the face of this conversation. Should she go in and interrupt or run the other direction? She was very much inclined to run, as Lady Mendleton had just now very casually pointed out her worst fear. Jasper was never here, he practically lived at his club now. And, it seemed to be his choice.

Oh, she knew that poor Lady Mendleton had gone wrong on one point—there was not an engagement in the works between Lord Langley and Lady Annabelle, not if Mr. Pottsgrove had anything to say about it. But Georgiana was afraid she was right in everything else. He was never here by his own choice. It was the fact that had been staring her in the face all along, and the fact she'd been trying to reason away.

A deep clear of the throat startled her and she spun around.

Mr. Perry stood staring at her. In a crisp tone, he said, "Do you require assistance, Miss Wilcox?"

"Goodness, no," she said hurriedly. "I was only going up to freshen myself from my walk in the garden."

She scurried past him and up the stairs, feeling his eyes on her back as she went.

Georgiana flew down the corridor, startling a housemaid as she went. Safe in her own room, she shut the door behind her and let out a breath.

Mr. Perry had caught her eavesdropping and she could not be more humiliated. God only knew what the butler took her for.

But what she had overheard! It was only what she had known in her heart, but to hear it spoken of aloud made it somehow more real, more irrefutable.

Jasper kept himself away very deliberately.

She could not escape the reality that swam in front of her eyes, A man interested in a lady does not avoid her, especially when she is conveniently located in his own house. There could be no circumstance to account for it. Her own interest, her love, if she were to be brutally honest, was entirely one-sided.

What a mess she'd made of things! How was she to go forward? She supposed she would return to her father, her prospects much the same as she had left him. What else could she do? Marry some poor fellow who did not realize that her heart would always be elsewhere? It would be too cruel. She could not do it, not even to secure a future.

Georgiana sat on the windowsill and watched the resident tree sparrows go in and out of their nest box. They seemed busy and well-satisfied with themselves, and Georgiana presumed there were hatched chicks in the box.

"Oh yes," she said to them, "things appear to go on swimmingly for *you*. As for me, I have made a mess of it."

As if he heard her, and understood her, the male sparrow paused to stare at her. His round black eyes seemed to hold little sympathy.

"You are right, of course," she said. "After all, whatever has befallen me has been caused by me, and nobody else. At least I've told nobody my secret and it can be mine to bear alone. Lord Langley never declared himself, it was only the way he looked at me..."

Georgiana paused, a glimmer of hope like a small candle out in a dark field began to flicker.

There had been looks. It had not been only her imagination. Lady Heathway had noticed looks. She had very specifically gone to Lady Mendleton about her concern over looks.

Then perhaps...but then perhaps not. Perhaps she should give up all hope, but then there had been looks.

She must just wait and see. She was ridiculous, she was certain of it. It was as if she were on a sinking ship and somehow holding out hope that it would sail on to arrive safely at port. And yet, she would wait and see. She could not bear to do otherwise.

THE STUART HAD taken a house in a prominent neighborhood and boldly walked into London society, though his handful of advisors had counseled otherwise. They might think he ought to hide himself away, but creeping around the shadows was anathema to him. They did not understand the fundamental thing he understood—the English were incredibly stupid and generally believed what they were told.

He'd taken his place with nary a raised eyebrow, though they were a pack of idiots to believe he was a lord who'd been lounging in Ireland these past years. Did nobody check patents? Did nobody have an ear for accents? The Tsarina would have taken apart his story in less than a day. For that matter, the Russian Noble Register would have done him in, as to be listed in it one must produce a veritable mountain of documents. But not here, no—he'd taken on the identity of a man recently dead, Lord Astur. Aside from being hard to check, as the man had been rather a recluse on a remote estate in Ireland, it had tickled him to choose that particular identity. When he was king, stories would be written of his ascent and the wit and daring of his selection would be understood. An extra *t* on the end would tell the tale.

Fortunately for him, the English were a dull-witted lot—wear the right clothes, put it about that there was money in one's pockets by losing one large bet at a club and laughing it off, and make oneself agreeable. These buffoons did not inquire further until a marriage contract was on the table.

He had been right about what he would find here. His instincts always were right, precisely why he ought to be king. No, he reminded himself, he *was* king. He had been king since his father died. That he had been denied his throne was a separate matter. He was a king ordained by God and by God he would get it back from those weak-minded Germans and hold dominion over these thickheaded Englishmen.

Much of the work had been tedious and he had felt himself quite out of patience at times. It had taken all of his self-control when some matron who thought very highly of herself would lecture him on some matter, or some fellow who was only an earl thought to air his politics. They would learn to bow before him.

There had been one bright spot, though. Miss Wilcox. How charming! How elegant! What a head suited for a crown. Did she not have the delicate features of a Mary Queen of Scots? Did she not even have something of a Scots nature? She was direct and sensible, so unlike those other flitty ladies who fanned themselves as if a constant breeze were necessary to keep them alive. He was also convinced there were interesting hidden depths to Miss Wilcox. The day he'd seen her launched over her horse and onto the ground, he'd known precisely what he was viewing—the lady was a fine horsewoman, but she'd never been on a sidesaddle in her life. He had first sought out her acquaintance only because of her residence in the same house with Langley, he had never imagined he would be so struck by her.

Miss Wilcox was also delightfully unlike the Hurko sisters he had left behind in Russia. Of course, at the time, the Tsarina thought she did him a great favor by making the match between him and Marianna Hurko. He'd even thought so himself. But then, he'd seen her sister, Evelina, who was far more pleasant to look at. Promised elsewhere, unfortunately, but could that not be undone?

As it happened, it could not. To add salt to the wound, his dwindling fortune had been entirely lost to an incompetent financier. The Hurkos were irate, the Tsarina furious. It had seemed as if all was up with him. Where would he go? How would he live?

He had fled with only his manservant, Marcus, to accompany him. But then, during the long journey out of that frozen wasteland, his real purpose had become clear to him. On a particularly dark night, their carriage struggled through the snow as they made their way toward the border. As he watched the endless flakes beat relentlessly against the windows, a sudden lightness overcame him.

God had not forsaken him! Of course God had not allowed him to marry Evelina! He was the rightful king of England. God had maneuvered him away from a pointless existence in Russia. God was sending him back to his realm.

He had always avoided thoughts of reclaiming the throne and tried to convince himself that he was content as he was. It was never true, though. Now that he knew his purpose, that he was born to rule, he would not be as stupid as his grandfather. He would not hang about Europe begging for armies. It had been a silly idea then and was even sillier now, there were far better methods available. He had watched how the Tsar and Tsarina managed their people—they controlled what the people understood. A hint of criticism and the unlucky criticizer was seen no more. He did not have the power to control everything just yet, but he could influence enough to turn things his way.

Once the English people were convinced that the Hanover's mental malady was inherited, combined with their visceral dislike of the fat and indulgent son, they would welcome a Stuart back to the throne.

At that glorious moment, he would reveal all to Miss Wilcox. The English people would rejoice to have one of their own made queen. The lady would be shocked when all was known, but not unpleasantly so, he was sure. He had cleverly dropped her some hints that she might reflect on when she understood who he really was. In that way, she would know she had always been his choice, long before his prospects had been raised to the skies.

In the beginning, his plan had unfolded smoothly and with little effort. Nothing had stood in his way. That was, until he became aware of Jasper Stapleton's, or Lord Langley as he styled himself, activities. At first, it had only seemed that he was a confidant of the queen and might perhaps funnel information.

However, it turned out the lord was spending his time attempting to identify the author of the various reports in the newspapers.

Fortunately, his valet had recently decamped to America and it was no trouble to slip Marcus into the role. He was kept well apprised of Langley's activities and had even garnered a few reports he could use.

But now, the rogue had found a way to stir up more trouble for him! The man had composed some sort of list for the queen to peruse. Marcus had copied it down, and his name was on it.

He did not fool himself that the list was a recommendation for any sort of accolades. No, not when he thought of the others on the list. It was an assortment of odd people that one only ran into at the less discriminating routs. And himself. Why should he be included in this list of mediocrity?

He was under suspicion and Langley was leading the charge.

Langley must be disposed of. The Hanover king was incapacitated and with Langley gone, dumpy old Charlotte would be left with no man at her right hand—there was not even a Lord Chamberlain at her disposal. One might think the son might be of some use, but Prinny, as they called him, was a pointless and cowardly specimen. That fat fellow would be on a fast boat out of England at the first sign of trouble.

Perhaps he would even find an opportunity to get rid of his problem this evening. He had been made aware that Langley went to the masque as Poseidon and so would be easy enough to identify. But then, he could hardly claim Miss Wilcox's supper *and* kill off Langley so perhaps that venture would have to wait.

Once Langley was got out of the way, he would be free to see that more and more outrageous reports appeared in the newspapers, and those reports would be about the regent. The public was already convinced of the king's madness, let them become convinced of the son's too and the final nail in the Hanover coffin would be hammered in. After that, subtle rumors of the good sense and grace of the Stuart, and then a report that the Stuart planned to visit England. He would sail to France and come right back again to be met at the docks by the masses and escorted to the palace. It would be a peaceful and quiet transition. He'd thought of killing off the Hanovers but that would be a mistake. They were stupid, uninspiring, and mad—why make martyrs out of them? They could go back to Germany and farm, it was all they were capable of and all they deserved.

It was a plan far beyond any his grandfather could have dreamed up and it was a plan that would work.

In the meantime, Lady Tredwell's masque was hours away. His costume was a private joke that none would understand until he took the throne. He would drop some further hints regarding it to Miss Wilcox though.

He would be delighted to see Miss Wilcox.

GEORGIANA HAD NO clear idea of how she was to be dressed until the very day of the masque ball. Lady Mendleton had taken great pains to have their costumes made, hiring a certain Mrs. Turnerton who was known for her skill in that direction. The lady had arrived at the house a week prior to take Georgiana's measurements, and had even pressed a sheet of softened wax across her nose and her eyes for an impression so that her mask would fit flawlessly. Lady Mendleton had taken delight in keeping her plans secret until the costumes were delivered for a final fitting.

Georgiana could not say she was disappointed with the result. Lady Mendleton had styled her as a damask rose for its message of purity. The mask itself was soft, dusky pink silk. Though it had a fine silk string attached to tie the mask round her head, Georgiana found that hardly necessary. There was a piece of thin metal cleverly sewn inside the mask that was bent to conform to the bridge of her nose to hold it securely in place.

The dress itself was a marvel. Made of a pale rose velvet, it had a fitted bodice and then a wonderfully full skirt. The skirt was made of rounded pieces of velvet sewn one atop the other and meant to resemble petals, with layers of petticoats underneath lifting the whole thing up. The effect was remarkably reminiscent of a blooming rose.

Lady Mendleton was to go as Leto, the Greek goddess of motherhood. Her mode of dress was a simple white silk, but the draping was exquisitely done. According to the lady, she had arranged for Lord Langley's costume too, as he could hardly be bothered with it.

This was the first definite confirmation that Jasper would attend and Georgiana felt her stomach flutter in nervousness. Would he avoid her there too? Or perhaps he would not. But then perhaps he would. He was to be dressed as Poseidon and so it would not be hard to spot him and understand whatever he chose to do.

How was she to act when she saw him? Should she pretend it was no great matter? Ask him if he avoided her? Assume indifference if he did not secure a dance?

She thought the likelihood of carrying off indifference if he did not ask to be low to nothing. If she was not careful, she'd end up weeping in the retiring room just as Lady Annabelle had done before her.

It had taken some doing to get herself and her voluminous skirts into and out of the carriage, and she was not at all sure how elegant she would look at supper with the massive skirt on her lap, but she had no thought for that now. She must see if Lord Langley had arrived.

Before leaving the house, it became apparent that nobody seemed to be certain what he was doing. She had assumed he would leave the house near the time they did, she even hoped she might encounter him on the stairs, but Perry had reported that he'd left long ago. The butler had some idea that he planned to change at his club. Lady Mendleton only hoped he had not forgotten his trident, as it was absolutely crucial to the effect of the costume. Georgiana had no such concerns about the trident, only wishing to know what was to be his attitude toward her.

Lady Tredwell's house on Berkeley Square was gracious and exceedingly similar to so many other London houses she had visited. Georgiana noticed that she had become inured to the grandeur of it all. The ponderous dimensions and the hand cut stone façade could not distract her from her worries. Not even the footmen dressed in black silk dominos could take her mind from Jasper Stapleton.

The ballroom was a near-overwhelming a sight—costumes of all sorts, some she recognized and some she did not. Lady Heathway was a shepherdess, and though it should have been a gentle costume, the lady looked rather threatening with a staff in hand. Lady Redfield had come as an Egyptian and Lady Featherstone looked decidedly Tudor. Lady Easton had dressed as a nun, and looked as if she had just as much fun as if she really were in a priory. The duchess had styled herself as Queen Mab, though Georgiana had needed that explained to her as she was completely lost in deciphering the robe covered in blooms and the heavy crown of purple flowers that seemed perennially in danger of slipping over her eyes.

Lady Annabelle was a forest faerie and looked every bit the part. She also seemed in better spirits than when they last met, and so Georgiana had every hope that she'd put her foot down regarding Mr. Pottsgrove. Her high spirits were pleasant to witness, though perhaps less pleasant was Lady Mendleton's enthusiasm over them. The lady was convinced they were due to Lady Annabelle's fondness for her son.

There were any number of gentlemen dressed in a domino, including Lord Bertridge who'd just put his name down on her card. While the cape and black mask over his eyes were suitable, they did not exactly disguise him and it seemed the smallest effort one could practicably make. At least others who'd dressed the same had donned their hoods, which cast their features in shadows and gave them a mysterious appearance.

There were a number of masters of ceremonies swanning about, introducing gentlemen to ladies, and even revealing who was who when pressed. This seemed a sensible idea, as some of the costumes were clever in hiding the identity of their wearer.

There were many more costumes to consider, but what Georgiana could not find was Poseidon. It had not gone unnoticed by Lady Mendleton either. Lady Annabelle's card had begun to fill, and Georgiana's patroness was beginning to fuss that her son would miss his chance with his intended. Or, perhaps more accurate, *her* intended for him.

Georgiana's own card had begun to fill, and she fretted about it. Supper had already been taken by Lord Gresham, Lady Heathway's nephew. This had surprised Georgiana, as she was well aware of Lady Heathway warning Lady Mendleton about her. By the looks of it, it surprised Lady Heathway too. Upon Lord Gresham writing his name down she had seemed to become agitated and her shepardess's staff swung in dangerous directions—Mr. Swanson had the foresight to duck as it came his way. Georgiana supposed Lord Gresham did not consult his aunt on his dance partners, but then she also supposed he'd hear about it later.

That incident should have been alarming, but her thoughts were too much taken up by Poseidon. What if Jasper did wish to put himself down and there was not even a dance left to take? Why must he be so late?

On the other hand, if he did not wish to claim her for a dance, it might be well that her card was filled. It might save her from embarrassment, at the least.

Lord Asturt approached, and Georgiana approved of his costume, as he'd clearly put a deal of thought and effort into it. He came as a king of old, with a stiff lace ruff, his sleeves cuffed in intricate lace, a scarlet velvet cape over it all and sweeping down to the ground. His crown was rather magnificent—trimmed in ermine and bejeweled over a cap of the same red velvet as his cape.

Though she was not unhappy to see him, she had begun to view any gentleman wishing to add himself to her card as highly inconvenient!

He bowed and held his hand out and she had no recourse but to give it to him.

Lord Asturt's brow furrowed as he examined it. He wrote his name down for the second and said, "I will not hide my disappointment, Miss Wilcox. I did hope to find your supper free. I see Lord Gresham has beaten me to it."

Georgiana did not answer as the only thing she could think to say would not have been appropriate—*your surprise could not hope to equal Lady Heathway's surprise.*

"Still," Lord Asturt went on, "I cannot be unhappy to see you costumed as an English rose. It suits you very well."

"I am afraid the credit must go to Lady Mendleton," Georgiana said. "She composed my dress quite on her own and I had no hand in it."

"Modest, how charming," Lord Asturt said. He bowed and moved off.

Lady Mendleton leaned close to her and said, "He does seem rather taken with you, my dear. Though, perhaps you might put him off for a bit, before anything is actually declared. I'd rather have you with me for a second season and certainly there is no hurry? Just think how bereft of company I will be when my youngest goes away to school and Jasper is married to Lady Annabelle. You would be a great comfort to me."

Georgiana did not answer that either. What was she to say? *Lady Annabelle is set on Mr. Pottsgrove and thinks your son ill-humored. Your son does not care a fig about Lady Annabelle. I, myself, am in love with your son, though I think I may be fast on my way to heartbreak. I believe you've misread Lord Asturt's feelings and you most definitely misread my own regarding him. There is nothing in any of this to provide comfort, unless you are Lady Annabelle or Mr. Pottsgrove.*

Fortunately, Lady Mendleton did not look for an answer— Queen Mab had arrived by her side to pronounce opinions on various of Lady Tredwell's guests. The duchess declared one charming, one misguided, one far too bold, one a wallflower, one a bore, and one not quite up to snuff, as Lady Mendleton nodded in agreement.

Georgiana was left to search the crowded ballroom, but nowhere was there a Poseidon.

JASPER HAD LEFT the ridiculous Poseidon costume safe in his dressing room where it belonged and where it would never see the light of day. He'd purchased a simple domino mask and cape—black silk, voluminous, and with an oversized hood. He'd got one on the short side so that the white stockings and black shoes with silver buckles that he'd added to the ensemble would be clearly visible. With the hood up and the Tredwell's coat of arms sewn on the breast, he looked as any other footmen at the ball. That left him free to move around the ballroom with nobody paying any attention to him.

Of course, some had paid attention to him. When they required something. He had not factored into his plans that he'd be running and fetching for people who would be on any other night delighted to find him at their table. On the other hand, it gave him an insight he'd not had before about how invisible a servant really was. Some of these people had known him for years, but when they ordered him about they did not talk to him. They talked at him, or past him. They never even tried to look him in the face. Convenient, but disturbing.

Miss Wilcox was also disturbing, though in an entirely different way. His mother may have aimed badly with his own costume, but she had hit the mark with her charge's dress. She was a rose and she was blooming. He also could not help noticing that she did not lack partners. Gentlemen were all too eager to secure her.

How he wished he could be one of them. He could not, but that did not stop him from viewing those who could in a very dim light. Especially Asturt. The fellow was all too keen and now there was the further question about him, or as the queen had termed it, *the mystery of his history.*

As Jasper had suspected, Lord Ryland had been tasked with investigating the list he'd put together, though he'd not been told particularly why. Most of the fellows on it were wrapped up and discounted as nothing but odd. Except Asturt. Ryland said that investigation remained in process and there seemed to be some confusion as to the spelling of his name, possibly an administrative error. That might mean anything or nothing. But what was his surname? What was his title, exactly? Was it Irish? He wondered if Asturt was some sort of insignificant Irish baron and had decided to style himself as a lord while he was in London.

Whatever he was, he was three things at the moment. One, he was not good enough for Miss Wilcox, despite the trouble she'd landed herself in. Two, he was not very subtle about his interest in the lady. Though he had moved off and no longer spoke to her, he kept looking in her direction. And three, he was ridiculously dressed as a king, crown and all. Just the sort of thing one who was low on the pole would do. Insecurity made a man try too hard and speak too loud.

As Asturt's history *was* still a mystery, and as Jasper had only vague ideas of whether he might discover anything useful by disguising himself at the ball, he thought he would keep an eye on him. Though, his primary attention must be on Miss Wilcox. Would anybody take an opportunity to pass a message to her? Would *she* take such an opportunity? Lovely as her dress might be, it had plenty of places to hide a slip of paper. She might have easily enough sewn a small pocket on the underside of one of the petals. Should he see her do anything strange—stand beside a potted plant or slip out to the balcony or make eye contact with one of the musicians—he would closely follow what came next.

Whoever she made contact with, he would like to throttle them for putting her in so much danger.

CHAPTER SIXTEEN

ERRY TOURED THE drawing room and library, assuring himself that everything was in order. The house was quiet, as all the family had gone out. Lord Mendleton was supposed to be home nursing his alleged gouty foot, but as soon as his lady was gone he'd made a remarkable recovery and gone to his club. Perry had no idea where Lord Langley had taken himself off to, but according to Marcus, he'd left his Poseidon costume behind. Marcus had seemed fairly distraught over it and had asked repeatedly if anybody knew if he'd got a second costume he might have taken with him to his club.

However distraught Marcus might be over it, Lady Mendleton was sure to be a deal worse, as she'd put quite an effort into it.

Perry had left the rest of the staff playing cards in the servants' hall. He had no inclination for amusement at this moment. His thoughts were too taken up by Miss Wilcox.

Perhaps his earlier suspicions had been just that, but now he'd caught her eavesdropping on Lady Mendleton and Lady Heathway! What was he to do about it? What had been her purpose?

He'd thought of going to Lady Mendleton with the information. He'd even composed and practiced what he would say, the drawing room he just now paced became his stage and the darkened room lent it a certain amount of drama.

He would stand here…no, here. He would decisively turn and say—

My lady, over the years, when certain matters have come to my attention, I have thought, is this the hill on which I plant my flag and die a hero's death? Will I sacrifice my livelihood and therefore my very life to cry out against what I know is an injustice? Will I sacrifice myself over yet another flea-bitten mongrel turned up at the door or another servant hired who manages to know nothing, or a housekeeper who drinks sherry at noon, or a cook employed who, frankly, overuses garlic? In all those cases, I have resigned myself to walk away from the hill and keep my own counsel. In all those cases, the injustice was done to ME. That, I could bear. But this! There is a game afoot involving the family I have sworn to serve and the interloper who has been brought into it. And so this, the hill of Miss Wilcox, is the hill I shall die upon.

It relieved his feelings to imagine himself giving such a speech and he practiced it for a full hour before discarding the idea. His lady was far too fond of the girl and, in any case, Miss Wilcox might invent any sort of fiction to account for her standing outside of the drawing room door. He would be blamed for accusing an innocent young lady.

However, he would not abandon the family to their fate! Whatever Miss Wilcox was up to, he would do his best to discover it. He would keep his eyes sharp as a hawk, his hearing good as a fox, and his guiding instincts as attuned as a cloud of barn bats.

Miss Wilcox would not out-hawk, out-fox, or out-bat him.

In the meantime, he was rather cheerful over how articulate and stirring he could be when he had a mind to.

THE BALL HAD begun, and it had become all too clear that Jasper would not come. There was no Poseidon in the room.

Georgiana supposed she must take that as her answer. He had been expected by his mother *and* the hostess, and still he had not come. Avoiding her must be the reason.

She had for a moment grasped at wild ideas that might explain his absence—perhaps he had been taken ill, or encountered a misadventure on the road, or been suddenly called to the queen's side. However, the sensible part of her mind would not allow her to cling to such fantasies. He'd left the house early and had never the intention of coming. He would no doubt excuse himself with some story.

The sensible part of her mind also told her she must throw over her fevered imaginations of Lord Langley. She had clung to the idea of wait and see, but she had waited and now she saw.

It was never to be, she had been foolish in thinking it might, and she'd best begin thinking of practicalities. She'd had the notion that if it could not be Jasper, it could not be anyone. She'd thought it would be too unfair to marry a gentleman when her heart belonged to another. Commonsense had crept in, though. If every lady disappointed in love never married, England would soon find itself short of people and families would overflow with spinsters. Commonsense told her that she would not relish looking back twenty years from now and realizing that she had been an idiot who had thrown away her chances. She must be steely-eyed rational and do what was right and what was expected of her by her father.

She must marry. Lady Mendleton had been a dear to suggest a second season, but that was not yet firm and she supposed Lord Mendleton might have something to say about it. He was very kind, but he might not be willing to have her as an endless houseguest. This season could very well be her only chance. She could not bear to disappoint her father by coming home just as she had left. He would think her so foolish, and he would be right.

As for herself, she did not wish for spinsterhood and could not afford it even if she did wish for it. Her father's estate was entailed, such as it was, and the heir was entirely unknown to her. She could not put herself at the mercy of some fellow in Cornwall who would be none too pleased to be saddled with a dependent after having inherited an estate that barely paid its way.

She could go back to her original plan, she supposed. She might marry a passing soldier. Though, she had begun to realize that idea had always been only a comfort and not a real plan. She'd not once met an officer at their local assemblies who she liked even a little. They always seemed too old or too young, too voluble or too silent, too coarse or too…no, none of them had seemed too refined.

There *was* Lord Asturt to consider. She did not dislike him, after all. She suspected he liked her, at least he seemed as if he did, and Lady Mendleton was thoroughly convinced of it. She did appreciate his indulgence toward her. He had been not the least put off to watch her sail over Minerva's back and did that not speak of a liberal temperament? He seemed good-natured enough and it was really no trouble to allow him to wax on about his research into the kings of England if he liked it. There were far worse hobbies he might engage in—it was not as if he were out collecting earthworms on the road and naming them.

His estate was in Ireland and she could not say whether that would be pleasant or no, having never been. But then, aside from her own neighborhood and now London, she'd never been to any other county in England. If a gentleman from Cornwall or Devon were to ask, was she to be put off because she'd never been? She might look at Ireland just the same. Well, perhaps not *just* the same. As an Englishwoman, she would not be particularly well-received, at least not by a sizable amount of the local population.

She was not unsympathetic to the rebels and their cause, though it verged on un-English to say so. After all, if Italians or Danes had confiscated her father's lands she supposed she'd be all for swift action with a sword. Though, considering the fairly recent strife, she did wonder why Lord Asturt had spent so much time there. Perhaps the situation was not what she had been led to believe it was?

All these thoughts had consumed her through the first dance, and she pitied Mr. Swanson. He'd been so keen to claim the first, seeming to think it a great victory, but she assumed he was rather less keen now. She had been far too quiet and not done him a justice at all and it would not surprise her if he gave her a wide berth going forward. Whatever he was to do, he appeared relieved to be done with the set.

Lord Asturt came to claim her and she felt suddenly awkward. She'd just been thinking of him in a manner she had not viewed him before and it had somehow affected her. Still, she was determined not to be as dull as she'd just been with Mr. Swanson. She also determined that if she were going to consider him at all seriously, she ought to find out as much as she could.

As they waited their turn, Georgiana said, "Lord Asturt, I know so little about Ireland, in which part do you live and how do you find it?"

"My estate is in County Wexford," Lord Asturt said. "Ballyhough Hall is a pleasant place, set on a hill and overlooking farms and pastures. Far more quiet than London, as you might imagine. Do you, Miss Wilcox, enjoy the quiet of the countryside?"

"Indeed I do," Georgiana said. "Though, your own neighborhood must not always have been quiet. The rebellion was not so long ago."

Lord Asturt's expression seemed to cast the supposition aside. "That was all too predictable," he said. "A rational king would have seen that the American and French revolutions would inspire those nearer to home to try the same. He might have toured or demanded Parliament hear their complaints. Many of us were disgusted with the lack of foresight. I do recall a lot of talk about how a restoration of the Stuarts would be preferable to the dull-witted Hanovers."

Georgiana had not been able to comprehend why Lord Asturt held such a negative view of the monarchy, but she thought she understood it now. She could not know what he'd witnessed during the rebellion, but he would have been a youth at the time. Old enough to perceive the danger but too young to fight. It had no doubt been frightening.

Thinking to pull his mind away from dark memories, she said playfully, "Well, the Stuart pretenders both old and young are long gone so I suppose that sort of talk is all for naught."

"They were never pretenders," Lord Asturt said, his voice suddenly sharp. He seemed to collect himself and said, "Of course, should England ever wish for a return of the Stuarts, Count Roehenstart is a direct descendant. He is currently in Russia, I believe."

"Goodness," Georgiana said, "I hadn't known."

"*He* has royal blood and is recognized by the Tsarina. What are the Hanovers?" Lord Asturt said derisively. "A bunch of German farmers prone to madness."

"Please do not say such things!" Georgiana said heatedly. She was very afraid that one day soon the lord would misspeak within earshot of the wrong person.

She had thought it would not be much trouble to listen to the lord's opinions on kings, and it would not be if he were talking of the ancient past. One might disparage King John or even Henry the VIII all one liked, but not the current king. Lord Asturt had twice now come close to sounding treasonous! Could she really consider a man who might do or say something so foolish and irrevocable? He might be stripped of his title, or worse.

Georgiana took in a deep and slow breath and reminded herself to be rational. It might be usual that those living in Ireland spoke with such disregard. Distance from the crown might result in less respect or more casual opinions, she supposed. She had heard that very thing regarding those who made their home in India. He must only learn to keep those opinions quiet while he was in London.

Lord Asturt seemed to recognize her shock over his words and said, "Please excuse me, Miss Wilcox. I did not mean to alarm you."

Georgiana had nodded and, to her relief, he did not return to the topic.

JASPER HAD TO concede that disguising himself as a footman had not turned out to be his cleverest plan. He'd been run off his feet and gained no new information whatsoever.

My God, these people were impossible to footmen! At first, he had complied with whatever nonsense they demanded. *This* lady wished to have a glass of champagne, but not too warm and yet not too cold. It should be the precise temperature of an early spring day. He had a great urge to inquire, "Which spring day, you tedious matron?" Instead, he got her a glass of champagne at the temperature it was currently kept, of which he had not the first idea.

Then, *that* gentleman required two pieces of folded paper the width of his pinkie finger, as it appeared his shoes were too big. He would place the paper in the gap between his heels and shoes. Jasper had been forced to explore half the house until he'd stumbled upon the library and acquired it, all the while wondering how Lord Morgan didn't notice he wore ill-fitting shoes before he left his house.

As if that were not enough, *this* pert Miss caught his eye and motioned him to her. When he arrived to hear what the lady needed, she pointed to a stray hairpin on the floor. He picked it up, suppressing the urge to stab her in the eye with it.

Finally, though, he realized he need not do anything for anybody. None of these people could tell one footman apart from another and so he just nodded at each new request and drifted away.

If he had gained any insight on this night, it was to mind how he spoke to footmen and forgo asking them for anything silly. Yes, they were paid to run and fetch, but it gave him a bit of a queasy feeling to know that the poor fellows must spend half their lives enraged. He wondered if his own footmen had ever gleefully imagined stabbing him in the eye with an errant hairpin.

He was a bit ashamed that while he had gained that insight, he had caused the real footmen some amount of trouble. Lady Landen was just now berating one of them for failing to mend her broken fan. She had, nearly a half hour ago, told Jasper that she'd dropped it and Mr. Lester had stepped on it. He'd mumbled something about needing to fetch the proper fan repair equipment and left her waiting where she stood. Naturally, Lady Landen had collared the nearest footman and assumed it was the one she'd originally spoken to.

The night was turning out long and tedious and he'd not discovered anything of value. Nobody seemed suspicious or attempting to make contact with Miss Wilcox. Miss Wilcox, herself, did not plant a note or stare meaningfully at anybody. Of course, she might have done so while he was roaming around looking for Lord Morgan's pieces of paper, but he doubted it.

He'd put himself to all of this trouble for nothing. Nothing but having to observe Miss Wilcox being admired, and dancing prettily.

At least Asturt was not taking her into supper. Jasper had watched them dance for so long that a footman who considered himself senior to the rest had actually elbowed him in the ribs and given him a tray of empty glasses to do he knew not what with. Probably take them to the kitchens, had he known where they were. As it was, he deposited them on a deep windowsill and shifted the drapery to hide them.

He would slip out and return home prior to supper. Attempting to prolong the ruse and serve at table would reveal him to be an imposter in a trice. He had not the first idea of how it was done, but it was always done so seamlessly that he was certain there was some sort of system. It would be as a well-oiled clock, each piece moving in synchronicity under the watchful eye of the butler. His efforts would only result in a jammed gear bringing the whole thing to a painful and embarrassing halt.

In any case, Miss Wilcox was being taken in by Gresham. He did not know what they would talk about, but it was certain to be circumspect. The fellow was sensible and he was Lady Heathway's nephew, after all.

At least it was not Asturt taking her in. That fellow hung around Miss Wilcox far too much.

She could not choose him, could she? She was so far superior to him in every way. Aside from embroiling herself in a treasonous plot.

⫸⫷

LORD GRESHAM HAD taken Georgiana into supper. She had been surprised that he had put himself down for it, as there was no particular spark between them, nor was she entirely at ease with him as she would have been with someone like Mr. Vance. Lord Gresham was handsome and seemed a nice gentleman, to be sure, but Georgiana could never quite forget that he was Lady Heathway's nephew.

Georgiana had fallen back on her old habit of inquiring into a gentleman's hobbies, certain she would hear about horses for the next hour, but Lord Gresham had not obliged.

"I have been, until recently, far too busy for entertainments," Lord Gresham said. "I have spent the past two years mostly traveling from place to place in service to our majesty's government. Now that I am retired from that duty, do you suggest any particular hobby for me, Miss Wilcox?"

"I do not," Georgiana said. "I usually inquire only to give a gentleman the opportunity to speak of his horses."

Lord Gresham had laughed, and Georgiana said, "But indeed, travel is far more interesting than hobbies. Where had you been sent to?"

"Oh here and there, mostly Ireland but to the Netherlands and Spain as well."

Georgiana's ears had perked up upon mention of Ireland. Perhaps she might learn more about the real state of things there.

"Had you been to County Wexford, my lord? Lord Asturt was just telling me of it."

"Once, a few years ago," Lord Gresham said.

"Oh, I see! Perhaps you met Lord Asturt there."

"Indeed I did not," Lord Gresham said.

"Well, perhaps not if you were only visiting once," Georgiana said, "his family resides at Ballyhough Hall. He tells me it is a charming place with good views."

Lord Gresham laid his fork down. "Ballyhough Hall? But I had been under the impression that the owner of that estate was Lord Astur, not Asturt."

Georgiana thought certainly the lord was mistaken. There could hardly be two gentlemen of such similar names residing nearby one another. But then, Lady Mendleton had made the exact same mistake. She began to think it was a matter of accent and pronunciation that caused the confusion.

"Well," she said, "the names are very like, I suspect they must be one and the same."

"Perhaps," Lord Gresham said. "Though I had also been under the impression that Lord Astur was in his sixties and his heir was a grandson, still a boy. Of course, my information may have been wrong."

Georgiana suspected that Lord Gresham's travels had muddled his memory a bit. She did her best to participate in the rest of the conversation and since she *had* mentioned horses, Lord Gresham took the opportunity of describing a pretty little mare he'd bought. She was a chestnut with white socks and he intended to institute a breeding program, and...she knew not what else.

She did, from time to time, allow her thoughts to drift. That they only seemed to drift in one direction was not particularly a surprise. Of all the things that she'd imagined could happen to her in London, being the ridiculous victim of unrequited love had not been in her wildest imaginings.

Still, that was what had happened to her.

She ought to be thinking about Lord Asturt. She ought to be considering whether he might be a suitable match. She ought to be turning her thoughts to whether or not she might create some affection in her heart for Lord Asturt. Instead, she was thinking about the unsuitable match. The match that would never be.

Where was he this evening? What did he do? Was he sitting somewhere, playing cards? Was he at the theater? Had he been taken with some lady and now sought to turn up wherever she could be found? What was he to say to his very disappointed mother? Would he tell Lady Mendleton the truth? That he stayed away to avoid Miss Wilcox?

Jasper Stapleton, where are you?

CHAPTER SEVENTEEN

A S THE BUTLER, Perry was well-used to setting the tone at the servants' table. It must be a firm hand, but not *too* firm a hand. Were one to allow anything and everything to be spoken of, the talk would get bolder by the day. But to allow nothing to be spoken of...well, one would only find staff in corners discussing the very thing that had been forbidden. It was a delicate balance. When something untoward occurred in the family they served, it *would* be discussed. As long as the talk did not go too far off the road, Perry was amenable to it. He rather thought of it as tradition and supposed even Athelstan's servants had formed their own opinions in those long-ago early days.

There was no lack of subjects to be discussed at this moment. Lord Langley continued to make himself unusually scarce, he'd failed to don the Poseidon costume Lady Mendleton had ordered made, and it was said he'd not even gone to the masque. Miss Wilcox was reported to be out of sorts, though this was generally attributed to her sympathy with Lady Mendleton, who was out of sorts with her son. Perry, having an understanding and falcon eye vastly superior to his staff, thought Miss Wilcox was out of sorts because her intended prey was never at home.

On top of all that, they were to host a ball in two days' time.

"So as I brushed her hair," Jenny went on, "I said, my lady, the Poseidon costume might be put aside and worn another time and you do dote on Lord Langley after all." Jenny sipped her tea with satisfaction. "Well, that seemed to soften her a bit and now she's really turned a corner. She's decided it was not her son's fault at all, but the queen's fault for calling him away on such a night."

"Though," Perry interrupted, lest the conversation veer off the road, "we, as Lord and Lady Mendleton's staff, will never breathe a word of our queen being at fault in any matter."

"No, a'course not," Jenny said. "Who would we even tell it to?"

"I cannot imagine," Perry said, "though you do seem to tell everybody you can get hold of absolutely everything you know."

"Is it as bad as that?" Jenny asked, looking rather surprised.

Perry nodded and Jenny blushed and said softly, "I'm like a faucet, it just pours out."

"But here's what I don't understand—there was no message delivered from the palace to call Lord Langley away," Marcus said. "Does anybody know for certain if he went to the queen or to the masque, or maybe somewhere else altogether?"

"He didn't wear the costume, we already know that. And, if *you* don't know where he went," Jimmy said, "how are the rest of us to know? Why don't you just ask him?"

"He wouldn't like it," Marcus admitted. "He doesn't like to be questioned."

"By his valet? I should think not!" Perry said.

"I just wonder about it, though," Marcus went on. "He could have worn a domino, I bet there would have been a hundred like it at the ball."

"Why would you imagine that Lord Langley would have disguised himself from his own mother at an event where he was expected?" Perry asked, now perennially suspicious of the valet's endless curiosity.

Marcus seemed embarrassed by the question and did not answer.

"Maybe," Thomas said, "he don't want to be Poseidon and he don't want his ma to know it. So he goes in disguise and then pretends the queen called for him."

"Thomas," Perry said, "if you ever again refer to Lady Mendleton as *ma*, you will be dismissed."

Thomas nodded gravely, as if this were a point he would file away for the future. He'd lived a rougher upbringing than most and was forever encountering mistakes he never saw coming. Jimmy patted his shoulder in solidarity.

"*If* we are done speculating on a subject we know nothing about," Perry said, "it would be an ideal time to discuss the ball."

An uncomfortable silence settled over the table. Perry was not ignorant of its cause—this was the first large ball the house had hosted in years. Oh, there had been routs and card parties and musical evenings. There had even been the ghastly scavenger hunt that everybody would like to forget on account of Lady Brathwaite breaking her leg on the stairs. Fortunately, the lady had been still young and the bone had mended, but poor Lord Mendleton had been called Break-a-leg-Benjamin for the rest of the season. Had the stairs been over-zealously polished? Possibly. Had Lady Brathwaite fallen because of her speed and competitiveness? Definitely.

Now, they were to embark on a project that exceeded anything they had done before. A ball…a very large ball. There would be extra footmen brought in and Jimmy and Thomas would be stretched to their limits in supervising them. An elaborate menu had been settled upon and the cook would be pressed to ever greater heights. Perry presumed he could look forward to a few breakdowns and threats of handing in notice. Musicians inside, and the traffic of carriages outside, all must be managed. The maids had been bringing him all sorts of lists about what was required in the ladies' retiring room and he did not dare ask the reason for half of it. Champagne was even now sitting in the cold cellar. Wines had been selected by his own hand in conference with Lord Mendleton.

The house must be readied and shine like it had never done before. The ballroom floor must be chalked so they had no repeat of the Break-a-leg-Benjamin fiasco. Perry shuddered to think what he would deal with when the artist turned up. The fellow was meant to chalk in Lord Mendleton's coat of arms and he'd sketched it out a week ago, but Lady Mendleton had changed her mind and now it was to be blooming roses. *He* would be left to deliver that delightful piece of news.

Perry surveyed the faces looking toward him, waiting for his guidance. He set his teacup down with deliberation. "Each of you will have a critical role to play. Each of you will play it flawlessly like a well-choreographed ballet. That ballet will be directed expertly by me." He paused for dramatic effect, allowing the silence to further imbue gravity to his words. "Directed by Mr. Aldous Perry—your butler."

The servants all nodded at this proclamation.

Jenny lifted her teacup in his direction and said, "Right you are, Mr. Perry."

Perry suppressed a sigh. Jenny had the remarkable ability to instantly take an inspiring moment right down to the common-place.

⊰⊱

GEORGIANA FLIPPED THE pages of *Zastrozzi* aimlessly as she sat in her bedchamber. When she was not pretending to read, she gazed out the window and watched the comings and goings of the two very officious sparrows in the tree outside as evening slowly stole over the Town. The two birds seemed to have a lot to do before they settled in for the night. Finally, they went into their box and did not come out again, leaving her to her book. *Zastrozzi* had become her standby prop to appear as if she was doing something, though she found the story rather dreadful and only read bits and pieces. As far as she could tell, everybody was going to die.

The dress she would wear to Lady Mendleton's ball had been

taken out of its linen wrappings and lay on the bed. If she did not have so much care upon her heart, what would it have been to gaze at such a miracle of a gown? Never had she seen anything more beautiful. It was the softest ivory silk, with a blush gauze overlay dotted with pearls that were tinged pink in the light. Those same pearls edged the bodice and the sleeves and Lady Mendleton had told her they were imported from the Caribbean. After the ballgown's usefulness expired, the pearls would be removed and made into a necklace. The whole thing must have taken weeks and an army of seamstresses to sew, and Georgiana could not even bear to imagine the cost.

It was lovely and she was cognizant of how lucky she was, but she could not put her whole mind to it. There was so much else to think about.

The days following the masque had been odd indeed. Lady Mendleton had been sorely affected by her son's absence at the ball. She'd gone to such trouble for his costume! Over the course of days, Georgiana began to understand that it was less the lady's own disappointment in the scheme and more having to face up to her friends. Apparently, she'd said quite a lot to them about the Poseidon costume. Lady Heathway, in particular, seemed loathe to drop the subject.

Then, of course, Jasper was less in the house than ever.

Lady Mendleton had eventually softened on the matter of the Poseidon costume and now entirely blamed the queen for it. It seemed that Jasper had told his mother that he had been called away by that great lady and had no choice but to go.

Georgiana did not really believe it, but at least Lady Mendleton *did* and had been mollified. She supposed she should be grateful that he'd not told his mother the real reason—that he had stayed away as part of his campaign to avoid his mother's foolish female charity cause from the countryside.

Now it was the evening of the ball. The sun had dropped and the sparrows were quiet in the darkness that enveloped them. How lovely it must be to live the life of a sparrow—no uncomfortable memories or feelings haunted them, and they were secure and at peace in their box. She did not know how sparrows went about choosing their mates, but she suspected it had been done with little fuss and there had been no wondering or wishing or regrets.

As the time ticked nearer for her to dress, Georgiana felt her stomach do little flips. She would dance with him.

Jasper might have stayed away from the masque, but he would not dare miss his own mother's ball—a fact that Lady Mendleton had pressed not a few times in conversation with him. He was to know that she would not be able to face her friends if he did, would be heartbroken forever, and she really did not care if the queen's hair was on fire and she needed him to come and put it out.

He would come. He would also put his name down on her card, for to not do so would be noted. He would not claim her supper, though. Of that she was certain.

She had not the first idea who *would* take her into supper. Lord Asturt had sent his regrets earlier in the day, having come down with a fever. Lady Mendleton might have taken it as a slight, had the gentleman not written a full two pages of regret in the most dramatic and high-flown language possible. In the end, the lady had been satisfied that he must be laid very low and devastated to miss a ball held for Miss Wilcox. The lady only hoped he did not actually perish as he might end up being a serious suitor.

Georgiana, herself, was not certain how she felt about Lord Asturt's absence.

There were others who she'd danced with prior who for one reason or another could not come. Lord Ryland had called off as soon as he'd received his invitation, as he was chairing a meeting of his criminal society that night. Lady Mendleton had not been at all offended as everybody knew that nothing short of a direct word from God would ever tear him away from his project. Mr. Cahill was escorting his mother to something or other and Lady

Mendleton could not care less. She had her doubts about whether the gentleman would ever marry, as he seemed far too married to his mama. As far as Lady Mendleton was concerned, a man who would never marry was useless.

Georgiana did have hopes of seeing Mr. Vance, one of the few gentlemen who had so instantly and completely put her at ease. Perhaps Mr. Vance might take her into supper?

Jenny bustled in and said, "Right, I've squared away the mistress, though don't ask me how I did it so timely what with all the ruckus that went on."

Georgiana smiled to herself, thinking that Jenny really was uniquely talented at hinting there was a story in the offing. She said, "Pray, what ruckus, Jenny?"

As Jenny heated the tongs to take Georgiana's curls from one way to another way, she said, "I was just finishing Lady Mendleton's hair when Lord Langley came to see her. She'd called for him because she was fretting that her lord had not overseen Perry's preparations close enough and she would put her son to the task. It's just nerves, you know, Mr. Perry knows what he's about. Anyway, that was all well and good, but then came the suggestion about Lady Annabelle."

Jenny had paused dramatically, tongs in hand, staring at the now dark window as if the sparrows had decided to come out of their box to hear her tale.

"And?" Georgiana asked.

Jenny nodded to herself and went on. "You see, she says to him that he ought to take Lady Annabelle into supper. Then he says he won't take anybody into supper. She nearly fell over. Can you guess why he won't?"

Georgiana certainly could not guess. What did he mean to do? Go in on his own? Take a plate above stairs?

"He tells Lady Mendleton that he's been summoned to the palace at midnight! Well, you can just imagine how she takes it! What could be so important that he's got to go there at midnight on the night of *her* ball?"

Georgiana, of course, could not know. Though her heart sank.

"Then, things get interesting and I was quiet as a mouse 'cause I think they both forgot I was there. Never, in all the time that Lord Langley has worked for the queen, has he ever said what he did. Now, though, he's faced with a mother on the verge of hysterics. So, he says, *the very crown may be at stake.*"

Jenny took to wrapping her hair round the hot tongs. Georgiana glanced up at the maid, reflected in the looking glass. "That sounds rather dire," she said.

"Maybe to you," Jenny said, "but Lady Mendleton was having none of it and told him that the queen could put down her horrible dill sandwiches and fix something on her own for once."

Georgiana thought if she was not so disturbed, she might have laughed at Lady Mendleton's mention of the dill sandwiches. They *were* horrible.

"Then he said something about duty and marched out and Lady Mendleton was in fits over it. She's better now, though. I got her a glass of Canary and she was calmed by it. She's decided she's going to advertise far and wide that her son was called away because the crown is at stake. She reckons that ought to satisfy the duchess and Lady Heathway."

Georgiana nodded, hoping her attempt at a serene expression did not belie her roiling thoughts. At first, she was distressed because Lord Langley would leave her ball and it would be noted. Then she was distressed that Lady Mendleton was so distressed. Finally, though, she was distressed because she wondered what sort of danger came along with a midnight meeting and the very crown being at stake. There must be something happening, it would be too absurd and unnecessary to use such a story as an excuse, only to avoid her. It was too elaborate to be a ruse.

Certainly, Jasper would not leave his mother in the lurch unless it was both serious and unavoidable. He may have failed to make a showing at the masque, but he would not abandon his mother in her own house. He would not offend Lady Mendleton so deeply in some further effort to avoid herself. In any case, there was no need to absent himself at supper to avoid Miss Wilcox, he simply need not take her in. He might have taken in Lady Annabelle and all would have been satisfied, except for himself and Lady Annabelle.

To upset Lady Mendleton in such a way spoke of something very significant. A circumstance that had not left him with a choice.

She wondered if something had happened to the king and it was being kept quiet. Perhaps there was a panic in the palace, as they did not know how the public would welcome the regent as their new king. It would not be a concern out of place—everybody hoped the regent would settle himself. It would be natural that the palace thought they had time on their side in that regard and had been taken aback to discover they did not. But if that were the case, what were they to do about it at midnight?

"Now then," Jenny said, "let's get you into that dress. I never did see anything so fine."

JASPER HAD ONCE again taken his neckcloth from his valet and tied it himself. He was becoming convinced that Marcus was never going to get it right. Though, his neckcloth was the least of his concerns just now.

"Tell Carstares to have my horse saddled at half past eleven," he said.

Marcus nodded and Jasper was grateful that for once the fellow didn't have a thousand questions. He was rather pleased by it, actually. Perhaps the valet was finally figuring out how to act as a proper valet—never question, never raise a brow, never admit surprise. Of all times to need a horse, it *was* rather surprising that it should be on the night of his own house's ball.

It could not be avoided though. He was getting very close to the Stuart. Just when he'd thought he had hit a firm dead end, Ryland had delivered information into his hands and had more still to give. Ryland wrote enough to make him certain they could close in on the Stuart, but had said he had to reveal it in person. He arranged a midnight meeting at the northwest corner of Gloucester's Riding House nearby Grosvenor Gate.

That, of course, was an inconvenience and rather ridiculous, though not particularly unexpected. Ryland had one of his Society for Advancing Criminal Knowledge meetings this night and Jasper was well aware that a team of horses could not pull him away from it. As well, he was certain Ryland liked the cloak and dagger aspect of meeting at midnight in the park. Jasper thought they could have just as easily met in his library, but he wouldn't dare communicate that opinion to Ryland.

Jasper dismissed Marcus and sat in his chair by the window to re-read Ryland's letter.

Langley—

A certain gentleman I have spent a great amount of resources to investigate does not appear to be who he says he is. I believe him to be the person we have had recent concerns about. I do not disclose anything further, for if the plot is as deep as I suspect, there are likely spies everywhere. Meet me at midnight at the northwest corner of Gloucester's Riding House nearby the Grosvenor Gate. Come alone and see that you are not followed.

Ryland

His mother was deeply unhappy that he would leave her ball just when supper would be served, but he would go forward all the same. This was his chance to find the Stuart. This was his chance to extricate Miss Wilcox from the dangerous situation she'd got herself into.

He would get her out, one way or the other, but what then? Well, if it were done neatly and quietly, he might re-engage with Miss Wilcox.

Jasper slowly shook his head, embarrassed by his own lies to himself. He would not just re-engage with Miss Wilcox. He would seek her hand. And, what if she were not extricated at all? That did not bear thinking about. She must be extricated, one way or the other.

He just had to get her out of the situation before she landed in the tower.

GEORGIANA PUT A smile on her face and was determined to keep it there for the rest of the night. The expense and effort required to put on such a ball had been enormous and she would not insult Lord and Lady Mendleton with any expressions that might hint at unhappiness.

She descended the stairs to Lord and Lady Mendleton and Lord Langley just as Perry opened the door to the first arriving guests.

Lord Mendleton came forward to take her arm as she came down the last stair. "My dear," he said kindly, "you are an angel come to earth to grace us."

Georgiana smiled gratefully; he really was such a generous soul. She knew perfectly well that if it had not been his wife's own ball, he would have gladly claimed a gouty foot—even if he could not quite remember which foot it was supposed to be.

She avoided Lord Langley's eye and he did not speak to her. She stole a quick glance at him—he was as handsome as ever in his dress coat, his cravat tied in a complicated and yet restrained and elegant knot.

If only things were different! They were not, though. She was as she was, and he was not at all interested. And now, he was walking into some sort of terrible situation. Was it dangerous, even? A midnight meeting did suggest it, but then her imagination might be taking her places there was no need to go.

She had no further moment to think about it, as guests began making their way in, one party after the other.

GEORGIANA HAD NOT considered that because the ball was in her honor, she would be the recipient of endless attention. It seemed, at times, as if all eyes were upon her. Including, discomposingly, Lord Langley's. She never looked directly at him, but she took her opportunities to glance at him and caught him glancing at her. What was he thinking? Did he admire her dress, or did he wonder what the ball had cost his father and how soon he could be done with it?

When her eyes were not taking in Lord Langley, she admired the room. What care had been taken! Just now, as lords and ladies poured in, all were doing their best to step around the chalked roses. They would fade to nothing as the evening wore on but for now they bloomed a deep pink under the hundred candles in chandeliers above them.

Jasper had, as she had expected, put himself down on her card. Also as expected, he had not taken supper or the first. Mr. Vance had put himself down for her supper, though Lady Mendleton would probably have steered him to another of the dances had she had the opportunity. Lady Mendleton liked the gentleman well enough, but she never could quite get over the idea that he was *new* on account of him being grandson to a gunmaker who had been given the title for his service to the king. Georgiana was relieved that she would dine with him, the evening was likely to be an odd combination of smiling and feeling fraught and at least supper would not be nerve-inducing with the amiable Mr. Vance by her side.

She did not know if Jasper would have taken the first set had he the opportunity to do so, though she doubted it. As it was, Lady Mendleton and the duchess had conspired together to arrange that the duchess' husband, the Duke of Stanbury, would lead her through the first. He was an older, paunchy gentleman, but he was not chosen for his looks or eligibility—he was the most senior in rank attending and it was meant to be some compliment to Georgiana. She assumed Lady Mendleton also would not mind talking about the duke insisting on leading her girl as she made visits to drawing rooms in the following days. She would conveniently forget that the poor fellow had been conscripted into service.

The dance had come off successfully and though the duke in his advancing years would not make any lady swoon, he was kind and gracious. Georgiana was grateful for it, as she could hardly keep her attention on the dance—the next was with Lord Langley.

CHAPTER EIGHTEEN

J ASPER HAD NOT danced with Miss Wilcox since he had discovered firm proof that she was being used as a pawn in the Stuart's game. He had studiously avoided her presence, as he was fairly certain that one of the things she had been directed to do was charm him and elicit any information she could in the process. He felt himself well up to the challenge, but he shied away from it like a hand on a hot stove. It would be too agonizing to be near her and know she was doing what she had been somehow forced to do. He would be far too tempted to shake her and demand the truth.

However, he could not avoid putting his name down on her card at his mother's ball. It would have raised eyebrows if he had ignored the lady, and as for his mother…well, she was already in a state after hearing that he would leave just before supper. If he snubbed her protégé as well, mere raised eyebrows would pale in comparison. His mother's eyebrows would fly right off her face and be on fire while they went.

So, he could not avoid it. He did not really want to avoid it. He only thought he *should* avoid it, had it been practical.

As he led her to their place, he could not help but think how lovely she was. She was always so, but the gown she wore made her look…his father had described it as an angel come down to earth and that was very close to the mark. Not the cherubs with their childish chubby cheeks, but the long and lithe depiction from a master. Caravaggio would have felt the honor of painting her.

Her hand trembled through her glove and he thought it must be what every miss underwent at their own ball. So many eyes upon one must shake even the most experienced of debutantes.

He had no words to say to her, though she kept glancing up at him as if she would speak.

Finally, she said, "Lady Mendleton said, well, she mentioned...a midnight meeting at the palace sounds very, as if there was some danger."

He could not tell if she were on a fishing excursion, hoping to elicit some information, or whether she was only curious.

"Not at all," he said.

"I only wondered," she said softly, "is the king dead?"

"Certainly not," he said, sternly.

Why should she say such a thing? Was the Stuart worried that the king was dead? Why would he think it?

Jasper got a very sinking feeling. As the queen had requested, he'd left an invented report on his desk of the king having been ambushed and bravely fighting off his attackers. He never thought he would see the report in the newspapers, and he had not. What he and the queen *had* thought is the Stuart might feel pressure to move more quickly and thereby make mistakes if he thought some other plot was in the works.

He must assume Miss Wilcox had passed on that report and had now been directed to be certain that the king still lived. The Stuart would wish to know if some other party planned something, and he would most certainly wish the king alive and mad. Were the king to die, the country would be plunged into mourning, memories of his madness would fade, and memories of the good days would come to the forefront. Mourning would also throw some cold water on the regent, and most likely make him appear more sensible and sympathetic. The Stuart would not favor any of those things.

As he led her through the changes, Miss Wilcox said, "I am glad. I only could not imagine what else would keep the queen up for meetings at midnight."

"Plenty keeps the queen awake," he said roughly. "There are always those villains who seek to throw the country into chaos."

Miss Wilcox did not answer, and he thought he had hit her very close to home. It was not likely that she had any real idea of the Stuart or what he was up to, but she would certainly understand that the information she passed along was meant to stir up trouble for the monarchy.

"I am surprised I do not see Asturt here," Jasper said. "He seems to be always hanging about the place."

He did not know why he said so. Was it spite for Miss Wilcox's irritating lothario? He'd seen Asturt in the club a few hours prior and had left because he had the unaccountable urge to punch him in the face. He *was* rather surprised the fellow was not here, as he seemed to be here every other day. Perhaps the fates had smiled upon the house and run the man over with a carriage.

"Lord Asturt sent a note to Lady Mendleton this morning," Miss Wilcox said. "It seems he's been taken with fever."

"Or taken with a better offer," Jasper said, telling himself to stop talking but unable to stop. "I saw him at my club not many hours ago and he looked fit as a fiddle."

Miss Wilcox's color was always rather rosy, but it now deepened to such a degree that she appeared to have a fever herself.

"Oh, I see," she said softly.

Upon viewing her distress, Jasper cursed himself for his lack of self-control. He was not a schoolboy and yet he had sounded decidedly petulant. To hint to a lady that a gentleman could not be bothered to turn up at her ball was ungentlemanly. And possibly unforgivable.

What was wrong with him?

He knew what was wrong with him, though it did not excuse his behavior. He wished to take Miss Wilcox in his arms, he wished to make her the woman who would travel through life by his side. Most of all, he wished she was not engaged in a nefarious business that stopped him from doing so. He wished to rescue her, but he was also angry at her for it. He'd lashed out with a verbal barb to punish her, and so he had punished. That he regretted it meant little.

Miss Wilcox slowly recovered her composure. Her red cheeks faded and her eyes, which had begun to look dangerously glistening in the candlelight as if there were tears ready to spring out, lost their telltale shine. By the time the dance ended, she was looking positively steely.

She might well hate him now and he had nobody to blame for that but himself. All he could do was meet Ryland, get his information, and put an end to the Stuart's plans. Only then could he attempt to repair whatever harm he'd caused.

⇒⇒⇒⇐⇐⇐

GEORGIANA WAS WELL aware of how close she had come to crying. *Actually* crying, at her own ball, on the ballroom floor in view of all. It would have made Lady Annabelle's weeping in the retiring room at Lady Featherstone's ball seem minor indeed. The horror of the humiliation of such a spectacle had been enough to quell her tears.

She was not particularly devastated that Lord Asturt had made up some fib about being sick so that he might go elsewhere. She was surprised, but not devastated.

She had been devastated by Jasper's intent. Or rather, she supposed she'd better think of him as Lord Langley now. He sought to strike at her. It had come on so suddenly, in such a disdainful tone. She could never have been prepared for it.

He had wished to wound her and point out to her how insignificant she really was. She was to know that she had imagined all sorts of admirers, but they turned out to be ephemeral wisps of delusion. He had certainly done a fine job of it.

She had composed herself and in so doing felt herself harden. Georgiana Wilcox would not be humiliated at her own ball, nor would she allow Lady Mendleton to be so. She had vowed at the very beginning of the evening to keep a smile on her face and now she was even more determined. She would not let him see that she suffered. Let him think she cared not one jot over who came to her ball or what their opinions might be, including himself and his own. Let him steal out before supper to see the queen, Miss Wilcox would not even deign to notice his departure. He would be nothing to her. At least, he would *think* he was nothing to her. There was little left to save but her own pride, and she would save it.

She was resolute.

So far, she thought she was succeeding. She'd managed to appear engaged when Lady Annabelle excitedly informed her that her mama had been overcome and Mr. Pottsgrove was now a sanctioned suitor. It had taken three days of crying jags and fits and refusing to eat, though she did creep down to the kitchens at night because she did not want to actually starve. Her father had thrown up his hands and her mother had commented that at least he was not a butcher or a farrier and that had been that. Good Mr. Pottsgrove himself would have had no notion yet of this interesting development and, as Lady Annabelle was rather afraid he might do a violence to himself on account of his doting, she had daringly sent him an anonymous letter. According to the lady, all it said was: *Don't give up hope, Annie.*

For all the sadness heaped upon her shoulders, Georgiana could not help but to laugh over the idea that Lady Annabelle had signed her name to it and yet thought it was anonymous. Mr. Pottsgrove was about to have quite the adventure with his future wife.

Now Mr. Vance led her through the dance preceding supper. Though Georgiana had no intention of noticing when Lord Langley made his departure, she could not help glancing about.

She saw Marcus at the ballroom door, no doubt come to tell his lord that his horse was saddled. Lady Annabelle was nearby the door too, looking as if she did not quite know what to do with herself. She'd earlier told Georgiana that she had not allowed all of her dances to be taken, in honor of Mr. Pottsgrove. They were, after all, practically engaged, though he did not know anything about it. When she saw him, she would regale him with how she'd said no to this gentleman and that gentleman, and he would be pleased to hear of it. For her supper, she had arranged to go in with her father, who was currently occupying himself in the card room. Now, though, it seemed as if she rather regretted her scheme as she looked about uncomfortably and clasped and unclasped her hands.

As Georgiana turned with Mr. Vance, she noted Lord Langley striding toward the door. Marcus stepped aside to let him pass, and he was gone.

As Marcus followed the lord out, something fluttered from his coat pocket to the ballroom floor. Lady Annabelle noted it and picked it up. She looked as if she would follow Marcus to return it to him, but then she stopped.

Georgiana pressed her lips together as Lady Annabelle opened the paper and appeared to read it. She supposed perusing a valet's laundry list of shirts and cravats *was* one thing to do to occupy oneself if one did not dance at a ball.

She was beginning to wonder why she had ever any enmity toward the lady. There really was nobody more eccentric and amusing.

Even more amusing, Marcus returned to the ballroom and looked around the floor. At the same time, Lady Annabelle had folded the paper and held it behind her back.

The poor valet was looking everywhere for his notes and for some reason, Lady Annabelle had decided to hide it from him. She really was delightfully odd.

As they moved through the dance, Mr. Vance distracted Georgiana with all sorts of wit and pleasantries in his usual easygoing style. Now the dance had concluded and it was mercifully time for supper.

So far, she had done well. All of Lady Mendleton's particular friends had been spoken to and even Lady Heathway had complimented her on her dress. They had all assured Lady Mendleton of the success of the ball.

Georgiana was doing her duty and getting through the ball

minute by minute. The main thing was to please Lady Mendleton and that she had done so far. It would not be too long now before she was blissfully alone in her bed and could give vent to the feelings she had kept under wraps all evening.

As she and Mr. Vance made their way toward the doors, Lady Annabelle hurried to her side and said, "Mr. Vance, you will not mind if Miss Wilcox escorts me into the ladies' retiring room for a moment?"

Mr. Vance, naturally, had no recourse but to claim cheerfully that he did not mind in the least. Georgiana was both perplexed and diverted. Were they to have another conversation about Mr. Pottsgrove? Or were they to review the valet's list she had pilfered and discuss the various shirts to be laundered? Or was it some other delightful idea that had occurred to the lady? Perhaps she was considering a second letter to Mr. Pottsgrove in case he did not comprehend the first?

Lady Annabelle hurried her to the doors leading into the retiring room. The place was not as elaborate as Lady Featherstone's, but it was spacious and comfortable all the same.

They sat down on a sofa together and Lady Annabelle said quietly. "I have been a snooper. Mr. Pottsgrove thinks my snooping very charming and says I might snoop all I like, but I think others are sometimes not as approving."

Georgiana nodded, having been a snooper herself in the not so distant past and not at all approving of herself for it.

"I don't usually find anything interesting, and well, I would not say this is interesting as much as it is...I think it a very odd letter for a servant to have! I am sure it is very odd."

Lady Annabelle handed over the paper that Marcus had dropped.

Georgiana unfolded it. She could not be certain what it might contain, but was rather afraid it was some missive from a lady-love that she'd really rather not know anything about.

Marcus—

The fool has agreed to meet me inside the Grosvenor Gate at midnight, see that he's on his horse in good time. If by chance Ryland turns up at the ball, send me immediate word. Langley thinks he's meeting Ryland and I will call this off if they encounter one another prior. There has been one minor slip up— Langley spotted me at the club though I claimed an illness to his mother to account for my absence. Keep your ears open on that front. He must not suspect and think to come armed. The crown may well depend upon the outcome of this night—we shall not allow those idiot Hanovers to prevail a minute longer than they already have. My destiny is at hand.

Asturt

Georgiana read through it again as Lady Annabelle chattered on. "You see what I say about odd. Midnight meetings and the crown and such. Why should Lord Langley's valet have a letter like that from Lord Asturt? What does Lord Asturt mean by it?"

What indeed did Lord Asturt mean by it? Of course, he and Marcus were acquainted, Lord Asturt had recommended the valet to Lord Langley. But that did not account for the contents of this letter.

As she read it over and over, she searched for meaning. She began to reflect on everything Lord Asturt had ever said to her. As she did so, the various threads began to come together. The letter was the warp and Lord Asturt's words were the weft—they weaved themselves into a whole cloth.

Lord Asturt had sent Marcus into Lord Langley's employ quite deliberately. They were in some sort of plot together and the lord wished Marcus to be in this house in particular because…

Because of Lord Langley's work for the queen. Lord Asturt always had questions about Lord Langley and she knew from Jenny that Marcus did the same below stairs. Marcus was excessively interested in the king's condition. Lord Asturt had several times hinted that the king's madness was a family condition, passed down through the generations.

Georgiana sat back, the letter fluttering to the floor. That day in the library, when she suspected Marcus was snooping and she had snooped herself. He had been spying for Lord Asturt. Then, did they not meet in the park that one morning and claim it happenstance?

The park! Lord Asturt had claimed that Marcus had told him of the latest report on the king from having read it in the newspaper. But he could not have. It was too early in the day and he had no paper with him. Perry took charge of all the papers that were delivered to the house and took them straight in to Lord Langley in the library.

And what about Lady Featherstone's ball? Lord Asturt had startled her with what had sounded close to treason. He said if the public knew about the inherited nature of the king's madness, the Hanovers would be finished.

Then at Lady Tredwell's masque, he'd talked of a restoration of the Stuarts. When she'd joked about the Stuart pretenders, he'd said they never were pretenders. He'd said a true heir was alive, a Count somebody or other.

And then both Lady Mendleton and Lord Gresham only recalling the lord of the Irish estate as *Astur*. Lord Gresham even thought the lord was very old and the heir was still a child. She had assumed them both mistaken, but what if they'd both been right? What if there were no Lord Asturt? Only an old man named Astur? But then, if Lord Asturt had taken on another's identity, why add the *t* to the end of the name?

Astur. Asturt.

Almost sounding as if she were far away, Georgiana heard Lady Annabelle say, "Are you all right, Miss Wilcox?"

"Yes, yes," she said hurriedly. She had bent down to grasp the letter again. She stared at the name.

Oh God, she was right. Asturt. The letters rearranged were…Stuart.

Lord Asturt did not just know of the count descended from the Stuarts. He *was* the count. He *was* the gentleman he considered a suitable replacement for the Hanovers, and a restoration of the Stuarts. At the masque, he'd even dressed as a king.

Now, he had arranged to meet Lord Langley at midnight, all the while claiming to be Lord Ryland.

She did not know why Lord Asturt would attempt something against Lord Langley, other than if the lord was getting too close to the truth. Whatever the reason, Lord Langley was walking into a trap. A very dangerous trap. What wouldn't a man who wished to be king try?

She leapt up and shoved the letter into her bodice. "Lady Annabelle, you must make my excuses."

"Excuses for what?" Lady Annabelle asked.

"For leaving the house rather than going into supper."

As she raced from the retiring room, she heard Lady Annabelle say, "Oh, dear, I am sure nobody will like that."

JASPER HAD MOUNTED his horse and turned him toward the park. He glanced at Marcus standing at the open doors to the house. What was the fellow doing? Why had his valet come to tell him his horse was ready anyway?

He supposed Perry and the footmen were being run off their feet and Marcus had decided to step in. Still, the fellow was odd, just standing there like that.

He kept his horse at a walk as he was in good time, it was not quarter to midnight yet. He must turn his attention to the matter at hand and away from Miss Wilcox! He'd acted abominably to her, that was all too true. But if she knew what he was doing this night, she might not mind it so much.

He was doing everything he could to catch out the Stuart and bring this ridiculous plot to a close. Once that was done, Miss Wilcox would be freed from whatever obligations her father had placed her under. Whoever was making contact with Baron Manley would disappear like a vapor, as if they'd never been there at all. The baron would not know why the contacts had stopped, but over time he would realize that they had stopped permanently. Miss Wilcox would be free.

The Grosvenor Gate lay just ahead. Let him get this bizarre meeting with Ryland done with so he could consider his next move.

⟫⟫⟫⟪⟪⟪

GEORGIANA RACED TO the back of the house toward the door leading into the gardens and the stable. She turned a corner and ran smack into Mr. Perry. A tray of champagne glasses crashed to the floor and the butler stared at her with some mixture of horror and outrage.

"Mr. Perry," she said, before he could comment on the destruction before him, "there is no time to explain, but Lord Langley is in grave danger and Marcus is not who he claims to be. Find Marcus and lock him up."

"I knew it!" Perry cried. "I had my suspicions all along."

Georgiana skirted round him and headed for the back door at a run.

"Wait!" Perry cried. "Who is he, then? What did I suspect? Where are you going?"

"To extricate Lord Langley," Georgiana called over her shoulder.

She did not hear clearly what Perry said next as she was already in the garden, but it was something to the effect that he would do his duty despite the world gone mad.

Georgiana picked up her skirt and sprinted across the garden, the stones on the paths poking painfully through her feeble ballroom slippers. It was no matter, she must just get there in time. She must get there before Lord Asturt, or whatever his name really was, did something that could not be undone.

She crashed through the garden's back gate, ran along the side of the stables to the door and threw it open.

At her noisy entrance, Carstares and the grooms burst out of the stablemaster's room to investigate the racket. One of the grooms held up a threateningly sharp-looking hoe in case she was a very loud horse thief.

"Miss Wilcox?" Carstares said, looking rather amazed to find her there in her ballgown and now very muddy slippers.

"Saddle Minerva," she said. "Lord Langley has gone to the park and he is walking into a trap. And give me the most lethal horsewhip you have. Hurry!"

For a moment, Carstares and his grooms stood like statues, as if they were attempting to parse the information she had just delivered.

"Hurry!" she shouted.

This jolted them from their stupor. Carstares turned to the grooms and said, "Saddle Minerva and Zeus, I will go too."

Georgiana was rather relieved at the suggestion. "Pistols, Mr. Carstares. Do you have pistols?"

"Jimmy! Fetch my pistols!" Carstares directed.

The stables became a hive of activity. Horses brought out, pistols loaded, horsewhips located. Georgiana chose a horrid looking specimen of a whip, the butt encased in silver, the braid long and thick, and small silver balls tied at the end of the braid. It was not one she would ever use on a horse and she hoped nobody ever had, but it would inflict very much pain on any man who happened to get in its way.

Jimmy handed over the pistols to Carstares while another of the grooms carried a saddle to Minerva.

"For God's sake, not the sidesaddle!" Georgiana cried.

The boy dropped it and ran back into the tack room.

It was not more than a minute before Minerva was saddled, the horse wild-eyed at this late-night turn of events. Georgiana mounted, and Carstares was already on his own horse. He patted the pocket holding his pistols, Georgiana took up the whip.

"To the Grosvenor Gate," she said.

They clattered out of the stable as the grooms jumped aside and they turned their horses down the mews toward the park.

CHAPTER NINETEEN

J ASPER SLIPPED OFF his horse and led him through the gate and
into the park. There had been no sign of a guard at the
entrance, which was hardly surprising. They were generally
either drunk at the gate or drunk at home, having been bribed by
those persons who wished to do their nefarious business
unobserved.

He did not see Ryland anywhere and hoped the fellow did
not have some plan to spring out at him like a footpad to amuse
himself. It would be just like Ryland—he was always going on
about being prepared and anticipating the enemy and never
letting one's guard down.

He suddenly heard a rustling to his right and placed his hand
on his horse's nose to still him. A man shadowed in darkness
emerged from the bushes and Jasper started. He was not nearly
tall enough to be Ryland. How stupid that he did not bring his
pistol, he might very well be on the verge of being set upon by
footpads while Ryland ran late.

The man approached and Jasper could see now that he did so
with his pistol raised. His idea of a footpad began to fade as his
instincts took over. They told him this was not a happenstance
meeting, this was not some thief delighted that he'd turned up
unexpectedly. This man had been waiting, this was a trap, and
he'd fallen right into it. Worse, it was a trap no doubt laid by the
Stuart, for if not, where was Ryland? The Stuart had decided he

was getting too close. He'd probably decided it based on whatever Miss Wilcox had fed to him.

That damn girl!

The man approached and the light from a streetlamp softly illuminated him. "Step away from the horse," he said. "I never shoot a good horse."

"Asturt?" Jasper said, failing to keep the note of incredulity from his voice.

"Charles Edward Augustus Maximilian Stuart, Baron Korff, Count Roehenstart, last of the Stuarts, and the true King of England," Asturt said, cocking his pistol.

My God, Asturt was the Stuart?

How could he have been so stupid as to not figure it out? Asturt had placed a valet in his house. Asturt had met Miss Wilcox in the park. Asturt had called on Miss Wilcox persistently. Asturt had even dressed as a king at the masque.

"You must be mad," Jasper said, carefully glancing around him and looking for some kind of escape route.

The suggestion of madness appeared to shake Asturt, and Jasper saw the gun waver ever so slightly. "*I* must be mad? You, who are so well-acquainted with the madness of the Hanoverians, are wondering if *I* am mad? I am a Stuart, we do not carry the disease. Move away from your horse."

Jasper could not see a way out. All he could do was hope Asturt's aim was not particularly good and that he did not carry a second loaded pistol. Once the first shot was off, if he was lucky enough not to be hit he'd have to move quickly.

The sound of galloping hoofbeats reached his ears and he stared at Asturt, hoping the fellow might become distracted by it.

"I said," Asturt shouted, "move away from your horse!"

It began to occur to Jasper that Asturt was not so intent on moving him away from his horse for the sake of the horse, but because he was shadowed by the horse. Asturt was wary of approaching closer and he wanted a clearer shot. The man might not be certain if Jasper himself had a pistol in his pocket, which would have been a very sensible thing to have. He patted his pocket as if he did have one.

The galloping hoofbeats that Jasper had been sure would pass by suddenly turned and came through the gate. "There they are!" a lady shouted.

And not just any lady, it was Miss Wilcox.

My God, what was she doing? Coming along to be sure he was dead?

Jasper took the distraction to lunge at Asturt. A blast echoed through the night. He felt a burning pain sear through his left arm, while Asturt turned and ran. Miss Wilcox galloped past him in pursuit. She raised a whip and brought it down upon the man.

Asturt cried out in pain and fell to the ground, his pistol rolling into the darkness. The rider of the second horse passed by Jasper and he was even more confounded to see it was Carstares.

Miss Wilcox had leapt off her horse and whipped Asturt as he rolled around on the grass shouting for her to stop and that she was meant to be his queen. Carstares dismounted and threw the reins over Zeus' back. He jogged to Miss Wilcox, pulled out a pistol, and stayed her hand. "That'll do, miss," he said, as casual as if he was indicating the amount of milk he took in his tea. "I've brought some rope along, I'll tie him up. Best go see if Lord Langley has been hit."

"Yes," Miss Wilcox cried. "Oh dear, yes!"

She dropped the horsewhip and ran to him. Jasper realized he'd been standing dumbly, watching this bizarre tableau unfold before him. What was happening?

"Are you hit?" Miss Wilcox asked.

"What?"

"Oh, I see you are," she said, ripping the bottom panel of her skirt away. "Yes, there," she said, as if she were talking to herself, "I can feel the blood seeping through your coat. It does not seem to be too much, though."

As she wound the fabric round his arm, Jasper said, "Miss Wilcox, what are you doing here?"

"Extricating you from a dangerous plot," she said, knotting the material.

"No, that's why *I'm* here. To extricate *you* from a dangerous plot," he said.

"Truly?" Miss Wilcox said, pausing her ministrations. "You came to extricate *me*? Truly?"

"Yes, truly," he said. "I caught you out some time ago. I know you were forced to spy, though I wondered if you knew it was a Stuart plot or that Asturt was the man at the bottom of it. I had to put an end to it before you landed yourself in the tower."

"You thought I would end in the tower?" Miss Wilcox asked, laughing.

"Why are you laughing?" Jasper asked.

Was he dreaming all of this? Like a dream, there was no logic to any of it—it just leapt from one strange scene to the next.

Carstares had tied up Asturt and got him to his feet. Now he marched him past Jasper and Miss Wilcox. "I'll lock him up in the tack room until you decide what to do with him," the coachman said. "I'll throw him over Minerva, if you don't mind."

Miss Wilcox had nodded her assent.

"You were meant for a crown," Asturt said as he was dragged past her.

"Enough of that, you heathen," Carstares said, shoving him to move him along.

Georgiana shivered. All along, she'd thought Lord Asturt might be a suitor. She'd even considered the idea. Now she was to know he'd schemed to overthrow the monarchy and drag her into it as well. Queen, indeed.

She put her mind back to the matter at hand and turned to Jasper, "Can you walk, Lord Langley? Or else, I can help you onto your horse and lead him back. He has not been hit and can easily carry you under my guidance."

"I can walk," he said. The sting and ache was coming upon his arm stronger by the minute, but he could walk. It might clear his thoughts to walk, and God knew his thoughts needed clearing just now.

⟫⟩⟨⟨

CARSTARES HAD MUZZLED Asturt with a handkerchief and thrown him upon Minerva. As they went ahead, keeping to the darkness as much as possible, Georgiana supposed poor Minerva had never had a night like it.

She, herself, had never had a night like it. What a wild thing she had done! But then, what else could she have done?

And then, after she'd subdued Asturt, or the Stuart as she guessed he really was, Lord Langley had said *he'd* come to extricate *her*. He said it so kindly too, not at all like his tone at the ball. He'd been afraid she'd end in the tower, of all things. She could not make heads or tails of most of what he'd said, but she at least understood that.

It was really something to think about—he disappointed his mother and came to this mad midnight assignation to save *her*. That she did not need saving seemed entirely beside the point.

"Miss Wilcox," he said, walking by her side as she led his horse, "I really must understand what has occurred here."

As they walked underneath a streetlamp and then into darkness and then into light again, Georgiana told him all she knew and what she'd put together from the note Marcus had dropped.

Lord Langley, Jasper, then told her all he *thought* he'd known, though he had been very much mistaken.

They passed the turn to the house, they both agreeing that they ought to go in from the mews lest they cause a stir amongst Lady Mendleton's guests. Jasper could not yet know what the queen would do with Asturt and the thing ought to be kept quiet until then.

They passed the turn to the mews as they were still talking, and then went down various streets, always turning to head back to the house and not quite getting there. It was only when

Georgiana began to get the feeling that Lord Langley grew tired from his injury, graze though it seemed to be, that she insisted on returning.

As they strolled along the quiet mews, Jasper said, "I hope you are not disappointed that you are not to be Queen of England, bride of the new Stuart king."

"Do not even joke of such a thing," Georgiana said.

"I did think, though, that you liked Asturt," Jasper said. "At least a little."

"Let us leave Lord Asturt behind, if you will. After all, there was never such a person existing," Georgiana said, holding out her skirt and peering down at the wreckage she'd made of it. "I do not suppose Lady Mendleton will be very happy over what I've done to this dress."

To her surprise, Lord Langley stopped her walking and pulled her close. "I don't care about the dress." He bent over her and softly kissed her.

Georgiana felt as if her body had become liquid, her knees no longer made of anything solid. She hoped his arms would keep her up and she would not fall on the cobblestones. She did think his embrace would keep her up, as it was far more powerful than she had imagined. It was powerful and rather perfect.

As she sank into the bliss of him, her very inconvenient rational mind kept posing the same questions. Did he kiss her from some sort of gratefulness? Was he really in his right mind? She could not bear to discover on the morrow that he had not been.

She pulled away gently and whispered, "I don't care about the dress either. But I pray you do not kiss me only out of a sense of gratefulness."

"Gratefulness?"

"For saving your life," Georgiana said. "Or it might be loss of blood and you are not thinking clearly."

"My God, Miss Wilcox," Jasper said softly into ear, "I have been in love with you since the moment you blew into this house with your shockingly bad playing and bad taste in books and I'm guessing bad sewing and drawing too."

Georgiana breathed a long sigh into his coat lapel. No gentleman out of his senses would recall how badly she played. "I think I have loved you all along, despite your incessant reading of newspapers and secretiveness and long absences and deranged suspicions and outrageous barbs."

Jasper loosened one of her curls and twirled it round his finger. "Yes, as to the barbs this night, that was unforgivable."

In truth, Georgiana could not care less about the barbs. It felt silly now, that she'd almost burst into tears on the ballroom floor. "My playing of the pianoforte is rather unforgivable too, so I suppose we just must put up with each other," she said, a soft laughter escaping her.

"Tell me what else I must put up with," Jasper said, nuzzling her hair. "I want to know it all and be delighted with it."

As Georgiana rested her cheek against his coat, she thought of how very good he did smell. She had hardly dared imagine herself in his arms, and yet here she was. She would have to admit all though, no matter how vexed he got over it. If they were to spend their lives together, it could not begin with a secret. There had already been too many secrets and misunderstandings between them.

She peeked up and him. "I must admit to reading a letter that was in your desk. When I went to the library for a book, Marcus was reading it and I…"

"You were only a nosy meddler, precisely as I'd hoped you were."

Georgiana nodded and continued. "As well, I fell off Minerva in the park because I've never in my life used a sidesaddle. I expect you think me a heathen."

"A delightful heathen with none of the tedious accomplishments a young miss is usually forced to carry round and subject everybody to. Rather, you set off into the night like a veritable Joan of Arc to rescue me, which I find a far more interesting accomplishment."

"I will hold you to that."

"Do hold me, in any case."

Georgiana did as she was bid, and gladly. She might stay standing in the mews all night. They both ignored Lord Langley's horse, who did not seem to see the charm of standing in the mews and had taken to irritating snorting.

Jasper suddenly started. "Good Lord, I am bad at this."

"What? What has happened?" Georgiana asked, silently praying he'd not changed his mind or suddenly remembered he'd declared for somebody else or realized a connection to her less than lofty family would not bring him any glory.

"Miss Wilcox," he said, "I presume you have agreed to become my wife? I should have asked very specifically, but then I kissed you instead. I suppose you'll want some sort of poem? Or at the very least, a list of your charms."

Georgiana smiled. "Well, you did get shot in your effort to extricate me from a treasonous plot—I suppose that's declaration enough. And, you'd better call me Georgiana. I have been thinking of you as 'Jasper' for ages."

"Georgiana," he said.

AFTER STAYING OUT on the lane far longer than they meant to and far longer than the horse had any patience for, Jasper said, "Come, let us face whatever awaits us."

They had paused at the stables to ensure that Asturt was held secure. He was, as was Marcus. After Georgiana had left for the park, Mr. Perry had lured Marcus out of the house with some tale of more champagne being delivered and left in the stables. He'd then slammed the tack room door shut and put the padlock on it to the amazement of the grooms. The grooms were particularly amazed that the butler could not explain exactly why he locked Marcus up. The valet was not who he said he was, but Perry did not have the first idea of who he actually was. Mr. Perry also seemed very much relieved to know that Carstares had accompanied Miss Wilcox to the park, though again he could not explain why.

Now, both Asturt and Marcus were under lock and key with three grooms sitting against the door and Carstares sitting in a chair in front of it with his pistols by his side. Jasper wrote out a note for the queen and sent it with one of the grooms to the palace, accompanied by the code word *meddle*.

Both Georgiana and Jasper were in agreement that they needed an outlandish explanation for their current outlandish appearances. They had concocted one so bizarre it was likely to be believed. After all, who would invent such a tale? It was a wobbly story if one peered too close, but it was all they had.

They slipped in the back door and made their way down the corridor. As they neared the front of the house, they could hear Lady Mendleton speaking to Perry.

"I do not understand," Lady Mendleton said, her voice full of handwringing and nerves. "Lady Annabelle said she'd gone out and you say she may have gone out but are not certain. Where is she? You don't suppose she eloped with somebody? She would not, would she? Do you know from what heights Lady Heathway will crow if the girl has eloped?"

"Calm yourself, Mother," Jasper said, turning the corner with Georgiana on his arm. "All is well. We only encountered a mishap."

Lady Mendleton was, for one brief moment, all relief. Then, her eyes took in the pair that stood before her. Her son's arm bandaged and her protégé's skirt being the bandage. A pearl from that bandage dropped and rolled across the floor.

Lady Mendleton staggered and Perry propped her arm to keep her upright.

"I only meant to go out to the garden for a moment," Georgiana said. "I needed some fresh air. But then I heard a shot."

"A shot," Jasper said, "from the mews. As I left to see the

Queen, I was set upon by armed footpads."

"Armed footpads!" Lady Mendleton cried. Perry led the lady to a bench in the corridor so that she might take the alarming news sitting down. Perry himself looked as if he might need a chair, as he was entirely lost.

"I raced to the scene," Georgiana said. "And found Lord Langley's valet was among them."

"Marcus?" Lady Mendleton said, her eyes nearly rolling back in her head. "Your valet is a footpad?"

"Miss Wilcox discovered me laying on the street, hit. Just a graze, though."

"I tripped Marcus and he hit his head and was unconscious," Georgiana said, "though the rest of them escaped. I am afraid Lord Asturt was in on it too and is some sort of fraud, as he was later found hanging round the end of the mews waiting for him. As you can see, I was forced to tear my dress to stop the bleeding on Lord Langley's arm. I'm very sorry I ruined it."

"But Marcus? Lord Asturt? Thieves? It seems impossible!" Lady Mendleton cried.

It might well seem impossible. It was the most ridiculous story ever told.

"Jasper, you are not terribly hurt? Georgiana, you should not have rushed into danger! Where were Carstares and the grooms?"

This, they had not discussed. Georgiana glanced at Jasper. Jasper said, "I did not wake them when I left, and you know they all sleep like rocks. Had Miss Wilcox not sounded the alarm, I would likely be laying in the street even now. Carstares was able to overcome Asturt and has locked him up."

Lady Mendleton clutched at Perry's sleeve. "A fan, and sherry. Get them for me."

Georgiana sat by Lady Mendleton on the bench and patted her hand. She dearly hoped the lady would not stop to consider what in the world Marcus or Lord Asturt hoped to steal from Lord Langley outside of the house, rather than inside it. Still, it was the only way to account for both of those rogues being tied up in the stable, which would never stay quiet among the servants. "It has all come out right in the end," she said encouragingly to Lady Mendleton. "Though, we might send for a doctor to dress the wound."

"The wound!" Lady Mendleton cried.

"It is just a scratch," Jasper said.

Mr. Perry hurried back with the items he had been sent for. Lady Mendleton downed the sherry, of which Mr. Perry had been exceedingly generous and brought the whole decanter lest it was not sufficient, while Georgiana fanned her.

"Also," Jasper said, looking meaningfully at Georgiana, "Miss Wilcox and I are engaged."

"Engaged?" Lady Mendleton said querulously, holding out her glass to be refilled. "To be married? On account of Marcus and Lord Asturt being footpads?"

"Something like that," Jasper said, appearing amused.

Georgiana thought he might well look amused, but she was rather quaking. She wouldn't wonder if Lady Mendleton took her to be worse than a footpad. She'd not taken *things*, she'd taken the lady's son.

"But what of Lady Annabelle..." Lady Mendleton whispered.

"I am afraid Lady Annabelle is entirely set on Mr. Pottsgrove," Georgiana said.

"Who is Mr.—"

"Now, you can have nothing against it, Mother," Jasper said firmly. "It would not matter a jot if you did. I will have my way in this matter. It is decided."

"Well of course, you must have your way, and Georgiana is such a dear, but I thought, well I suppose your father will be agreeable, but...what will Lady Heathway say? We were all very set on Lady Annabelle, we were all in agreement, it really was quite a settled thing..."

"Mother, I do not care what Lady Naysay or the duchess or the rest of them say about it and neither should you," Jasper said. "But since you do care, slap whatever face on it that you will."

"Slap a face on it…" Lady Mendleton murmured.

Georgiana could see that the wheels began to turn in Lady Mendleton's mind. She very much hoped they were turning on the idea of managing Lady Heathway and not on the credibility of their flimsy story or how she might still convince her son to marry Lady Annabelle.

"Now of course," Lady Mendleton said slowly, "Georgiana has just saved my son from murderous footpads and the queen does hold her in rather high regard…"

"You are not angry with me, then?" Georgiana asked, holding the lady's hand.

"It is just such a shock," Lady Mendleton said, gulping down her second glass of sherry. "My head can barely keep up. My mind was very set one way and now it's to go another way. I really had not thought, Jasper practically avoided the house, so of course I told Lady Heathway it was her own imagination…"

"Mr. Perry," Georgiana said, "perhaps you could send for a doctor to dress Lord Langley's arm while I take Lady Mendleton above stairs to rest."

At this, Lady Mendleton shook her head. "Oh, no, my dear. I cannot retreat in the face of this…turn of events. As Jasper said, a face must be put on it!"

Georgiana had no notion of what Lady Mendleton wished to do about this turn of events. She was only relieved that the good lady did not seem too angry with her.

Lady Mendleton's eye twitched and she pressed on it to make it stop. Then, she slowly nodded to herself.

"I know what to do, it is the only course. I will gather myself and go into the dining room. I will tell everyone the tale of Miss Wilcox saving my son from footpads and that Lord Asturt has been unmasked as a fraud."

Lady Mendleton's nodding picked up speed. "Of course that is what I ought to do. There will never have been a ball like it! Absolutely everybody will wish they'd been here or crow that they had been. Let Lady Heathway consider *that!*"

As Lady Mendleton rose, appearing to have regained her vim and vigor, she suddenly paused. "Goodness, I just thought...now I really will be your mother, Georgiana."

"So you will," Georgiana said, "and I could not imagine a one better."

Jasper kissed the top of his mother's head and said, "Go in and spin your web round your friends, mother. Perry, I'll take that decanter of sherry. Miss Wilcox and I will restore ourselves from our adventure in the library."

GEORGIANA AND JASPER had taken themselves off to the library while Lady Mendleton went back to the dining room to spin her web. They could not hear the entirety of the performance, but the occasional word did reach them. There was an outcry over the mention of footpads, a further outcry over the devious Lord Asturt, and gasps and bravas which they presumed was related to Miss Wilcox's daring rescue of Lord Langley. They supposed there had also been mention of an engagement as there was a gentle clapping heard. They might have heard more than they did if they had not entwined themselves on the sofa.

Between kisses, they agreed that if they were asked about the night's events, as they most assuredly would be, they would claim they had vowed to never speak of it again. It was a story that would not hold up well under any sort of scrutiny. It had been necessary, though, to allow the queen to decide what, if anything, would be revealed about Asturt's plot.

The doctor arrived and, much to his embarrassment and Perry's, Jasper and Georgiana were quite oblivious to the sound of the door opening. A loud clearing of the throat set them disentangling themselves. Georgiana did not know what sort of state she was in, but between her ripped dress from bandaging Jasper's arm and the hairpins scattered on the sofa, she could not imagine it was anything less than shocking.

As the doctor set to cleaning and dressing the wound, Jasper helpfully informed him they were engaged. This, fortunately, did seem to lessen his surprise at what he had found when he'd walked in.

The wound was more than a scratch, but it would heal, in the end. As the gentleman did his work, Georgiana and Jasper made various arrangements between them.

"I'll ride to see Baron Manley on the morrow," Jasper said. "You don't suppose he'll withhold his approval for any reason?"

"Indeed, no," Georgiana said. "He is a sensible man and you will like him."

"I look forward to meeting Lady Manley too," Jasper said.

Georgiana thought she'd allow him to look forward to it, though the feeling might not hold after actually meeting her. Then again, one never knew what emotion might overtake her mother. She might be put out that somehow it was not herself to become a countess someday or she might revel in the amount of bragging she might do in the village over the match. Only time would tell.

"We'll need our own house, of course. In the country, I stay in a hunting lodge on the estate's grounds, it will not be at all suitable. You shall wish to be mistress of something larger."

"Shall I?" Georgiana asked. "I rather like your parents. I would not mind staying under their roof. Unless, of course, you would not like it?"

"I would not mind it," Jasper said. "In the country, we might take over the west wing. But you do know my mother is a bit of a meddler?"

"As am I," Georgiana said, laughing.

Jasper smiled. "Two meddlers under one roof might seem insurmountable. Until I remind myself that I have been far worse than a meddler. I have been an accuser of treason against an innocent lady, all from my own fevered imagination."

Georgiana nodded, though she found she could not care less about his fevered imaginations at this moment. His fevered *feelings*, of which she had been thoroughly convinced of while they'd been on the sofa, were all that mattered now.

Lady Mendleton came in with Lord Mendleton behind her.

"I am told there is an engagement?" the lord said. "Is it true? Or has my wife gone mad in her wishing for a daughter?"

"I hope you do not mind it, my lord," Georgiana said.

"I certainly do not," Lord Mendleton said. "I was rather terrified of finding Lady Annabelle under my roof—a lifetime of London air on hair complaints would have done me in."

Georgiana would have very much liked to explain that it had been Lady Annabelle who had been the key to everything. If she had not been snooping into Marcus's note, Jasper would be lying dead in the park just now. She could not, though. They could not reveal anything that would lead to more questions.

Instead, she said, "The lady has been unhappy and is not as you think her, but all that will come right when she returns home to see a certain gentleman. The banns will be read in no time, I think."

"As will yours," Lady Mendleton said. "I suppose you'll rent a house somewhere, do not make it so very far away, Jasper. I did hope to have Georgiana under my wing for at least another season."

"We rather thought of going nowhere for the time being," Jasper said.

Lady Mendleton clutched the arm of a chair and sank down into it. "You will stay! With us? Well, I hadn't thought...goodness, just imagine! Georgiana, we will shop and have tea and I shouldn't wonder at all if your playing becomes very good with more practice. We might even have a musical evening some time in the future."

Georgiana looked at Jasper ruefully, lest he get the idea that sweet music was even a remote possibility for his future. He looked away, suppressing his laughter.

"What a night this has been!" Lady Mendleton said. "My son has survived a scheming fraud and dangerous footpads, and dear Georgiana has saved him and is to be my daughter forever. And, while you did not witness it yourselves, I do not think I flatter myself when I say my speech to the guests was a triumph. Was it not a triumph, Husband?"

Lord Mendleton, the dear good-humored man, nodded and said, "Indeed. Lady Heathway appeared most unhappy at its happy reception, so it must have been a triumph."

Georgiana could not know for certain what sort of triumph Lady Mendleton had managed, but she felt rather triumphant herself.

⇒⇒⇒⫷⫷⫷

BARON MANLEY HAD given his consent to Lord Langley with alacrity. He liked the fellow and thought his dear Georgiana could hardly do better. If the Stapleton household remained in the dark about what had really transpired between the couple, Baron Manley remained in the dark with a blindfold tied on for good measure. As far as he ever knew it, it had been a quite usual courtship.

Jasper, upon spending the night as Manley's guest and having a look round the estate, could see how and why things had fallen into disrepair. There was a general rundown look to the place, and to the baron for that matter. After a ghastly dinner with Lady Manley, he guessed her husband was too tired to provide much energy to the estate. The lady was by turns flirtatious and petulant, proud and sulking—her moods changed as fast as the courses.

Jasper was determined to right the ship and he arranged to send his own assistant steward to whip the estate into shape, including the judicious selling of wood from the rather extensive woodlands that the baron had not done a thing with. It would put the estate on far firmer footing than it had been and allow Lady Manley to have the dresses made that she seemed to pine for. One could only hope it was enough to bring the baron some peace.

GEORGIANA HAD PERHAPS had some little trepidation over Jasper visiting her father's estate, as one never did know what her mother might do or say. However, he returned all cheerfulness and only described her mother as an *interesting lady*.

He had somehow convinced her father not only that they should marry, but that one of his own stewards should be instated at Manley Hall for the foreseeable future. Jasper had all the confidence in the world that the estate could be righted, and so did she.

Lady Mendleton had taken Georgiana's trousseau in hand and a flurry of dressmakers had flown about the house, generally looking exceedingly harried. After the measurements were taken, Georgiana had little to do with it. Lady Mendleton, or *mama* as she kept hinting she ought to be called, was a mother duck chasing her ducklings ahead of her. Georgiana was glad of it as she and Jasper had their own schedule to keep before the wedding. Breakfast in the library with the newspapers, rides through the park, the occasional visit to the queen, and seeking out a cozy corner wherever they could find one. The amount of hairpins Georgiana lost during these interludes was positively criminal.

The wedding breakfast came off smoothly, primarily because Lady Manley stayed home with a cold. Though a head cold was posited as the excuse, Georgiana received a letter from the lady explaining that she refused to be looked down upon by such persons as a duchess and a lady this and a lady that until she had a wardrobe suitable to hold up against it.

The baron *did* come and he and Jasper's father hit it off wonderfully. Georgiana fully expected to see her father at Lord Mendleton's next shooting party.

Neither Jasper nor Georgiana wished for an extended wedding trip to the continent, as they both preferred to be on hand if the queen had need of them, but a fortnight's trip to Ramsgate was taken.

Lord Ryland had lent his house there and it was charmingly situated on the cliffs overlooking the sea. There, with the salty breeze blowing in through their bedchamber windows, they stayed abed half the day.

On the afternoon before they were set to return to Town, they still had not come down. The servants, who had become well-acquainted with their brow-raising habits, had sent up a tray and discreetly knocked on the door and left it so that Lord Ryland's peculiar friends would not actually starve.

Jasper brought the tray in, a lovely set up of a light German wine, sandwiches, fruit, biscuits, and the cook's rather wonderful blackcurrant jam.

Georgiana stretched out on the bed, her hair loose on the pillow, and said, "I am afraid the staff is well and truly scandalized."

Jasper laughed. "I have been rather scandalized myself at times."

"I see, now you regret that you did not marry a more indirect miss. Perhaps a lady shy and retiring who would fan herself and look for the hartshorn as soon as the bedchamber door closed."

"Never," Jasper said, feeding her a strawberry. "The Society of Sponsoring Ladies has done me a great service in providing me with my beautiful heathen bride."

"Ah, the society," Georgiana said, laughing. "I wonder what they will do next?"

"Though we are too far away from London to hear their plotting, I can almost hear their plotting."

"Oh yes, let them plot away. Some lucky girl has no idea what's in store for her."

THE TON WAS always a herd of gazelle nervously hoping to blend in and avoid being singled out by a powerful predator, though the powerful predator that could take one down was the *ton* itself. Therefore, nobody was entirely sure of their opinion of the match between Miss Wilcox and Lord Langley. After all, she was the granddaughter of a tradesman and practically a charity case living on Lady Mendleton's largesse. Now, she was to marry the eldest son?

Most of those thoughts were thoughts only, as everybody waited for somebody else to step away from the herd and make some pronouncement about it. After all, it would take somebody bold indeed to go against the cabal of middle-aged women led by a duchess who'd put together a society to sponsor young ladies.

Somebody did finally make a pronouncement about it. The queen, who was one of the few people who knew what really occurred that night, was firmly in Miss Wilcox's camp. The queen told all and sundry that it was Lord Langley who ought to be grateful that Miss Wilcox had consented. According to the queen, Miss Wilcox was one of particularly fine sensibilities and there was not a more clever girl in England.

That was that. Even Lady Heathway, whatever her private thoughts may have been, was convinced to celebrate the match. She could at least console herself that she'd been right, she'd suspected an attachment all along.

Lady Annabelle returned to Mr. Pottsgrove and wrote Georgiana a charming letter regarding their reunion. It seemed that Mr. Pottsgrove *had* divined that the anonymous letters signed Annie were from her and had waited patiently for her return. He'd called the same day he'd seen the family's carriages arrive and he'd lifted her onto her horse with one hand and they'd ridden down the local lanes discussing their future.

Georgiana was delighted to understand that along with the prior arrangements of a small white dog on her lap and plentiful marzipan on hand, a sitting room was to be redecorated exclusively for her use. It was to be very pink, as they both agreed that color particularly set off her complexion. As well, they were to expand both the ballroom and the dining room. Mr. Pottsgrove had promised that all Lady Annabelle would be required to do was throw parties and he was determined to keep his word. Lady Annabelle had felt a moment's pause about this, as she wondered if the housekeeper would like all the rest of the household duties and decisions falling upon her shoulders. As it happened, Mrs. Broadstart was delighted with the idea.

Georgiana thought delight was probably the wrong description. She suspected Mrs. Broadstart was relieved. In any case, as Lady Annabelle's only work would be to plan parties and balls, the neighborhood would find itself far more entertained than it ever had done.

Mr. Perry went on having no clear idea of what actually occurred the fateful night of the ball. It seemed that Miss Wilcox planned to go to the park but ended in the mews? Lord Asturt and Marcus were in a gang of footpads? And then, the grooms said both Carstares and Miss Wilcox were on horses. None of it added up. That led him to believe there was a secret about it. As one of the grooms had been sent to the palace with a message, that led him to believe it might be the queen's secret.

His staff were all abuzz with speculation until he decided it ought not be discussed further. If the queen were involved, he would lay down his life to protect the great lady. He hinted that he knew all the particulars and it was enough that he knew it. All he would say was that it must have been obvious to everybody that he'd kept his eye on Marcus all along. Further talk on the subject was banned, else he would *take steps*.

For himself, he congratulated himself on keeping his private thoughts private. Had he denounced Miss Wilcox as he had so often thought about in satisfying terms of drama and pathos, he would have landed on the wrong side. Aldous Perry never landed on the wrong side. As it was, he was rather relieved to be done with the whole thing. Now, he could go back to his usual activities of managing the foreign cook and his bizarre sauces, shedding a private tear over how many dogs were just now roaming the estate, and wondering if Mrs. Ripperton would be inebriated when he saw her next. All was as it should be.

Jenny finally gave up questioning Georgiana about that night, as Georgiana claimed it was too upsetting to think of. In any case, Jenny was easily distracted and Lord Langley had hired a new valet. Roberts appeared to be a sensible fellow, but who really knew? Jenny had her eye firmly upon him lest it be discovered that he also was in a gang of footpads.

The queen decided the best course was to deal with the Stuart privately. As she said to Jasper, "You see, there were only two solutions. A public trial for treason which would put the king's malady and the Stuart's claims of it being inherited on trial too. Or, my second option, which is a quiet end to this plot. While I would have liked to kill him secretly and thereby be done with the Stuarts forever, we could never have kept it quiet – it would get out somehow. I would have made him into a martyr and there would be some who would accuse me of regicide."

The queen had walked to a window and gazed out, as if she surveyed the kingdom that had so recently been in peril.

"All would have condemned me for overstepping my rights, even my own son who knows nothing of anything of this. This way, I have provided Roehenstart with enough income that he may live comfortably and have something to lose if he makes another move. I have sworn to him that I will assassinate him if he does, and I can assure you he believes me. I do not think he will bother us again."

As for what society thought of the nefarious Lord Asturt who was discovered to lead a gang of footpads, they had not much that was actually a fact to think about. The fellow disappeared and nobody ever did know his true identity. However, having generally too much time on their hands, stories began to circulate and be embellished as they went from person to person. It was no time at all before Lord Asturt became a veritable Dick Turpin who might turn up again at any moment. On occasion, somebody who traveled to the continent came upon Count Roehen-start and remarked on his striking similarity to Lord Asturt. Though, they promptly put aside the idea that they could be one and the same. After all, why would a respected count be in London working as a footpad?

Georgiana and Jasper, to the delight of Lady Mendleton, did in fact remove to the country estate. Though Georgiana was not always certain of the veracity of Jenny's stories, she did find that her description of the housekeeper, Mrs. Ripperton, was all too accurate. The lady was forever unsteady on her feet or missing and found to be abed. Georgiana might have wondered why Lady Mendleton put up with it if she had not grown to understand the lady's nature. That nature would also account for the ten dogs and counting that had been taken in, the housemaids who appeared never to have seen a house before, or the recently hired footman with a constantly running nose and a preference for sleeves rather than handkerchiefs. If there were ever a lost soul in Lady Mendleton's vicinity, she would be sure to find them.

Though it was still some years away, an infant girl would finally make her appearance at Mendleton Hall. The trunk that had lain forlorn in the attic, filled with all the pretty things Lady Mendleton had collected when she'd had hopes of her own, would be joyfully unpacked.

As a matter of course, nannies and governesses would be hired, but those ladies would find themselves with much free time on their hands—Lady Mendleton could not be kept away from the nursery.

Never had a girl been so doted on and indulged by a grandmother. And a grandfather too, for that matter. It was only a shame that she was found to have a rather tin ear. Three musical instructors quit in fast succession and the pianoforte was finally relegated to a room nobody used. She was, after all, her mother's daughter.

Of course, that was still years away. For now, Georgiana and Jasper continued with their shocking habit of staying abed all morning while the rest of the house pretended not to notice it.

Lady Mendleton's attention was thankfully soon turned to the society's latest project. Lady Heathway had discovered a late viscount's daughter now living in a ramshackle cottage on the estate her father had once occupied. The girl was to be rescued and launched properly the following season.

Lady Heathway had sent a letter to the girl's mother, outlining her plan. Though, so far it had not gone as smoothly as one might hope...

The End

About the Author

By the time I was eleven, my Irish Nana and I had formed a book club of sorts. On a timetable only known to herself, Nana would grab her blackthorn walking stick and steam down to the local Woolworth's. There, she would buy the latest Barbara Cartland romance, hurry home to read it accompanied by viciously strong wine, (Wild Irish Rose, if you're wondering) and then pass the book on to me. Though I was not particularly interested in real boys yet, I was *very* interested in the gentlemen in those stories— daring, bold, and often enraging and unaccountable. After my Barbara Cartland phase, I went on to Georgette Heyer, Jane Austen and so many other gifted authors blessed with the ability to bring the Georgian and Regency eras to life.

I would like nothing more than to time travel back to the Regency (and time travel back to my twenties as long as we're going somewhere) to take my chances at a ball. Who would take the first? Who would escort me into supper? What sort of meaningful looks would be exchanged? I would hope, having made the trip, to encounter a gentleman who would give me a very hard time. He ought to be vexatious in the extreme, and *worth* every vexation, to make the journey worthwhile.

I most likely won't be able to work out the time travel gambit, so I will content myself with writing stories of adventure and romance in my beloved time period. There are lives to be created, marvelous gowns to wear, jewels to don, instant attractions that inevitably come with a difficulty, and hearts to break before putting them back together again. In traditional Regency fashion, my stories are clean—the action happens in a drawing room, rather than a bedroom.

As I muse over what will happen next to my H and h, and wish I were there with them, I will occasionally remind myself that it's also nice to have a microwave, Netflix, cheese popcorn, and steaming hot showers.

Come see me on Facebook! @KateArcherAuthor

CPSIA information can be obtained
at www.ICGtesting.com
Printed in the USA
BVHW040040210222
629654BV00011B/762